FEEL MY LOVE

FEEL MY LOVE

GAIL R. DELANEY

PRAISE FOR GAIL R. DELANEY

"I can't rave enough about this book! Gail Delaney does an amazing job bringing these characters to life in a way that makes you laugh and cry with them. There's just so much heart in this, and how very touching to learn the real-life story that inspired this amazing fictional account!"

— ESTHER MITCHELL, AUTHOR OF THE
PROJECT PROMETHEUS SERIES

"I have to say: Oh my gosh! Who wouldn't want a love like this -- and a guy like Lee Henry! I'm tempted to read it again just to feel that love again!"

— READER, 5 STAR REVIEW

"This book left me with a sigh and a smile..."

— READER, 5 STAR REVIEW

#SupportArtistsNotAI
www.GailDelaney.com

Thank you to William Scarborough, a precious friend and an artist in many mediums. He wrote for me the lyrics to "Getting Started on Forever" that Lee sings for Missy.

Thank you, my precious friend. I am blessed to have you in my life.

THE ORIGIN OF THE STORY

This novel is dedicated to my parents, Hank and Maxine Hughes. This novel is a modernized, loose, and fictional retelling of their love story. I brought their story to a contemporary setting and had to change some details because, in truth, their love story would read as completely implausible within the pages of a book. Sometimes, the truth is stranger—or more beautiful—than fiction.

There was an eighteen-year age gap between my parents, my dad being the younger of the two. He was 21 years old and Mom was 39 when they met and married. I didn't have a typical childhood with typical parents. I was raised between two generations with parents even from different parts of the country, and I loved it. I had the benefit of many influences. Even though I lost my mother when I was relatively young—in my early twenties—I wouldn't change a single moment I had with her for a younger mother.

When you hear the whole story, which I'll tell when you're done, you'll understand without question why I love writing romance. I grew up with it. The details vary, depending on who you ask—

neither my mother nor father would admit to being the pursuer, always the pursued—either way you look at it, their story is beautiful.

For anyone who might have been first-hand witnesses to my parents' story: No, I don't intend for this to be a true-to-life telling. Don't read and think, "That didn't happen that way..." Since I wasn't there, and I'm an author with poetic license, I'm winging it.

Thank you to my brother Mark Brow, for being the one to introduce them, even though he probably had *no* idea what would happen when he asked Mom to bake a cake. Thank you for telling me parts of the story neither one of them ever mentioned.

BOOK CONTENT EXPECTATIONS

I do my best to provide a disclaimer for any of my readers who might not wish to read about certain storylines or story elements. Without divulging too much of the story itself, please be aware the following topics, discussions, and scenarios take place in both significant portions and less significant portions: loss of a spouse due to illness, military service (honorable discharge), family trauma, unfaithfulness (not applicable to the primary characters), physical altercations, and the mention of loss of a child from miscarriage.

Please note, that the last item is not part of 99.5% of the story, mentioned near the end but not within the narration of this timeline.

"FEEL MY LOVE" SPOTIFY PLAYLIST

Do you like having a soundtrack to the books you read? I've created a playlist for "Feel My Love" on Spotify.

I miss Mom and Daddy every day, but have are videos of Daddy singing. This is "Sing Me Back Home," recorded during a Tribute to Country concert just about a year before Daddy died. If you're reading in print form, follow the QR code below. I hope you enjoy.

CHAPTER ONE

A NEON BLUE SIGN FLASHED "LOW PLACES", THE LOWER CURVE OF THE 's' flickering with the threat of going out completely, the obtrusive sign planted on top of the flat, windowless honkytonk. Missy stared out the pickup windshield, wondering how she'd managed to get here; other than giving in to the nagging of her little brother and his wife in a moment of weakness.

Thayne touched her arm and she looked at him, blinking to clear the filament image of the neon sign dancing in her vision. "You look like I'm dragging you to your execution," he said with a lopsided smirk. He looked like Daddy when he smiled like that.

"It's been a really, really long time..." She trailed off, not sure how to even categorize what it was exactly she'd avoided for so long.

"Since you kicked up your heels with your brother?" he said with a shrug. "Damn straight it's been a long time."

"I know, but—"

"The kids are fine," Susan said, leaning forward so Missy could see her from the other side of her brother. She draped over the steering wheel, the blue of the neon light shining off her blond hair. "They're having a blast with Becky. If I can step out for a night of fun and leave my little baby girl, you can very well come along and suffer with me."

Missy laughed and shook her head. "Fine. I'm over it. Let's go."

She opened her door and hopped out of the Dodge Ram, her brother following her out the passenger's side. The air thrummed with the hard baseline reverberating from the building. She couldn't differentiate any "music" in the sound, just the pounding of the beat. She and Thayne met Susan in front of the truck, and her brother took his wife's hand.

Thayne draped his arm across Missy's shoulders and walked her toward the bar entrance. She curled her hair behind her ear as they walked, instinctively finding the tiny volume control on her right hearing aid, automatically adjusting the sound in both, and then switching programs from a button on the left to a more appropriate setting. The pounding immediately reduced to a low hum until they opened the door to Low Places, then the base thud against her chest like a rubber mallet on a snare drum. The bar was to their right, the stage past it at one end of a sunken dance floor lined on three sides with tables and chairs, the center empty for dancing. A mass of people danced in front of the stage. Multi-colored stage lights strobed and flicked across the dark space, drawing everyone's attention to the men and women on stage. The lead singer pounded hard on his electric acoustic and sang about "House Rules". Before she could focus on any one of them, Thayne pulled her down the steps to the sitting area and toward a booth in the corner farthest away from the mounted speakers.

Thayne's friends Leone and April already sat in the booth, and waved at them as they approached. Missy was thankful to slide into the booth with her back to the stage, muffling the sound a little more. The thudding wasn't uncomfortable, but the idea of not having the full use of her hearing aids made her heart pound a little too rapid. She still felt compromised when she couldn't hear clearly, despite her best efforts. They all talked back and forth, and Missy did her best to follow the snippets of conversation by looking from face to face. She'd gotten very good at reading lips in the last few years.

"When will you be moving out to the new house?" April asked, turning to face Missy straight on. "More importantly, are you glad you decided to stay?"

"A couple of weeks," Missy said and nodded, setting down her sweet tea. "There is some work I want to do first, nothing major, just painting, some new appliances, that sort of thing. And yes, I am. It's so different from Boston."

"And that's a good thing?"

Missy tamped down her first answer. She loved Boston, but Boston was full of memories, and it was a pleasant relief to be somewhere she wasn't reminded of what was no more at every turn, from the restaurants where she ate dinner to the grocery store she shopped at on the way home with her boys. Instead, she simplified her answer. "Yes, it's a good thing. It's nice to be back in Oklahoma."

April smiled and nodded, and went back to her conversation with Susan and Leone. Thayne met Missy's look across the booth and winked, grinning. She smiled back, loving her brother for loving her enough to make her come. When she and Daniel had been newlyweds and Thayne was still in college, they'd gone out dancing every Saturday night. When Jude was born, she'd used dancing to get back in shape, but Wyatt came along, then Jeremiah, and Levi, and Saturday night dates were replaced by Saturday afternoons at the park and early nights of sharing the events of the day while lying in bed out of exhaustion.

The music pounded inside the small bar, pausing only on occasion to be interrupted by over-amplified, muffled voices and applause to resume again with foot stomping and whoops and hollers as people kicked up their cowboy boots to the thumping beat. Missy twisted in the booth to look back at the dance floor, a familiar draw urging her to join in the choreographed dance. A touch on her hand drew her reluctant attention back to the group at the table.

Thayne pulled back his hand, grabbing a handful of peanuts from the bowl in the center of the table.

"You want to dance?" he asked before popping the nuts in his mouth.

She nodded and shrugged one shoulder. "Maybe later." She shifted enough to draw her phone from her back pocket. "I'm going to check on the boys."

She saw the counterargument form on his lips, but he stopped short of saying anything and shook his head. He had to know better. Maybe she was overprotective. Maybe she shouldn't worry so much. In the last couple of years "maybe" had become the lion's share of her existence. She never thought she'd be a widow at thirty-seven, left to raise four sons alone. She never thought she'd leave Boston, but then again, when she was young she never thought she'd leave Oklahoma. And yet, here she was back in Oklahoma looking for a permanent home for herself and her four sons, all on her own.

Oklahoma was where Daniel's family was from, where she was from, and where Thayne settled after separating from his military service, so somehow Oklahoma felt right.

Her mama always told her "Never say never, Missy. It's like asking for the universe to prove you wrong."

She slid from the booth and headed toward the glowing neon sign pointing down a narrow, wood-paneled hall to the restrooms. A single payphone, battered and scratched with decades of telephone numbers, hung on the wall between two doors. The first door said "Gents", but she moved past both doors to two wooden chairs set at the end of the hall. Both were empty, so she sat in one and tapped open her text program.

Jeremiah and Levi would already be asleep, and Wyatt should be in bed but he probably wasn't. He'd be curled up on the couch, fighting sleep, just to hang with his big brother Jude. She'd told the babysitter to mention bed to Wyatt, but not to press the issue as long as Jude didn't mind. Jude usually didn't mind.

After a few minutes of texting with Jude, she sat back in the creaky wooden chair with a smile and closed the chat window. Jude was only thirteen, but he was the wisest soul she'd ever known, especially since he lost his dad. He told her, in no uncertain terms, they all loved her and it was time she went and had some fun.

A man rounded the corner into the narrow hall, heading right to the payphone; tall, probably over six feet, and the way his faded jeans and black tee shirt hugged his lean build only helped to accentuate his height. Dark hair spiked away from his tanned forehead, slick and damp with perspiration. Every bit of exposed skin on his arms and neck glistened. Missy couldn't look away for several moments, mesmerized by the way he moved, fluid but with an undeniable strength in the slow roll of his limbs. He lifted the handset off the archaic phone and wedged it between his sharp lantern jaw and his shoulder, shoving his hand into his front pocket.

His lips moved, and she assumed he mumbled under his breath so she diverted her eyes. Missy shifted on the rickety chair, hoping he made his call quickly so she could escape back to the table without having to brush past him in the tight space. Widow or not, she never lost the ability to appreciate an attractive man.

"Excuse me."

The clarity of his baritone voice, something she hardly ever experienced even when her aids were turned up, made her gasp and she jerked her head up with such force she barely avoided slamming the back of her skull into the old wood paneling.

"Whoa, I'm sorry. I didn't mean to startle you," he said, crouching slightly with his hands held up. "I thought you heard me walk over."

Missy shook her head, trying to will away the heat in her cheeks. "No," she said with a nervous laugh.

He smiled, the simple expression reaching all the way to his blue eyes. "I wondered if you have any change." He hooked his thumb over his shoulder toward the payphone. "I forgot to charge my phone, and I need to call my brother."

"I'll do you one better," she said before she decided against it and held up her hand, her smartphone on her open palm. "Use mine."

"Seriously?" She nodded and he swung around to sit in the chair beside her, taking the phone from her hand. His legs extended several inches farther than hers into the tight hall. "Thanks, I appreciate it."

Missy crossed her arms and slouched in the chair, keeping her chin tucked to her chest while he dialed whomever it was he needed to reach, watching through her hair when he held the phone to his ear. The subtle scent of his cologne, something earthy and musky, mingled with the aroma of a warm body and wrapped around her senses. Sitting this close, she took the opportunity to take a good look at him. He was very tan, like he'd spent days in the sun, and all angles from his jaw to his brow, even his cheekbones were pronounced and sharp. Not in a harsh way, but clearly enough Missy knew he probably was in his mid-twenties...maybe. She suddenly felt every bit of her thirty-seven years.

"Hey, Ricky. Yeah, sorry." He turned to her, and mouthed, "What's your name?"

She whispered back, "Missy Colton."

"Yeah, the lovely Missy Colton here was sweet enough to let me borrow her phone." He winked at her, then nodded at something the disembodied Ricky said. "Mark and I've got another set at ten, but I've got that favor I've got to take care of first." Pause. "Yeah, well, I'm not big on blind setups, but when a friend asks for a favor..."

He trailed off and listened for the next couple of minutes before confirming he'd be leaving the club by two at the latest, then ended the call and handed the phone to her again. Missy took it, avoiding direct eye contact, and slid the phone into her back pocket.

"Thanks," he said, holding out his hand. "So, I know your name is Missy. Guess it's only polite to introduce myself. Lee Henry."

Missy took in the smallest of breaths before she let his large, calloused, strong hand envelope hers, long fingers wrapping easily around her wrist. He didn't shake it, he just held it. Her heart did a funny little jerk behind her ribs. She immediately tamped it down and decided to ignore it, rattling off a dozen reasons in a single heartbeat why she had no place even entertaining the *slightest* attraction to the man. Then again, she hadn't felt a zing like that since the first time Daniel had taken her hand. Missy blinked and withdrew her hand.

He watched her a second longer than needed to make her feel self-conscious, then chuckled softly and looked down the hall. "I've got to meet a friend in a few minutes—"

"The setup?" she asked, and he looked back at her. "Sorry, couldn't help hear."

Lee nodded. "Yeah, the setup. In the meantime, do you want to dance?"

"I probably shouldn't," she said but realized she smiled too easily to convince anyone. "But I'm going to anyway."

Lee stood. Missy tipped back her head to watch him and held her breath when he offered his hand to help her stand. Fortifying her shaky resolve, she decided to do exactly as her son had urged her and have a good time. She slid her palm over his and his long fingers curled around her hand, drawing her to her feet.

In the short walk from the chairs to the end of the hall, where the volume of the jukebox amped up to a chest-thumping level, Missy ran through all the reasons it wasn't a big deal. She'd been in Indian Prairie for two months and had never seen Lee; the chances were they wouldn't see each other again, so what was the harm in a dance? He'd asked her, not the other way around, so it wasn't like she was the "older woman" chasing down the younger man. What was it they called that? A cougar. She wasn't a cougar. She was a widow, not dead, and she knew how to slap leather on the dance floor. And besides...dancing was great exercise.

Sure.

He led her onto the floor just as a new song began, the kind of song that called for old-fashioned face-to-face dancing but with a boot-stompin' kick. She knew the words by heart, and after four beats her feet and hips remembered the moves. Missy was intensely aware of Lee's large hand on her left hip, and the warmth of his grip as his fingers curled around hers. He knew how to dance, and once they found their rhythm together, Missy let go and enjoyed the pleasure of dancing like she hadn't in several years. She focused on him and let the pounding rhythm of the song guide her steps. As the song thundered to a close, Lee pulled her against him and spoke near her ear, "Dip," just in time for her to shift her weight and let him roll her back. She came against his chest, laughing. His deep rumble cut through the muffled sounds of the crowd, the clarity setting chills up her spine.

"Missy Colton, you are one hell of a dancer."

She smiled and tried to catch her breath. "I'm an out-of-practice dancer."

"Could have fooled me." He took her hand and led her off the dance floor as the next song began. Once off the floor and back at the entrance to the hallway, he turned to face her. The music was loud, so she focused on his mouth as he spoke. It wasn't as necessary as she expected; his voice rang clear over everything else. "Will you be here for a while?"

She shrugged. "I don't know how long we'll stay. I'm with friends."

"I'm playing in a bit," he said, leaning in closer as was usually necessary in honkytonks like this. "I'd like to see you before you leave, though."

Shouldn't she say no? "I can try."

Lee smiled, slight dimples popping in his stubble-roughed cheeks. "Okay." He winked. "I've got to go—"

"The setup," she finished, nodding. "Not sure if I should wish you luck or not."

His grin made her cheeks heat, and she glanced away. When she looked back, he watched her with an expression she couldn't quite interpret, only that it did funny things to her stomach. Then he squeezed the hand he still held, and let go before heading toward the stage.

Missy waited until he disappeared into the crowd, then drew in a deep breath. His cologne clung to her clothing. She huffed and shook her head, maneuvering through the crowd toward the table where she'd left her brother and friends. They had ordered more drinks and bar food, a tray of wings, and a basket of tortillas in the middle of the table. Thayne popped a chip, dripping with salsa, into his mouth as she slid in beside April.

"You were gone a while," he said around the food.

"Long text," she answered, avoiding the rest.

Thayne looked past her into the crowd, then slid from the booth with a grin, apparently greeting someone as they approached and extended his hand. "Hey, man. Good to see you."

In her peripheral, Missy caught sight of someone reaching the table just behind her, approaching from the dance floor. She turned to look, but Thayne blocked most of her view. A tall man, wearing dark clothes...

Missy's eyes popped wide and heat infused her from toe to hairline.

"Lee, you know Leone's wife April, right?"

"Oh, yeah," he said with a wide smile, his voice clear and sharp. He extended his hand to Leone on the other side of the table from Missy. "Good to see you, man." Then he turned enough to see April.

And Missy.

Lee's casual smile eased into a grin that melted Missy's toes. She was sure she might burst into flames with her next breath. His smile was enough to warm her by its power alone, but that warmth battled with the fury at her brother when she realized *she* was the dreaded "setup."

"Lee, this is my sister Missy," Thayne said from past Lee's shoulder.

"We've met." Lee leaned over at the waist, pressing his warm lips to her burning cheek. She closed her eyes, and tried not to make a sound when he whispered just loud enough for her to hear, "Best setup ever."

CHAPTER TWO

LAUGHTER AND SHOUTS BOUNCED OFF THE TALL WOODEN FENCE surrounding Thayne and Susan's backyard, mingled with the playful spray of water and loud splashes as kids cannonballed off the pool edge into the deep end. Missy smiled as she cut up fresh melons and strawberries for fruit salad. She didn't need to turn around and look out the kitchen window to enjoy the backyard party in full swing. Her daddy had always said the best reason for a party was no reason at all, and that was exactly the reason for the gathering of friends and family around the pool.

The backdoor creaked open and slammed shut, followed by the rapid, wet slaps of small feet on the linoleum. "Mama! Mama!"

Missy looked down at Levi and chuckled at his spiked, white-blond hair and rivulets of water running down his flushed cheeks. He was soaked through, leaving puddles and drops of water from the door to her side, but it was hard to scold when he looked at her with such bright, happy eyes.

"Mama, I jumped offa da edge wight inta da watur," he declared, pointing through the screen door to the backyard. He pulled his lower lip over his top and blew away a stream of water, then grinned. "Wanna see?"

"Absolutely. As soon as I'm finished with the fruit salad, I'm going to come out and sit in my favorite chair and watch you jump in, okay?"

He flashed another toothy, genuine smile—so much like Daniel—and bolted to the backdoor, amazingly avoiding a slip on the wet linoleum. As soon as the door slapped shut behind him, Missy picked up her dishtowel and crouched down to wipe up the water before someone fell.

"It's a good thing your new place has a pool," Susan said as she came into the kitchen from the hall, baby Betsy balanced on her hip. "Your boys sure do love the water. It's not even officially summer yet."

Missy stood and dropped the damp dishtowel on the counter, looking out the window to the yard. "Day after tomorrow they'll be in sweatshirts. Of course, I need to get the pool usable first."

Susan laughed and handed Betsy off to Missy so she could pour a glass of sweet tea. Missy gladly bounced the little girl, and straightened her yellow gingham dress, getting a toothy grin from the ten-month-old. She loved her boys, and wouldn't trade them for anything, but a small part of Missy's heart ached for a curly-haired little girl in Mary Jane shoes and frilly dresses.

"Are you still sore at me?" Susan asked. "Because Thayne sure is."

Missy kept her attention on Betsy, chuckling when the little girl broke into a wide, pure grin. It had been three days since their night at Low Places, and Missy had managed to let go of most of the initial anger at her sister-in-law for her sneaky tactics. Not even Thayne had known about Susan's plan to introduce Missy and Lee. Lee had been good-natured about the whole thing, but Missy had fumed with embarrassment the rest of the night.

"No, but you should have asked me if I even wanted to be setup, Susan, before you asked an Army buddy of my brother's to 'do you a favor'." She mocked the final words, feeling heat rise in her cheeks again at the memory of Lee on the phone, saying much the same. "I'm not desperate to be with a man. I've been without Daniel for over two years."

"I didn't think you were desperate, Missy. But you're not some old woman widowed after fifty years of marriage. You deserve—"

"Not the point, Susan," Missy cut her off, finally looking up from Betsy's giggling grin.

"You and Lee seemed to have hit it off pretty well before you found out, though." Susan tried to smile, but it was more question than anything else.

"Which is exactly the problem."

"So, why did you take off faster than a scalded dog when he joined us? You didn't even wait for us to take you home."

The doorbell chimed, and Missy silently thanked the universal intervention. "I'll get it."

Lee set his guitar case against the house and pressed the glowing doorbell button. Excited cries of children mingled with laughter and the distinct sound of splashing water from the backyard. The smell of charcoal and barbecue sauce made his mouth water. Thayne's Ram was in the driveway, along with Susan's minivan and a Jeep Cherokee he didn't recognize. Of course, he didn't recognize most of the vehicles along the curb in front of Thayne's house.

He entertained the idea one of them might belong to Missy Colton. Thayne had mentioned his sister a couple of times but hadn't told him much other than his sister was in Oklahoma, with the possible intention of staying. He'd left off the part about her being beautiful. Lee wondered what else Thayne had left out.

And then wondered if he cared.

The door swung open, and Lee knew immediately there was no question. He didn't care what Thayne left out, because he intended to find out on his own. Missy stood in the doorway, wearing a pretty yellow, cotton sundress with a scooped neck and no sleeves, falling just short of her bare knees. Her blond hair was pulled up in a haphazard twist and clipped to stay in place, leaving tendrils, curled by the humidity, to fall around her freckled cheeks. Betsy, Thayne's baby girl, balanced on her hip, blond hair sticking out wild from two tiny pigtails on either side of her head. Missy's blue eyes widened and color bloomed in her cheeks, accentuating her freckles.

"Hey, Missy," he said and winked.

She took a step back into the house, holding the door all the way open for him. "Come on in. Did you need Thayne?"

He reached to his right and picked up his guitar case, stepping into the house. It was a good fifteen degrees cooler inside the house, a relief from the hot sun and wind. Yesterday it had rained, today it baked. Missy moved back, her hand on the inner doorknob, to let him pass.

"He invited me a week or so ago to come by for a barbecue today. I didn't realize it was such a party until I got here." He looked back out to the rows of vehicles. "Looks like quite the shindig."

"He must have invited you before he knew about Susan's plan," she said with a smile. "It's not family only. Some friends of theirs are here, too."

Lee leaned in and kissed her cheek, just as he had at Low Places. She smelled of roses and coconut, a strange mixture but enticing. Her skin was smooth and warm, and her hair tickled his cheek. Missy leaned into the kiss, just a little, and he smiled. "It's good to see you again," he said before drawing back.

She cleared her throat and looked him in the eyes before she shut the door and shifted Betsy on her hip. "I'm living temporarily with Thayne and Susan," she explained, motioning for him to follow her down the hallway. "So, show up at any time and I'm probably going to be here."

"Good to know."

Missy glanced back at him over her shoulder and offered a delicate, nervous smile. When she turned away again, he caught sight of the bud in her ear, about the size of the end of his thumb, flesh-colored for camouflage. Hearing aids. Nothing about the way she spoke or the way she acted at the bar ever gave away to him she had problems hearing; then again, wasn't that the point of hearing aids? Lee had a vague memory of Thayne telling him their mother had lost much of her hearing as an adult. Did he say it was hereditary? Lee couldn't remember.

He and Thayne had known each other for several years, stationed out of the same base in Oklahoma. They did one tour together in Kabul a couple of years earlier. Conversations on base often turned back to family at home, but with the echo of artillery fire in the background, it was sometimes tough to remember the finer details. He wished now he'd paid more attention, or tried harder to remember.

They reached the kitchen, and in the loud chaos of Susan offering him sweet tea and Thayne shaking his hand, Missy passed Betsy off to Susan and slipped out the kitchen door to the backyard. Lee set his case against the wall and glanced out the window to see at least half a dozen kids, ranging from toddlers to teens playing in and around the water. Leone and April were amongst the guests, and he recognized Lucas Brent and his girlfriend. Her name escaped Lee.

Lee tried again to remember some of the Bingham family details Thayne had let slip over the three years they'd known each other, but he and Thayne had both been in and out of Indian Prairie much of that time with several stretches serving in Afghanistan. They always caught up when both were back in Oklahoma.

Thayne had ended his stint nine months before just after Betsy's birth, and Lee was officially a civilian again in about two weeks. Chances were they'd talk a lot more. And if Missy was moving to Oklahoma...

"She's madder than a wet hen in a tote sack over the other night."

Lee looked back to Thayne. "Why?"

Thayne glowered in his wife's direction. "Gee, I wonder. Maybe because she's a wi—"

"Thayne Bingham, get off your damn high horse," Susan snapped, scowling back with an equal vengeance. "Missy deserves to have some fun. That's all I was going for."

"By going behind everyone's back? What makes you think Missy, or Lee for that matter, would want to be setup with each other?"

"Hey, now," Lee said, holding up his hands. "Look, I'm not mad. Not even bothered. It's fine."

"Not the point," Thayne practically growled. He hunched up his shoulders and shook his head. "Look, Lee, don't take this personally but you two aren't exactly compatible."

"Who are you to decide that?" Susan demanded.

"Why are you being so pig-headed stubborn over this, Suz?"

"Why are *you*?"

Lee pushed his hands into his pockets and crossed to the sink so he could look outside, turning his back on the arguing couple. A wide awning covered the portion of the lanai closest to the house and about one-third of the in-ground pool on the shallow end. Missy had slipped into one of the shaded lounge chairs, watching the children play. A little boy, maybe three at most, ran around the edge of the pool, leaving wet footprints behind. He ran straight for her, talking all the while, but with all the other noise Lee couldn't hear what he said. She nodded and smiled and he took off again, meeting up with a teenage boy of about thirteen or fourteen.

"Don't you think it was maybe your reaction, Thayne, that got her back up? She didn't leave until you made your fourth or fifth stupid comment about her being your *older* sister like that should make all the difference."

"What has she said about all this?" Lee asked, not turning from the scene outside the window.

"I said the two of you seemed to get along fine before she found out," Susan said, joining Lee at the window. "She said that was the problem." She looked up at him and tilted her head. "You're scowling, Lee."

"Let's just say if this whole thing were a song, the harmony would be way off tune." Lee offered Susan a smile, knowing he probably didn't make much sense either, but he was beginning to understand. Maybe. Thayne and Susan probably didn't know about his conversation with Missy before the dance, and his reluctance to be setup. Better left that way, he figured.

"Jeremiah, don't splash your brother," Missy called from her chair, drawing Lee's attention again. "You don't want him to splash you, so don't splash him."

A young boy, though not the youngest of the group, bowed his head in proper admonishment. "Yes, Mama."

Lee leaned against the counter and took in the grouping. Four young boys, all towheads, formed a small cluster about midway to the deep end. The oldest of the group seemed to be the oldest of the kids as a whole, maybe thirteen or fourteen. On his back was a younger boy, maybe ten, hanging on tight but with a smile that said he wasn't afraid. Maybe because his big brother had him? Jeremiah, the splash offender, sat on the edge of the tile beside the littlest boy, the one who had run to Missy for attention and approval before returning to the pool.

Four boys, the pieces fell into place, and Lee remembered. He shifted his weight back on his heels and closed his eyes. *Dang it.* Probably about two years earlier, maybe not that long, he had been home on leave and stopped by to see Thayne. Thayne and Susan had only been married a few months and had just come back from Boston, where they had gone to be with Thayne's sister because her husband had died. Sister with four children, one still in arms at the time.

Missy Colton.

"Missy is your widowed sister..." Lee groaned out, then rubbed his face with his palms. "Geez, how did I forget that?"

"How many sisters do you think I have?" Thayne asked.

"I don't know." Lee shrugged. "Dang it, Thayne, in the last couple of years I've had a hard time keeping track of how many sisters *I* have, let alone anyone else." He turned away from the sink and walked halfway across the kitchen, hands on his hips.

"Doesn't matter now," Susan huffed. "She doesn't like setups any more than you do, so you're both off the hook." She nudged the handle of the backdoor with her elbow enough that it opened, and used her foot to leverage it all the way. Susan shrugged before stepping outside. "And I'm out of trouble. No harm. No foul."

Sure. No harm. No foul. Except the minute Missy had looked up at him in the hallway of Low Places, a switch had clicked in the back of his brain that said "get close", and when she danced with him, that same switch had turned to "get closer." After leaving her, he'd dreaded finding Thayne and Susan because he didn't want to feign interest with one woman when another was already on his mind, and he'd thanked God for His providence when the two ended up being one and the same.

The fact she was a little older had registered when he saw her, but that switch in the back of his head hadn't cared. Didn't care now. But, a widow with four sons? What kind of baggage was he willing to take on for a beautiful woman?

He remembered having a similar conversation a few years earlier, except then it wasn't him doing the considering.

"Come on out," Thayne said, holding open the door. "You can relax now, buddy."

Lee drew a deep breath and followed his friend out the door. As soon as his boots hit the cement lanai, Missy turned and looked at him. A tentative smile curved her lips before she looked away again.

The click was now a tug, and he knew before he was halfway to her he wasn't about to relax. He wasn't about to forget it. He didn't care how much baggage he had to lift and carry. He wouldn't toss off the chance to know Missy Colton. Something told him she would be worth it.

CHAPTER THREE

THERE WAS SOMETHING ABOUT THE WAY LEE HENRY MOVED—LOOSE AND easy—that refused to let Missy look away until he reached the lounge chair beside her and sat on the edge, facing her. She tried to focus on the scuffs on his well-worn boots, or the way the hem of his faded jeans hit the tops of his boots just right, but she lost the battle and shifted her gaze to look him in the eyes.

"You took off out of the house mighty quick," he said, leaning forward over his bent knees, his hands hanging loose. He was tall enough that the low lounge forced his knees higher than his hips, and he had to hunch to be able to look at her.

"You came to see Thayne and Susan, not me." Missy tried to keep her voice level, but it wasn't easy. "Besides, I promised Levi I'd come watch him jump in the pool."

Lee looked toward the pool, and smiled with a small chuckle. "Which one is Levi?"

"The youngest. He's three." She pointed in the direction of her boys, speaking generally. "Jeremiah is seven. Wyatt is ten. My oldest, Jude, is thirteen."

"Four boys." He made a clicking sound in his cheek and looked back at her with a wink. "You certainly have your hands full, Missy Colton. My mama had four of us boys, and three girls, and I'm pretty sure the nurses at the hospital knew her voice by the time John Junior was six."

Missy smiled, watching the boys as Jude lifted Levi from the edge of the pool and held him against his chest to ease his little brother out toward the middle of the deep end. Wyatt had joined Jeremiah on the pool edge. Levi didn't look the least bit nervous, but had a strong hold on his big brother, his water wings half-blocking Jude's face. Both boys were smiling and laughing. Sometimes, when she watched her boys, her heart swelled up with so much pride it hurt and brought tears to her eyes.

"They are good boys," she managed to say without her mama pride getting the best of her emotions. "I don't have to worry much. Except maybe for Jeremiah. He's the daredevil."

When she glanced back at Lee her breath hitched in her throat to find him studying her. Suddenly aware of his appraisal with a flash of heat up her throat, she raised a hand to curl behind her ear some of her stray hair from around her face, but stopped short, realizing she would expose her ears more. She tried not to be self-conscious about the hearing aids, having accepted years before they were necessary for her and always would be, but having the full attention of a man as young and attractive as Lee Henry made her feel very much like Mrs. Robinson. By any other standard, she was far from *old*. But he wasn't nearly *as* old, and adding something so often intrinsically connected to age as hearing aids just made it worse. Missy dropped her hand into her lap and shifted her legs to tuck her ankles against the back of her thighs, twisting her body to settle back onto the chair.

"Susan didn't mention I had four children," she said, trying to put some space between her and Lee's intensity. "Did she?"

"Not directly, no." He looked down at his hands and rubbed his palms together. The sound of callused skin against callused skin sent gooseflesh over Missy's arms. "I'm guessing she thought I'd remember. Thayne told me about you a couple years back, after..." He winced and looked her in the eyes again. "I'm sorry for your loss."

Missy had heard those same words hundreds of times in the last two years, but very rarely had she heard true sincerity behind them. Lee meant it. "Thank you," she said softly.

"Missy!" Thayne called from the grill, ready to slap on the steaks. "Medium, right?"

Missy nodded, wincing at the volume he shouted. Missy's hearing had begun to fade in her early twenties, even though she hadn't realized it herself, but everyone around her had gradually adjusted to speaking louder and often repeating. It hadn't been until shortly before Daniel's death that she finally admitted the loss was substantial and would just get worse if she didn't accept the inevitable. Thayne hadn't unlearned yet. She loved him for trying, and remembering.

"How did he die?"

The backyard was filled with laughter, conversation, children's shouts and giggles, splashing water, music, and activity, but through all that Lee's voice was sharp and clear. Whether it was his tone, or the way he projected his words, it cut through the chaos so vividly she could never deny hearing him. Missy rubbed her lips together and squinted into the sun, then took a slow, fortifying breath and answered.

"He had a brain tumor. There was an accident at work, stupid accident, and he had a head injury. They cleared him of anything more than a concussion, but months passed and the tumor developed." She had to pause, swallow, and take another breath. "The tumor was inoperable and eventually..." This time she couldn't finish. Missy swung her legs off the side of the lounge and stood, now towering over Lee, He leaned back and tipped his chin so he still looked up at her. "I'm going in to see if April needs any help."

"April came out with Betsy—"

She didn't give him a chance to finish, and moved away. Lee caught her wrist and he stood, now so close she was the one who would have to tip her chin to look at him. But she didn't, she couldn't. This was crazy. Her pulse hiked up, and she knew color flushed her throat and cheeks. It was insane. Absolutely insane. He was a young, single, *young* man who couldn't rationally ever be interested in a widowed mother of four. She didn't assume she'd be alone forever, but when she chose to be with someone again it would never be a man who was probably her eldest son's age when her eldest son was born.

Wow...that put things into perspective quick.

"Missy, I—"

She dared a glance at him; the honesty in his blue eyes made her heart jump. "We both know the other night was neither of our ideas. I didn't go there even knowing Susan had done it, and you told me yourself you weren't big on setups. It's ridiculous anyway. You don't need to work so hard."

He slid his hand down from her wrist until their palms were warm against each other, and laced his fingers through hers. Lee leaned closer so when he spoke, she was the only one who would hear. "The setup may not have been our idea, but that meeting in the hallway had nothing to do with Susan's plan. Me asking you to dance had nothing to do with Susan. Wanting to see you again had *nothing* to do with Susan."

"That was that night—"

"No, that's right now."

"Are you going to sing for us, Lee?" Susan called, interrupting them. She had slipped back into the house without Missy noticing because she came back out with Lee's guitar case in hand. She looked between Lee and Missy, then down at their joined hands.

Missy pulled free and headed toward the pool. "Boys, you need to come out and change before we eat. You can go back in the pool later if it stays warm."

A chorus of "Yes, Mama" preceded the four scrambling out of the pool. Jude lagged behind, making sure the three younger made it clear and headed toward the house before he followed. Levi diverted as he ran past, and hugged her legs, leaving wet splotches on her cotton skirt, then bolted again. She smiled at Jude, ruffling his wet hair, as he followed his little brothers into the house. To avoid heading back to the shade and the chairs, where Lee had found an Adirondack chair to perch on the edge of with his six-string balanced on his thigh, Missy went to her brother under the pretense of overseeing his cooking efforts.

"Hey, everything cool?" Thayne asked when she reached him.

"Sure. Why?"

"It just looked like you and Lee were getting intense. Is he bugging you about the other night?" Missy shook her head but didn't get a chance to answer before Thayne continued. "Sissy, I'm really sorry. Susan didn't tell me what she was planning, and if she had, I would've told her to mind—"

Missy laid her hand on his arm, smiling at his use of the name he'd given her when he was just a baby and couldn't quite get out Missy, and she preferred to ignore her full name outright. "It's okay, Thayne. I know Susan's heart was in the right place." She leaned up and kissed his cheek.

He smirked and flipped the steaks. The sweet sound of strummed guitar strings carried across the yard, drawing her attention. Lee spent a few moments tuning the instrument, playing random melodies beautiful in their simplicity. Missy loved music and always had. Her daddy had played guitar, and she'd known many musicians, especially in college, so she knew Lee was warming up before he played in earnest.

When the specialist had confirmed her hearing was indeed failing, and couldn't offer any guarantee she wouldn't lose it completely, her two greatest fears were that she would lose the ability to hear her children's voices and that she would no longer hear music. The aids changed how she heard herself and heard the world, but at least she heard. The audiologist assured her he believed the loss would slow once she began using the hearing aids, but the fear still niggled at her, especially when she heard something exceptionally beautiful.

She left Thayne's side and crossed the lanai, ducking under the awning for shade where she could stand to the side and watch. Lee was a skilled guitar player, his long fingers moving along the neck and string to produce melodies and cascades of notes that captured her attention and wouldn't let her go. Lee had his head down, his attention toward his right hand on the guitar's neck, but not focused on it. His eyes were partially closed and he swayed slightly to the music. He was wrapped in his music; she had seen that expression on the faces of many musicians through the years.

Then Lee raised his head, opened his eyes, and saw her. A slow smile spread his lips and reached all the way to his blue eyes. He sat up straighter and shifted the guitar on his thigh, and without looking away from her, launched into a fast beat melody, his fingers sliding and picking at the strings and his boot heel thumping on the cement patio. The distinct beginning of a song drew the attention of everyone seated around, and although some came to sit or stand close by, Lee kept his focus on her.

Then he began to sing.

She recognized the melody, and once he sang the first few lyrics, she knew it was "Somebody Like You" by Keith Urban. She already knew most of the lyrics, and heat crawled up Missy's chest to her throat, and flared in her cheeks. She blinked and looked away, anywhere but at him. Across the lanai, Missy caught her brother's deep scowl as he glowered at his friend, a beer clenched in his fist. Susan stood beside him and leaned closer to say something but Betsy's head hid her lips. Thayne's scowl deepened and he shook his head.

The more Lee played, the more the music wrapped around her and vibrated in the air. It was tangible. Beautiful. Thayne looked from Lee to her, and Missy turned away, hoping he didn't see the color in her cheeks from where he stood. Despite herself, she focused again on Lee and the way his long fingers slid and shifted over the strings, the way he swayed back and forth with the upbeat music and the way his boot tapped out the beat while he sang.

"*I want to love somebody, love somebody like you...*"

He finished the song with a quick relay of notes and a final flourished strum, and everyone around clapped. Lee still hadn't looked away from her, and she only managed to break eye contact when Levi skirted through people and chairs to slam into her legs, Jeremiah not far behind. Jeremiah stopped beside Lee, staring at the guitar.

"Was that you playin'?" he asked.

"Yep," Lee answered with a smile, his arms folded on the top curves of the guitar body. "Are you Jeremiah by chance?"

Jeremiah nodded and Lee winked, then took the guitar in hand and started a new song. "Jeremiah was a bullfrog, he was a good friend of mine..."

Jeremiah laughed and sat on the lounge where Missy had been, watching Lee play with wide-eyed wonderment. Missy picked up Levi and settled him on her hip so they could listen, thankful for the distraction.

"You want to tell me what the hell that was all about?"

Lee set his guitar case behind the seats of his truck and slammed the extended cab and passenger's door before turning to Thayne. "What the hell was what all about?"

"You and Missy."

Lee shrugged and walked around the front of his F150, his friend right behind him. "You're going to have to be more specific, Thayne. I've spent the last four hours here."

Thayne scowled and shoved his hands into his pockets, glancing back toward the house. "You know damn well what I mean. Susan's setup was a mistake. You gotta quit playing along like it meant something."

Lee rested his arm on the open window edge of his driver's side door. "Maybe it did mean something. Thayne, Missy and I met at Low Places before I even knew she was the woman Susan wanted me to meet and before I knew she was your sister. Hell, it was before she knew she'd even been setup." Lee shook his head and motioned back toward the house where he knew Missy was inside. "Man, you're sister is a beautiful woman."

"You don't think I know that?"

"Do you?"

Thayne huffed. "She decided to move out here to rebuild her life."

Lee scowled. "Just what do you think that means, Thayne? Yeah, I get that she lost her husband, and no one should lose someone they love, but does that mean she's not supposed to live?"

"Yeah, but not with—"

"Me?" Lee arched his eyebrows and stared at his friend. He shook his head. "Thayne, do you have issues with Susan setting Missy up with a guy, or is your issue with *me* being the guy?"

"No, man, don't take it like that. It's just..." Thayne marched away from the truck, and spun back when he was a few feet away. "You're younger than *me*, and Missy is..."

"Older?"

"Yeah."

Lee shook his head and yanked open his truck door, swinging up into the cab. By the time he slammed the door shut, Thayne had come back to the side of the truck. He didn't look happy, but at least now he looked more contrite than pissed off. Lee draped his hands through his steering wheel and stared at the Ford emblem in the center, trying to decide what to say. He didn't want to risk a friendship, but he'd be damned if he gave up a chance to know Missy.

"This isn't high school, Thayne," he finally said, looking out the window. "Are you asking me not to date your sister?"

Thayne looked out across the flat prairie leading away from the cluster of houses. "What if I am?

"Then I'm going to say that's up to Missy. You're the one pointing out her age; I think she's old enough to make up her own mind." Lee started the truck, the 8-cylinder engine roaring to life. "This isn't about Susan and her setup. You've got some personal demons to deal with."

"This has nothing to do with me." Thayne looked toward the house, looking for the world like he was afraid they would be heard even though they were thirty feet from the front door. "Don't go there."

"That goes both ways."

Thayne said nothing more. Lee put the truck in reverse and backed out of the driveway. He offered a final wave before driving away, a wave Thayne didn't return.

CHAPTER FOUR

"THIS IS A GORGEOUS HOUSE, MISSY."

Susan turned a full circle in the center of the massive kitchen in Missy's new home. Rich, red, two-foot square tiles covered the expanse of the floor and through most of the uniquely styled home. Four sections of the home formed a large square around a center garden courtyard. A pool took up half the courtyard, the other half both tiled lanai and lush grass with large canvas shade panels. Each section of the house served a different purpose, the north main section holding the kitchen, dining rooms, and foyer. The west section had four bedrooms, each with its own bathroom. The south section had a fifth bedroom and an impressive master suite, along with an office den. The final east section held a family room, living room, and game room.

The kitchen was well appointed, but the house itself had an authentic Santa Fe feel, designed to appear older than it was. Missy fell in love with the home immediately, but not so much with the decorating.

"I keep waiting for the downside," Missy said, going to the six-foot, paned sliding doors that opened from the breakfast nook area into the center courtyard. "It really is gorgeous, and hardly needs any work other than refreshing the pool and painting some walls. More cosmetic than anything."

"There has to be a downside?"

Missy chuckled and shrugged. "For the price I paid, yeah. I kept waiting for them to demand more than the asking price. Or for something to blow up."

"I wouldn't look a gift horse in the mouth."

Missy turned to her sister-in-law. "Do you know anything about them? The McNeils? I mean, is this place haunted or something?"

Susan laughed and walked back across the furniture-free space. Betsy played on the floor with some toys Susan had brought along, and Susan crouched beside her, looking up at Missy. "Not haunted near as I can tell, but we've only lived in Indian Prairie a couple of years. Someone from here might tell you better." She grinned wide. "Like Lee. He's lived here his whole life."

The sound of a heavy-duty truck coming down the driveway interrupted her before she came up with an adequate response. Missy headed out of the kitchen toward the front foyer. "Must be the supplies I ordered."

"Speak of the devil," Susan mumbled, but when Missy looked back, Susan's attention was fully focused on Betsy.

Missy opened the main of the double mission-style front doors just as Lee Henry came around the front of his truck parked beneath one of the old Oklahoma Buckeye trees around the house. His head was turned to the left, and he appeared to be taking in the details of the house, squinting slightly in the intense sunlight. Missy leaned her shoulder into the doorjamb and crossed her arms, waiting for him to look toward the door. When he did, he flashed a wide smile and his step quickened toward the shade offered by the covered entry porch.

"This is a pleasant surprise," he said, skipping the two steps leading onto the porch, his long legs spanning the height with ease. "I wondered who had bought this place."

Missy nodded. "My name wasn't on the delivery request?"

"Nope. Probably since Ed Elkins, your contractor, put in the order." He took a deep breath and released it through his nose. "It really is nice to see you again, Missy."

"It's been all of two days—"

"I'd see you every day if I had my way."

He had a compelling knack for making her blush, probably because she knew she shouldn't place any value in his flirting. Missy cleared her throat and looked past him to the truck. "So, do you work for..." Then the emblem on his tee shirt, reading *John Henry and Sons Hardware, Feed and Seed, and Ranch Supplies*, registered. "Oh."

Lee chuckled. "Yes, ma'am. In a manner of speaking." He looked into the house. "Don't suppose you'd mind if I took a look around? It's been a lot of years since I've been here."

"Sure." She stepped back into the house to let him pass. "Did you know the McNeils?"

"Sort of." He crossed the foyer and looked right and left down the corridors leading to either the kitchen or the dining room. "My brother John Jr. was a grade ahead of Jack and Isabella O'Neil, the kids of the people who owned this house." He took a right and headed for the kitchen, and Missy followed. He went all the way into the huge space before stopping, taking in the details of the hand-carved cabinetry and custom tile work. "Gorgeous."

"I fell in love with so much of the house when I saw it."

Lee nodded. "I understand why."

"I was just telling Susan..." She looked around, seeing no sign now of her sister-in-law. "I was curious why the price was so low. Makes me wonder why they gave it up for so much below the value. Is it haunted?" she asked with a small chuckle.

"Nah." Lee leaned against the counter edge, hands in his pockets and his ankles crossed. "They decided to move to Maine to live near their daughter. She moved there a few years ago when she married Jesse Mitchell. He's from here, too. His mother and step-father used to have a place a couple of miles from here."

Missy nodded and came around the counter to stand conversationally close, but not too close. She wasn't blind to her attraction but had decided she was mature enough to not let it override her common sense. *Mature*. Now, there was an apropos word. "I forget what it's like to live in a small town where everyone knows everyone."

"Your people are from near Oklahoma City, right?"

Missy nodded and crossed her arms. "Indiahoma. It's really kind of between Oklahoma City and Wichita Falls, and about the size of Indian Prairie. I suppose that's why it feels comfortable here, even though I've been in Boston for so many years." She tilted her head and tried to look scrutinizing. "Speaking of small towns, Mr. Henry." That earned her wide eyes, arched eyebrows, and a wide grin. "Why is it I've been here over two months and I never saw you once, yet in a handful of days our paths have crossed three times?"

"I just came home," he answered without pause. He looked at her, then away with a squint at the corner of his eyes. "I've been in the Army the last six years, serving in Kabul mostly. I'm separating from service officially in another week or so."

Missy drew in a slow breath and released it through her nose before speaking. "I'm probably not the first to say this, but thank you."

He turned back to her. "For what?"

"Serving." Missy smiled. "My husband was a Navy man, but he left shortly after Wyatt was born. Said he'd already missed too much of Jude's childhood and didn't want to miss any more. My daddy served in Viet Nam; Army, like you. I appreciate what you gave up to serve."

"You're welcome." He sniffed, looking uncomfortable, and stepped away from the counter. "Looks like you're doing work before moving in."

"I figured it would be easier that way. With four boys, I would rather not have tools...and paint...lying around. I'd invite you on a tour before you unload, but since you've been here—"

"Sure," he said with a wide grin that set off a dimple on each cheek. "It's been a while."

With a flash of heat up her throat, Missy realized asking Lee to stroll through her new home with her might be a very bad idea. Especially because she knew inevitably they would run into Susan, and she didn't trust her sister-in-law to hush up. She loved Susan, but sometimes Susan lacked any tact whatsoever.

The kitchen gave way to a short hallway with the laundry and storage room extending off the side of the house. A door there led to the side yard that was fenced in like a pen like perhaps the previous owners might have had a dog, and the garage. The hall rounded the corner into the bedroom wing. The bedrooms were on the interior side of the house, with each having sliding doors that opened into the courtyard. She had ordered braces and locks because she didn't want the boys, especially the younger ones, to be able to get into the courtyard without her knowing it. Not until they were all very profi-cient in swimming. Large, led-glass windows lined the exterior side, allowing light patterns to dance along the walls. The bedrooms were grouped two and two, with a short hall between them and another door to the courtyard. The yard could be accessed easily from nearly anywhere in the house.

"I brought the boys by yesterday," she explained as they passed the open doors. "They worked out amongst themselves who would have each room. Jude and Wyatt on one side, and Jeremiah and Levi on the other, the youngest closer to my bedroom."

"I bet they liked that."

"Mmmm. I figured they had been wonderful through all the chaos of moving out here in the middle of the school year, leaving the only home they've ever known, and staying with Thayne. They deserved to have some choices."

She nearly jumped, but hid her surprise in her step, when Lee's hand pressed to the small of her back. It was an unassuming touch, but it had been so long since a man had walked beside her like that, it caught her off guard. "It must have been tough for them, losing their daddy."

The familiar lump formed in the back of Missy's throat, but she forced it down and nodded. "Jude and Wyatt especially. Jeremiah doesn't remember much of Daniel, and Levi wasn't old enough when Daniel died to ever have his own memories. Some days I'm glad for that because he doesn't miss someone he never knew. Some days it breaks my heart that a child of Daniel's won't remember him."

Lee stopped and turned to face her, and she instinctively turned with him but kept her face turned down. She knew she hadn't tamped down all her emotion, and it would show in her eyes.

"You are an amazing woman, Missy."

The weight of his voice pressed against her, made her heart feel cramped in her chest. She moved away and back down the hall again toward the next bend and the next portion of the house. She cleared her throat before she could speak again.

"I love the fact each boy can have his own room, and we still have a space for guests. My folks are gone, but Daniel's parents can come whenever they want to visit. They live in Wichita Falls. This much space is so different compared to our townhouse in Boston. The boys were doubled up, and Jude and Wyatt slept in what used to be a den. I guess that's why I like this house so much. So much space."

A voice in her head whispered she was talking too much and too fast, but she couldn't seem to slow herself down. She walked past the open doorway of the guest bedroom and caught sight of Susan and Betsy sitting in the middle of the queen bed she'd purchased with the house. Overall, the house wasn't furnished, but the McNeils had said there was far more furniture in the house than they needed and offered to let Missy keep whatever she wanted. The extra room furnishings helped out, and she didn't have to worry right away.

Susan looked up and winked, and smiled wider when Lee stepped into the doorway beside Missy.

"Hey, Susan. I didn't know you were here." He raised his hand in greeting.

"Oh, don't mind Betsy and me," she said with a wave. "We're just checkin' things out, aren't we, baby girl?"

Betsy didn't really care. She was stretched out on her back with her feet in the air, babbling to herself. Missy gave Susan one more "Please hush up" look before moving away from the door. The master suite took up more than half of the section, set between the guest bedroom and an office den on the other side. The eight-panel, extra-wide, double doors were open, with the patio doors to the courtyard open to let the air flow through the house. It had been closed up for nearly a year before Missy bought it, and although the realtor had been in, she liked the fresh air.

"This is the master suite," she said with the intent of walking right past the open doors. "It's way too big for—"

She stopped, realizing Lee no longer followed but had turned left into the room. He crossed the large space, void of any furniture, his boot steps echoing off the tile floor. Lee stopped in the open patio doorway, his hands pushed into his back pockets.

"I don't think you have a bad view anywhere."

"Can you see now why I keep waiting for the other shoe to drop?" She stood in the hall just outside the bedroom. "It's just too good to be true."

"Don't worry." Lee turned on the heels of his boots and grinned. "Honestly. Mr. McNeil pretty much built this house, bit by bit, over the last thirty-five years. Everything you paid him was pure profit in his pocket, and he didn't care about making the most they could. They cared more about being with family." He sighed and looked around the room. "He built it for his family, and once his family wasn't here anymore, it didn't matter."

"That's beautiful, Lee."

He chuckled and shrugged, crossing the bedroom back to her. "Spend your life singing country songs and you develop a sentimental streak." When he reached her, he took her hand, not looking away from her face. "Come on, show me the rest."

By the time they reached the next corner, her heart had slowed to a staccato. She took him through the game room, with the slate pool table she'd inherited with the house. She imagined a jukebox in the corner and some games for the boys. They toured the family room and another living room before they reached the dining room and foyer back to the door.

"Well, I'll get your delivery in. Dad is probably wondering what's taking me so long."

"I'm sorry to keep you—"

"I'm not," he stopped her, grinning down at her with the smile that had melted her insides more than once. Lee looked toward the open front door, then down to their still joined hands. "I'm playing Thursday and Friday night down at Low Places. I'd like it if you came."

Missy folded her free hand around their joined ones and sucked in a breath when his grip tightened. She licked her lips and pressed them together, trying to find a way to ask what she needed to ask. "What are we doing here, Lee?"

"We're holding hands." He stepped closer, until the scent of wood and molasses on his clothes wrapped around her. "And I'm asking you on a date."

Missy raised her head, her pulse almost violent at the base of her throat. "And that's where I get confused."

"Nothing confusing about it, Missy." His lips drew her attention when he spoke, and Missy had to blink to look away. "I can pick you up at six. We'll go to dinner first."

"I should say no..." She looked into his blue eyes instead. "But I'm going to say yes anyway."

CHAPTER FIVE

"Mom?"

Missy jumped and gasped, turning enough where she sat on the edge of her clothing-littered bed to look toward Jude. He stood in the open doorway of her bedroom, hands pushed deep into his pockets, a deep scowl digging across his forehead.

"What's up, sweetheart?" she asked, hoping she sounded calmer than she felt. She'd just had another argument with Thayne, and her nerves hadn't calmed down yet.

Jude came into the room, still scowling, and eyed the stacks of clothing. Her search for something appropriate to wear had instigated the argument; one more chance for her little brother to inform her of his opinion regarding her date with Lee. She'd told him to mind his own business, but in truth, Missy wasn't sure her heart was in it. Hadn't she come to Oklahoma to be with family? Why alienate them now? Was the thrill of being around Lee Henry worth the fighting?

"Are you going out?"

Missy sighed and glanced at the clothes around her. She was

being foolish. How hard was it to pick out something to wear? "I was going to...but I don't think I am now."

"Is that what you were arguing with Uncle Thayne about?"

"Oh, I'm sorry you heard that, Jude." Missy looked away and rubbed her fingers across her forehead. "It was, yes."

"He doesn't think you should spend time with Lee Henry." It wasn't a question anymore.

"No, I guess he doesn't."

Jude sat beside her, and not for the first time, Missy marveled at how much he had grown. He was eye-to-eye with her now, and since his Dad was tall, Missy had no doubt Jude would be tall, too. The thought of Daniel tightened her throat, and she wondered if she'd ever think of her lost husband without the same reaction.

"Do you like Lee?" he asked, looking her in the eye.

Part of her was surprised Jude knew as much as he did, but then again, Thayne hadn't exactly been subtle. She reminded herself Jude was no longer a little boy, and since Daniel's death, he had grown far beyond his thirteen years; a truth that saddened her, because he deserved a childhood. Missy smiled and took her son's hand, squeezing it.

"I don't know Lee all that well yet," she answered as truthfully as she could. "It's hard to tell, but I think I might."

"And Uncle Thayne doesn't think you should?"

Missy laughed and shrugged. "I guess. I don't know. I can't figure out your uncle right now, sweetheart. I've tried, but he sounds an awful lot like your grandfather. *Because I said so,*" she said, dropping her voice low to mimic her father.

Jude chuckled, and that made Missy smile. Then just as quickly, Jude's expression was serious and he squeezed her hand. If anyone were to show up at the bedroom doorway, he'd probably drop her hand like a hot potato, but she welcomed his simple affection. Someday soon he might consider himself too old to hold his mother's hand.

"Mom, I don't think Dad would mind."

Instant tears burned her eyes and Missy had to swallow hard. She looked away, across the room at anything but the mirror over her bureau. How could a thirteen-year-old boy nail so eloquently the doubt that had kept her from sleeping well for two days? Missy swiped her fingertips across her cheeks, smearing her tears over her skin.

"I didn't mean to make you cry."

"I know," she whispered. "It's not you, sweetheart. I just...my heart hurts sometimes."

They sat quietly for a few minutes, Jude tense and still beside her while Missy tried to make sense of the thoughts in her head and the emotions in her heart. After a bit, Jude leaned until his shoulder touched hers. "Mom..."

She sniffed and tried to smile, looking at her eldest son.

"I think you should go."

"You said your dad wouldn't mind," she repeated. "What about you, Jude?"

He shook his head. "I don't mind." Then he smiled. "I kind of like Lee. He plays the guitar really good."

Missy laughed and wiped away the last of the tears from her cheeks. "Well, if I'm going to go I'd better get changed. You go check on your brothers, okay? Make sure they aren't giving Aunt Susan too much of a hard time."

Jude nodded and stood, heading to the door. Halfway he stopped and turned back. "You don't have to get all dressed up to look pretty, Mom. Just wear jeans and..." He paused, scanning the stack of clothes, then pointed. "...that white shirt. You'll look great." He didn't wait for her reply before he bolted again for the door.

Missy smiled and drew in a long, slow breath before she picked up the shirt her son had pointed out. She pursed her lips and nodded. "Not bad. Not bad at all."

"What did you expect me to do, man? Sit at the curb and honk?"

Lee stared down Thayne, waiting for him to provide a sufficient answer, but all he got was a dark glare from his friend of nearly six years. Thayne pressed his lips together into thin lines, his jaw clenched. Lee shook his head, a humorless laugh the only thing he could do.

"Okay, maybe you *did*."

Susan called from somewhere in the back of the house, and after a few more long moments, Thayne turned away and headed for the kitchen without another word to Lee. With his way cleared, Lee stepped into the house and shut the door. The evening had turned cold and a wind blew through the neighborhood. Moments later, Susan came into the foyer, shaking her head.

"I'm sorry, Lee."

Lee sighed and pushed his hands into his pockets. "Tell me, Suz, does he really expect me not to see Missy just because he doesn't like it?"

"Today?" Susan shrugged. "Yeah, I guess he does. But, he'll get over it."

"Will he?"

She smiled and winked. "He's going to have to unless he wants every female in this house ticked at him."

"Well, I'm not going to sneak around, pretending like I'm ashamed for wanting to see Missy. I already told him this isn't up to him."

"I know," she said with a wry smile and laid her hand on Lee's arm. "I'll go tell Missy you're here."

He nodded his thanks, and she headed up the stairs, meeting Missy's two oldest boys halfway. Jude led the way, with Wyatt not far behind, a pattern Lee had noted days earlier when he'd been at the barbeque. Wherever Jude went, Wyatt was sure to follow. It reminded Lee of him and his brother Rickey, three years older than him, except in that case, Lee had been the shadow until they were both in their teens.

"Hi, Mr. Henry," Jude said, hopping to the floor from two steps up.

Wyatt considered it but took the last two steps instead.

"Hey, guys" Lee answered, smiling at the boys. He saw a lot of Missy in both of them. "You can call me Lee. It's okay."

Jude nodded, and when Wyatt saw him nod, he nodded as well. "Mom will be down in a few minutes. She's almost done."

On cue, Lee heard footsteps at the top of the stairs and looked up. His breath caught in his chest. Every time he saw Missy Colton, his pulse did this funny jump. Something as simple as faded blue jeans, the kind that hugged her curves in all the right ways, and a white, loose-fitting shirt tied at her waist was as enticing as lingerie. Her blond hair fell loose to her shoulders, with natural waves and curls framing her face. He had to look appreciative because color bloomed in her cheeks as she came down the stairs.

"Come on, Wy," Jude said, grabbing his brother's arm. "Have fun, Mom," he called as he drew Wyatt into the kitchen. "Goodbye, Lee!"

Missy stopped at the bottom of the stairs, her hand still on the banister. "Hi," she said softly, then glanced back up as Susan came down with Betsy in her arms.

"Oh, don't mind me," Susan gushed, sliding between them when she reached the landing. "You two have fun. Don't do anything I wouldn't do." She stopped and looked over her shoulder with a grin. "Which leaves the evening wide open."

As soon as Susan disappeared around the corner, Lee closed the space between them and took her hand, leaning in to press a kiss to her cheek close enough to her lips that he felt her breath. Lee held his cheek to hers, unwilling to break the contact quite yet. That funny little switch that had been playing havoc with his head all week pointed out to him how easy it would be to move just a little to the right and kiss her lips instead.

"I've missed you," he whispered before pulling back.

"It's only been two days," she said with a smile, a beautiful splash of color on her cheeks.

"No, it's been two painfully long days."

It would be so easy to lean back in and touch those lips...

Lee stepped back but kept her hand in his. As annoyed as Thayne was over Lee coming into the house to pick up Missy, Lee figured a kiss in the foyer might send Thayne over the edge.

"Ready?"

She nodded, and still holding her hand, Lee opened the house door and led her out. He glanced back at the house as they walked to his truck parked along the curb, and caught sight of Thayne standing in the front room window, watching. Lee refused to slip into any kind of antagonization`, but he didn't drop Missy's hand either. Susan was right; Thayne had to get over it.

He opened the passenger door of his truck and offered his hand to help her in. Once again, Lee had to fight the urge to lean in and kiss her. He wondered if she knew what she did to him, how she drew him, like a moth to flame. He'd wanted to kiss a woman before, but not with this persistent pull. Once again, logic told him that the driveway of her brother's house wasn't the time or place.

But there would be a time and place...soon...or Lee might just go insane.

CHAPTER SIX

"Can I ask you something?"

Missy paused in her fork exploration of the last of her bread pudding dessert and looked across the table at Lee, the candlelight dancing over her features. She was so damn beautiful. "Haven't we been asking questions all evening?" she said with a smile.

Lee chuckled and nodded, wiping his mouth with his napkin. "I reckon we have."

Missy set down her fork and sat back, her hands in her lap. "Let's see...you know I studied English—a near pointless degree—in college, and I know you went directly into the military out of high school, but you are working on a degree in business management under the GI Bill. You know I met Daniel just before I left for college while he served in the Navy, I know your first serious girlfriend was Rebecca Sampson your senior year in high school. You know I learned to dance back in the dark ages, when I was in high school—you know, when you were in elementary school—" Lee shook his head and chuckled at her exaggerated expression. "And I know you taught yourself to play guitar starting when you were eleven and your brother Mark gave you his old Ibanez flattop." She paused and tilted her head to look toward the ceiling, mocking a deep look of thought. "You know I'm planning on possibly putting that degree to good use one of these days, maybe write a book or something, and I know you plan on taking over your father's business full time within the next two years because none of your siblings seem particularly interested in the business end. I know you were born and raised here in Indian Prairie, just like the last three generations of Henrys, and you know I grew up in Indiahoma, also three generations strong." She smiled and winked, and his stomach did a funny clench. "We're both Okies, born and bred."

"I guess we *have* covered a lot of ground."

"I'm not done yet. You're the youngest of seven children. Shelley is the oldest, then Beatrice—but I'll call her Bea if I know what's good for me—John Junior, Mark—whom I'll meet later tonight because he's in the band—Rickey, Ellie, and then you. The baby."

"You're very good."

Missy tapped her temple. "Memory like a steel trap. Oh!" she said with a pointed finger in the air, then ticked off each new name on a new finger. "I know you like Johnny Cash, Tim McGraw, and George Strait, can't stand chick country, but love Adele and Allison Kraus."

Lee laughed so loud that people three tables over turned to look in their direction. "There's nothing else you need to know about me. My life is an open book." He spread his arms, then dropped them onto his thighs.

"No, that's good. Helps me figure you out." Missy lifted her glass of wine, the same glass she'd nursed all evening, and watched him over the rim as she took a sip. The way she rubbed her lips together as she set the glass down made his insides warm. "So, to ask permission to ask, this must be a whopper of a question." She flipped a wave of blond hair behind one ear, revealing the hearing aid nestled inside; the source of his question. "Go ahead."

Lee sat forward and rested his arm on the table, pausing one more beat before asking, "How much of your hearing have you lost?" He immediately hated how the question sounded and tried to compensate. "I don't think you've always—" Lee stopped short and shook his head. "Okay, I'm going to shut up now. I'm sorry," he said and reached his hand across the table to take hers.

She met his hand halfway, and he loved how small and warm it felt in his. The first time he'd reached for her hand at the beginning of dinner, he'd noted her glance around, as if making sure no one was watching. She didn't look around this time.

"No, it's okay." She laughed, but it didn't hold much humor. Pity, maybe, for his bungled attempt at asking a simple question. "I've heard worse. One person once told me I couldn't be losing my hearing because I *sounded normal*. As if when you lose your hearing, you suddenly lose the ability to speak." She shook her head again and sighed, focusing on him. "About thirty percent. It started when I was in my late twenties."

He squeezed her fingers, wishing he could do more. She huffed and drew back her hand to adjust the napkin in her lap. Although she met his gaze, she'd just as quickly looked away, and explained further while staring at the salt shaker.

"I'll answer the inevitable question so you don't have to ask," she said with a smile that didn't quite reach her eyes. "It's hereditary, a condition called otosclerosis. It's a malformation of the bones in my middle ear." She tapped her cheek just in front of her ear. "Most prevalent in women, so hopefully my boys won't have to worry about it." She chuckled and shook her head. "Sorry, that's probably more than you wanted to know."

"No, I—"

"Can I get the two of you anything else?"

Lee looked up to Callie Hayden, not their original waitress, and returned her smile. They'd gone to school together, and dated casually when he was back in town a couple years after he'd enlisted, and with an internal wince, he remembered she had emailed him, and told him to call her when he got back into town for good. He looked across to Missy, who shook her head.

"No, we're good. Thanks, Callie. Did Meredith leave?"

"Nah, she's just on break. I'm covering for her." Callie waved in the general direction of the back of *High Steaks*, the only steakhouse in Indian Prairie. Not exactly high class for a date, but short of driving to Tulsa, it was the best he could do for the night. "I didn't realize you were back for good. Are you back for good?"

"Yep. It's official come next week." Lee paused and extended his hand toward Missy, who he noted hadn't said a word since Callie came up to the table. "Callie, this is Missy Colton. She's new in Indian Prairie."

"Hey," Callie said and set her hand on Lee's shoulder. "Lee and I are old friends, hope you don't mind me butting in." She pointed at Missy, squinting her eyes. "I think I've seen you 'round here and there. You got a parcel of boys, don't you?"

Missy folded her hands in her lap under the table and looked up, her smile strained but still honest. "Yes, four."

"Well, ain't that sweet of Lee to show you around. Did you and your husband transfer here to the base?" She didn't give Missy the chance to answer before she looked back to Lee and slid the bifold out of her apron. "Did you want the check split? Meredith said all her tables were date couples—"

Lee snatched the bifold from her hand. "No split. Thank you, Callie." He slid a glance at Missy. The candlelight did little to disguise the bloom of color in her cheeks.

"Split is fine," Missy said, reaching for her purse on the back of her chair.

"No split," Lee said again.

"Oh, okay," Callie said softly and cleared her throat.

Lee shifted and took his wallet from his back pocket, retrieved his Amex, and handed the bifold back to her. "Thanks."

As soon as Callie walked away, Lee reached across the table for Missy's hand, but she diverted away and stood, lifting her purse from the back of her chair.

"Missy—"

"I'll be right back," she said with only a quick glance at him before she stood and headed for the restrooms at the back of the restaurant.

Callie returned a minute later, bifold and his card in hand. She looked contrite when she glanced at Missy's empty chair and set the bifold on the table. "I didn't mean anything by what I said, Lee. I thought maybe Meredith had it wrong, but she just came back and said the two of you were real friendly; I just thought since she's—"

"She's my date, Callie. Let's just leave it at that, okay?" Lee added the tip to the bill and signed it, putting the card back in his wallet. He saw Missy weaving her way back through the tables, so he stood as he handed the bifold back to Callie. She still looked apologetic. "Don't worry about it, just don't say anything else. Okay?"

Callie nodded. "Okay. I really am sorry."

Missy met up with them, but instead of reaching for her hand, Lee moved past Callie and wrapped his arm around Missy's waist, drawing her against him. Her eyes shifted to look past him to Callie, but he turned them just enough so Callie was out of sight and Missy had to look up at him. "Ready to go?"

"You're subtle," she said with a soft laugh, but he got his reward when she slid one arm under his and laid her other hand against his heart.

"There's nothing subtle about wanting to get my arms around you." Lee raised his hand to touch her cheek, one of her curls tickling his fingers. "I will admit to one regret, however."

She arched her eyebrows. "Oh?"

Lee leaned in so he could speak softer, near her ear. "I regret I've never kissed you, Missy Colton, because that's all I've wanted to do all night...and in the middle of High Steaks isn't exactly where I intend to start."

He heard the undeniable catch in her breath, and her fingers curled into his shirt, the simple reaction stirring something strong and powerful in him. When he leaned back, she looked up at him, color once again staining her cheeks. There was something intensely sexy about Missy Colton's blush; it drove him to distraction.

"When do you intend to start?" she asked in a whisper.

"That is a very good question," he answered. "I don't rightly know, but trust me, when *I* know, *you'll* know."

The patrons of Low Places cheered and shouted, singing along with the chorus that seemed to be the theme song for the bar while Lee belted out the words and hammered his guitar.

"...think I'll slip on down to the—" He paused and grinned when the entire population of the bar cried out "Oasis!", then went back to the mic. "Oh, I've got friends in low places!"

The energy in the bar was tangible and contagious. Missy stood on the edge of the dance floor, clapping and sometimes singing along, at least until the sound got overwhelming and she had to take a step back. She hadn't paid attention the first night she'd been here, and although she knew Lee had played, she didn't remember this kind of churning fervor.

One thing she knew for certain, Lee Henry—on stage—singing his heart out, forehead slick with sweat, his entire body involved in the performance, had to be one of the most arousing things she had ever seen and stirred many, many memories from her younger years. He caught her eye more than once across the heads of his screaming fans, and would always wink or smile so she knew he'd seen her, and every time her heart jumped a beat.

Regardless of his effect on the crowd, and her, the distance of the span of the bar had given Missy some perspective she lacked, it seemed, whenever Lee was within touching distance. How had it become so easy to take his hand? To flirt mercilessly? To let him hold her close? How did three chance meetings lead to a tactile familiarity she couldn't deny? She let him bring her close, let him touch her and tease her, and more than that, she *wanted* him to be that close.

Then she gained distance and perspective.

Thayne had pointed out, more than once, the age difference between them; he failed to realize she wasn't blind to the reality. She was aware of it every time she looked at Lee, and wondered what he saw when he looked at her. Although Thayne had pointed out the obvious, she hadn't felt the sting of reality quite as sharply as she had tonight when the waitress at the restaurant had innocently assumed they couldn't possibly be on a date. A man like Lee Henry dating an older woman—a widow— with four children, seemed preposterous to even her, and she was the one with him.

And yet, she knew if he were to come to her right now, she'd welcome his hand over hers or his arm around her waist.

The idea of kissing him sent her pulse racing.

He finished the song and the crowd cheered, their thunderous clapping enough to make Missy wince. Places like this were a strange kind of torture for her. She loved the music, loved the dancing, loved the life...but no matter how much her hearing aids were supposed to buffer excess sound, there was only so much they could do, and they were, after all, created to enhance and magnify sound.

"Thank you," Lee shouted into the mic to be heard over the crowd. He braced the neck of his guitar with his left hand, and raised his right, asking the crowd to quiet. They died down slightly, but not completely. He wiped his forehead with the back of his arm and chuckled when some female voice on the other side of the room shouted out her love. "Okay, one more song then we're going to take a short break." The crowd booed, and Missy laughed. So did Lee. "I said short. We'll be back in half an hour." He stepped back and said something to his bandmates, then started strumming his guitar before returning to the mic.

This melody was slower and softer, and the crowd immediately adjusted. Couples paired off and came together on the dance floor, swaying to the ballad tune. Lee leaned into the mic, waited until Missy looked at him, then grinned and began to sing.

"Hey, pretty girl, won't you look my way?"

Missy swallowed hard and delicious heat crawled up her body to her throat, and into her face.

He continued to strum the cords, but stepped back from the mic and motioned for his brother Mark to step toward him. Still playing, he said something to his brother, who grinned and nodded, and Lee slipped the guitar strap over his head, handing it to his brother. Mark stepped to the mic, and Lee hopped down from the stage into the crowd. Missy lost sight of him. Then he stepped through the crowd, his full attention on her, as Mark picked up where Lee had left off; his deeper voice taking over.

By the time Lee reached her, Missy thought her heart would pound its way out of her chest. She saw the appreciative stares of the women Lee passed, but he never once looked away from her. When he was close enough, he reached for her, and Missy stepped into his arms. Lee pulled her close, his hand pressed to the small of her back, and he swayed them to the music. Now she didn't hear his brother at all. Only Lee's voice, singing softly near her ear.

"Hey, pretty girl, it feels so right. Just like it's meant to be. All wrapped up in my arms so tight..."

Missy raised her arms and wrapped them around his shoulders, lacing her fingers into his damp hair. Heat radiated off his body, but it didn't keep her from wanting to be as close to him as possible. Every reservation, every hesitation she'd been so clear on just minutes before disappeared in the tenor of his voice.

Lee stopped singing, his cheek rough with stubble brushing hers. The hard pounding of his heart competed with hers, his chest pressed against her breasts. He said her name, and she curled her grip in his hair. She felt lightheaded and as giddy as a child, hoping he would end the anticipation, yet terrified he would do just that. Lee brought his hands to her face, cupping her jaw, and pulled back to look down at her. His blue eyes were dark and intense.

"I don't think I can take it anymore," he said, his voice cutting through the cacophony around her. "God help me, Missy, I'm dying to kiss you."

Missy managed to swallow and licked her dry lips, his gaze shifting down to her mouth, and she swore she felt his breath shorten. "Is this where it starts?" she asked, trying to smile, mimicking his words from earlier in the evening.

He grinned, dimples forming on his cheeks. "I sure as hell hope so, sweetheart."

Missy wrapped her arms around him and pressed her palms to his damp back as he leaned in. He paused, his open lips hovering over hers, for one torturous second before he finally covered her mouth with an open kiss. Missy leaned into him, her whole body suddenly heavy and her head light as he kissed her with slow, deliberate, strokes of his tongue and lips. One of them might have groaned; she didn't hear it, but she felt the vibration through the slick connection of their mouths, and it was nearly her undoing.

Right then, she wanted to be anywhere other than a crowded dance floor. Anywhere she could be alone with Lee, and kiss like this forever.

Lee broke the kiss and held his forehead to hers, their rapid breaths mingling in the space between them. "I think that may have been the most dangerous thing I've ever done," he said with a raspy chuckle.

Missy laughed, hating how nervous it sounded, and forced her fingers to relax the grip she had on the back of his shirt. She fought the powerful urge to tip up her chin and touch her lips to his again. "I think I like danger."

Lee groaned and kissed her again, harder and more vehemently than the first, stealing her breath and her strength completely. She tasted the salt of his sweat and the heat of his mouth, and completely ignored the tiny, annoying voice way in the back of her head that said this was a bad, bad idea.

The crowd around them erupted in clapping again, and Missy realized the song was over. So did Lee, because he slowed the kiss again until he ended it with a series of brief touches of his mouth to her cheek, her jaw, and the side of her neck, sending a thousand butterflies to flight in her lower stomach.

He drew back enough to look into her face, a wide smile on his lips and slid his hands down her arms until he could take her hand. "I'm pretty sure I could do that every day for the rest of my life, and it wouldn't be long enough."

CHAPTER SEVEN

Lee's voice and a cool breeze across her face stirred Missy from her sleep, and she groaned at the cold intrusion on her warm cocoon. She buried her nose and refused to open her eyes. Warm fingers brushed her cheeks, and warm lips pressed a kiss to her forehead, then her cheek, flirting with her mouth.

"Wake up, Little Missy. Wake up," he sang softly to the tune of an old Everly Brothers song, and she smiled, still refusing to open her eyes. "Wake up, Little Missy. Wake up."

With a long moan, Missy snaked her arm from beneath her warm cover until she made contact with Lee's arm. She slid her palm over his shoulder until she could hook her hand behind Lee's neck, opening her eyes for just a second before pulling him to her for a kiss. He had told her he knew once he kissed her, he'd want to keep kissing her, and Missy agreed completely.

"If you're trying to convince me to let you stay, I'm an easy sell, sweetheart," he said against her lips, and she felt his smile.

Missy finally relented and opened her eyes in earnest. The front porch light of Thayne and Susan's house backlit Lee, but the interior light of his truck let her see his face. The more she woke up, the more the cold night air bit at her skin and she tugged Lee's jacket closer to her chin.

"What time is it?" she asked, reluctant to move from the warm interior of his cab. The heat still blew, fighting to stave off the chill of the night.

"Nearly one," he answered. "I'm sorry to keep you out so late."

With a long sigh, Missy sat up and let the leather jacket slide, immediately regretting it when the cold air hit her full force. Lee pulled the jacket around her shoulders until she was again bundled in its warmth. She slid her arms into the sleeves, the scent of leather and Lee wrapping around her again.

"It's okay," she said, scooting toward the door, and accepting his hand to help her out of the truck. "I didn't mind."

Once her feet were on the ground, Lee wrapped her in a firm hug before letting her go so he could shut the truck door and lead her toward the porch. "I'll give you a call tomorrow afternoon. Even if I can't see you until Saturday, I want to talk to you." They reached the porch and he curled his hand around the front door knob but didn't open it yet.

"Mmmm, you're sweet."

She turned her back to the door, putting her between Lee and the wood, and looked up at him. The way he watched her, seemed to study her, made her stomach flutter not for the first—or twentieth— time of the night. Lee raised his arm and rested it on the doorframe, moving in until his body pressed to hers and she had to tilt back her head to look him in the eyes. One corner of his mouth tipped up in a slow smile, and Missy couldn't help but smile back.

"You know we're crazy, right?" she said in a whisper.

"Crazy is just a state of mind." His voice was rough, and low, and Missy fought the shiver when he raised his hand and ran the rough pad of his thumb over her lower lip. "I don't think there's anything crazy here, Missy. No crazier than anyone else."

"I notice you tend to avoid the obvious."

He shook his head, his focus still intent on her mouth. "Not avoiding anything, sweetheart. It doesn't change how I feel." His gaze shifted up so he looked into her eyes. "Does my age bother you that much?"

"It's not about your age bothering me, it's about my age—"

He grinned, and she realized what he'd done. He'd turned her own argument around on her. Missy drew in a slow breath and released it. "Okay, I won't say it *bothers* me—our age difference in general—but it is something to consider. Lee, I'm a mother of four. That alone is something significant to be considered if this continues."

"If?" He arched his dark eyebrows. "Missy, I'm not considering anything about us an 'if'."

"How can you say that having known me a week?"

He grinned wider and shrugged. "I know a sure thing when I see it." His expression hardened and grew more serious. "Sweetheart, if the last several years in the Army taught me anything, it's to not let anything good get away. You might lose your chance tomorrow."

His words hit home, brutally so, and the intense tightening of her chest caught her by surprise. She didn't have enough warning to tamp it down, and it had to show on her face because Lee immediately reacted by taking her face in his hands and pressing a long kiss to her forehead.

"I'm sorry, baby," he whispered. "I'm an ass."

"No," she said, shaking her head in his hold. "I just understand better than most." Missy tipped back her head and saw the honest regret in his eyes. She smiled, hoping it was convincing. "I still think you're crazy, and don't understand why you wouldn't be with someone—"

He effectively silenced her with a kiss that stole her breath along with her ability to argue. Missy gave in to the kiss, and let him take her along for the ride. He kissed thoroughly, deeply, leaving her oblivious to everything else.

Until the door opened behind her and she nearly fell into the house. Lee moved quickly and caught her before she landed on her backside.

Lee growled, glared at Thayne, and hung on to her arms until Missy gained her balance again. Thayne deliberately looked at his watch and arched an eyebrow.

"Thought I heard something. Didn't think you were still out. It's nearly one."

"I know what time it is, Thayne," Missy said, fighting her sigh. She was growing sick of Thayne's passive-aggressive—sometimes blatantly aggressive—attitude about Lee. She moved into Lee's hold and tipped back her head, touching his chin so he would look at her. "I'll talk to you tomorrow." She grinned. "Or, later today."

Lee's features relaxed before he took her up on her offer and kissed her again, though far more subdued than any other time in the evening. He released her and took a backward step out the door. "Goodnight, Thayne," he said, giving a casual salute before heading for his truck.

Thayne shut the door and locked it before Lee reached the end of the walkway. Unwilling to get into it again with Thayne, she turned and headed for the stairs. Thayne called her name when she hit the bottom step, and although she was tempted to keep walking, she stopped and turned, resting her hand on the banister. The sleeves of Lee's jacket hung past her wrists, but it felt good to be enveloped in the smell and warmth.

"What, Thayne?"

He walked to the stairs, hands shoved into his pockets. "I know you think I'm being a jerk—"

"I don't think anything. You *are* being a jerk."

He pressed his lips together and looked away into the dark living room off the foyer, then back to her. "Sissy, I don't want you to get hurt."

The sincerity in his eyes softened Missy's anger but didn't wipe it away completely. She closed her eyes and rubbed her forehead, the jacket sleeve bunching around her wrists. "That's sweet, Thayne, but you don't know I will be."

"Don't you think it's inevitable?"

She opened her eyes again and looked at her brother. "Inevitable? Why would it be inevitable?"

"Do you need me to spell it out?"

"Yes, I do," she snapped, then shook her head and held up her hand. "No, you know what? I don't. I don't want to know your reasons. I want you to trust I know how to make decisions about my own life. I lived for two years in Boston all by myself, Thayne. Just me and the boys. I know how to take care of myself, I know how to make my own choices."

"And you think Lee is a good choice?"

"Why would he be a *bad* choice, Thayne?" she demanded, throwing out her arms. "Give me one good, *viable* reason why I should never see him again. Is he a drunk? Is he a violent man? Is he a womanizer? What?" She pointed a finger at him. "Don't you *dare* tell me it's because he's younger."

"You said it, not me."

"If we can get past it, why can't you?"

Thayne stared, his lips pressed together in a tight line.

Missy threw up her hands and started up the stairs.

"Are you really past it?" he called when she reached the top landing. He waited until she turned and looked down again before continuing. "Tell me, Sissy, honestly. Are you completely okay with the fact he's over a decade younger than you?"

Missy crossed her arms and swallowed, looking away before she focused again on her brother. "Of course not. I can't wrap my head around why he..." She stopped and shook her head. "No. But I'm not so lost in the fact I'm not willing to give it a try."

"Give *what* a try, exactly?" Thayne started up the stairs, and with each step closer, Missy's stomach clenched tighter. "Sis, I swear to you I'm not trying to be cruel. I'm trying to be realistic. Do you honestly, in your heart, in your head, believe a twenty-four-year-old guy wants to take on four kids not his own? Some of which he's not even old enough to have fathered if he wanted to?" He shook his head and sighed. "It sounds cold, but it's reality."

Tears burned Missy's eyes, but she met her brother's stare. "Maybe not *any* twenty-four-year-old, but Lee—"

"Is different? How do you know that? You've known him a week."

Every beautiful, light emotion that had filled her that evening seeped away, leaving Missy feeling empty and cold. "And you've known him a lot longer." Missy swallowed and squared her shoulders, facing Thayne straight on. "I've answered you honestly, Thayne. Now you answer me. Don't talk about other men you've known; only Lee Henry. Your friend for a long time. Do you think Lee is the kind of man to hurt me like that?"

Thayne drew in a breath through his nose and released it. "I've never known him to be a bastard."

Missy nodded and pressed her lips together before she turned away to walk to her door. "You've given me a lot to think about." She didn't turn around again and closed the bedroom door behind her.

The Henry house was dark when Lee pulled into the driveway, and he turned off the engine to drift the last few feet, hoping not to wake the dogs, and thus the whole house. He slid the Ford into neutral behind the Henry and Sons farm truck and eased open the door. Charlie was old, but he had bionic ears and a loud bark.

Just as gingerly, he opened the front door, finding it unlocked as he expected. A light shone into the front hall from the kitchen in the back, a habit Mama had gotten into when Shelley hit her teens, and in over fifteen years, she hadn't stopped as long as there was a chance one of her children would come home late.

Lee made his way through the hall to the kitchen, and stepped wide or to the side to avoid the creaky spots in the floor. The house was over a hundred years old and had more creaky floorboards than not, but the art of avoiding them had been passed down from oldest Henry child to youngest. In the kitchen, he retrieved a glass from the cupboard and a carton of milk from the refrigerator. Mama had made a roast for dinner, the remains on a plate on the top shelf, and Lee stole a pinch of tender meat when he put back the milk.

"Still think you can sneak in the house without your mama hearing?"

Lee grinned and shut the refrigerator door, turning to his mother where she stood in the kitchen doorway, wrapped in her favorite purple chenille robe and wearing the silly bunny slippers his niece Rachel bought her for Christmas the year before.

"Not sneaking. I figure Charlie needs his sleep."

Mama chuckled and looked down at the old basset hound at her feet, his face covered with more white hair than brown. "He was waiting up for you, too." She crossed the kitchen and sat down at the small table tucked under the window. The dining room had a table big enough for nearly the whole family, grandbabies included, but this was traditionally the table for early morning and late night talks. "Mark was home an hour ago."

"I took Missy home," Lee said, taking his glass of milk to the table to sit across from his mother. A plate of peanut butter cookies sat in the middle, and he snagged one. He'd probably eaten a couple hundred cookies since getting home, but in Kabul, he'd missed nothing as much as his mama's cookies.

"Yes, Missy. Mark mentioned her." Even in the dim light of the kitchen, Lee saw the gleam in his mother's eyes.

Lee chewed and swallowed, taking a deep chug of the milk. "Did he now? What did Mark say?"

"That she was pretty, and seemed very nice." She winked and grinned. "And that you seemed completely smitten."

"Mark said smitten?"

"Well, that's my interpretation." She set her elbow on the table and rested her temple against her curled fingers. "Tell me about her."

"Ahhh..." Lee paused, wondering where to begin, and what to say that wouldn't make him sound as smitten as Mark implied. Then again, maybe he was. No...he was. There was no doubt. "She's new to Indian Prairie, moved here a couple of months back, but she's originally from Indiahoma up north of here." His mother nodded, smiling. "She's Thayne's sister."

"Oh!" his mother said with enthusiasm. Thayne and Susan had been out to the ranch on several occasions and were no strangers to the Henry family. Though, Lee wondered if that would change if Thayne didn't adjust his opinion and attitude. "That's nice."

"Um..." Lee realized he was grinning like a fool, and might as well give in to the description of smitten. "She's beautiful. She's funny. She's wonderful." He shrugged and tapped his fingers on the table, looking at his mother. "I guess Mark is right."

"Do you think you could love her?"

"No, I don't think so." Lee shook his head. "I know. Is that crazy, Mama? I mean...I met her a week ago. But, yeah, I'm pretty positive I'm completely in love with her already."

His mother's aged face looked almost dreamy. Erin Henry hadn't had her first baby until she was thirty, and Lee's oldest sister was thirty-eight. Despite the wrinkles on Mama's face, her eyes were still young, her heart was still young, and sometimes even her children couldn't keep up with her.

"I'm happy for you, Lee. I don't think I've ever heard you speak of a girl like this."

"I've never felt like this." Lee drew in a long breath through his nose and released it. "Mama, there's more you should know. It seems to be a big deal to Thayne, and even though she won't admit it, I think Missy worries about it, too."

"What's that, honey?"

He slouched back in his chair and linked his hands together in his lap. "Missy is a widow. Her husband died two years ago."

"Oh, that's terrible," Mama tsked and pressed a weathered hand to her chest. "Bless her heart."

Feeling antsy, Lee shifted forward again and set his hands on the table, looking into her face. "Mama, Missy has four children." His mother's eyes widened, but she didn't say anything. "Her oldest, Jude, is thirteen and the youngest is three."

Mama brought her hands down to her lap and sat quiet for a few moments, and Lee watched, waiting. As much as he was willing to ignore Thayne's bullheaded attitude, he wasn't sure he wanted to fight against Mama if it came to that.

"I suppose it's safe to say there's a decent age difference."

Lee chuckled at his mother's simplified statement. "It's safe to say, yes. But, honestly, I don't know exactly how much. I haven't asked, because it doesn't matter to me, Mama. Yes, I know she's older; old enough to have married after college and have a teenage son." He shrugged and held his hands out, palms up. "Doesn't matter to me."

Mama smiled and reached out to take Lee's hand. "Baby, as long as she's a good woman and she loves you as much as you love her, then it doesn't matter to your daddy and me either."

Lee came out of his chair to lean over and press a kiss to his mother's cheek. "Thank you, Mama."

She sighed and smiled when he sat again. "I could have me four instant grandbabies."

Lee laughed. "Could be. I'm heading to bed. Work in the morning. Love you, Mama."

He kissed his mother's cheek again, and when he glanced back from the hall, she still sat at the table, a warm smile on her lips. Lee inhaled, and let go with the breath some of the niggling worries he'd refused to acknowledge, even though they had been there. Not the worries Thayne had, or even Missy, but without his family Lee knew everyone else's doubts would have been a heavy load to carry. With his family, he could do anything.

Especially for Missy.

Yep, he was smitten.

CHAPTER EIGHT

"I appreciate you comin' down, Miz Colton," Ed Elkins said as Missy climbed out of her Cherokee in the parking lot of John Henry and Sons. "I know you said we could just pick up the new front lock, but since they don't have a match to the one you got now, you'll need to see what they've got."

"No problem, Mr. Elkins." Missy opened the back passenger door and unbuckled Levi from his car seat. "You'll need to narrow it down for me, though."

"Sure thing. John can point us in the right direction, and if he can't, one of the boys will."

Missy's stomach did a pleasant flip at the mention of the Henry boys, and she wondered when Lee said he was working today, if he meant at John Henry and Sons. She supposed she would know soon enough. She set Levi on his feet and took his hand so he would walk beside her, and they followed Mr. Elkins into the store.

The inside of the store was huge, and she knew this wasn't every-thing because she had seen at least four outbuildings, including a wood mill, when she pulled in behind Mr. Elkins. The store interior smelled like gear grease, molasses grain, and metal, but not in an unpleasant way. The floors were wide, polished wood planks, as were the walls, and the ceiling was open with massive beams spanning from front to back.

Levi yanked on her hand. "Mama!" he cried and pointed toward a display of toy John Deer tractors lined up on low shelves. A definite smart marketing ploy by someone.

"Not right now, Levi. We need to help Mr. Elkins with something. I'll let you look when we're done."

He tugged on her hand one more time, but when she didn't relent and headed in the other direction, he followed. She didn't have to look down to know the littlest of her brood was probably pouting.

"The locks are back this way, ma'am," Mr. Elkins said, leading her past the end of three rows before turning left to head toward the back of the store.

Every few steps, Levi's hold on her hand tugged at her as he saw something else his little boy mind screamed to play with, but she kept him moving along behind Mr. Elkins. A young man, probably fresh out of high school in the last year or two, stood behind a counter tucked in the back of the store with blank keys of every size and style hanging on a display. Mr. Elkins headed straight for him.

"Hey, Ethan. Is John in today?"

"No, sir, Mr. Elkins," Ethan answered. "He had to go up to Tulsa. John Jr and Lee are here today."

Gooseflesh shifted up Missy's arms and she smiled before she could tell herself to do anything different.

"Could you get one of them for me, son? We need some direction on a front door lock for Miz Colton here."

"Sure thing," Ethan said and lifted a hinged portion of the counter to get out of his small corral and headed down the aisle.

"I'm pretty sure which ones you want to look at, but they keep a record here of all their customer purchases," Mr. Elkins explained. "John Jr. or Lee should be able to tell us which one the McNeils bought before you, and maybe get the same one again. Since you said you liked it, and all."

Before she could say thank you, a familiar voice carried from around the corner just before Lee came into view. "Hey there, Ed. It's been a whole three days since you were in here."

Mr. Elkins laughed and extended his hand, which Lee took in a shake. He then glanced past Mr. Elkins and saw Missy. Heat crawled up her throat at the way his smile—which had been friendly and cordial for Mr. Elkins—spread into a wide, appreciative grin.

"Miz Colton here needs a new front door mechanism," Mr. Elkins began, but Lee had already shifted past him.

"Hey, sweetheart," he said and didn't even glance around before leaning in to kiss her. It was brief, and chaste, in comparison to the night before, but enough to make her face bloom hotter.

Mr. Elkins cleared his throat but said nothing.

Lee crouched to be eye-to-eye with Levi. "Hey there, buddy."

"Dey have toy tactors," Levi said, skipping right past any hello, and pointing back the way they came. "Gween ones."

Lee laughed. "We sure do. Maybe we can check them out when your mama is done." He stood again and moved to Missy's side so he could press his hand to the small of her back. "Let's see what we can do for you two first."

Most of the conversation between Lee and Mr. Elkins for the next few minutes went right past Missy. She understood the front door knobs and mechanism on her new home had been discontinued, so she couldn't get the same set to replace it; however, the store could order something very similar from the original manufacturer. It would be in within a week, she said that was fine, and easy as that they were done.

"I'll walk you to your car, Miz Colton," Mr. Elkins said, and Missy couldn't help the quick glance in Lee's direction.

Lee stepped toward Missy. "Can you take some time?"

"I can," Missy answered with a nod and turned to her contractor. "Thank you, Mr. Elkins, for all your help."

Ed nodded and walked down the aisle they'd used to get there, and as soon as he stepped away, Lee grabbed her hand and pulled her to him for a longer kiss than his one of greeting, but still respectable for public consumption.

"He didn't say a thing," Missy said once Ed was out of earshot.

"What would he have said?" Lee asked with a grin, his hand on the small of her back holding her close. "You think Ed Elkins hasn't seen a man kiss a woman in public before?"

"No, but—"

He kissed her again.

Missy giggled when he paused in the kiss. "Are you going to do that every time the subject comes up?"

Lee ran his thumb across her lower lip. "Maybe." He shook his head. "Not everyone will have an opinion, sweetheart. In fact, I'm willing to say most won't. But, if I have to kiss you every time you need convincing, I'm up for the task." As proof, he kissed her again and she decided she might not mind his form of persuasion. "I was going to call you in a bit," he said when he stepped back. "This is better."

"Can we go see da gween tactors?" Levi demanded, slipping into the space between Lee and Missy, tugging insistently on the untucked tail of Lee's flannel shirt.

"Absolutely, little man."

Lee surprised her when he swept Levi off the floor and set him on his hip, holding him with one arm so he could take Missy's hand with the other. "Why didn't you text me and tell me you were coming in?" he asked, leading them along.

"I realized I wasn't sure you meant here when you said working today," Missy explained. "I mean, I know you worked for your dad, but I didn't know if you worked anywhere else. And I didn't want to interrupt you if you were busy."

"Don't ever worry about that. You can text me any time." He squeezed her hand. "Okay?"

Missy nodded, smiling as they passed some customers and Lee

called out a hello. He seemed completely comfortable and at ease with walking through his own place of business holding a woman's hand—kissing her—and carrying her child. His ease let her relax somewhat and silence the niggling voice, which sounded suspiciously like Thayne, that had kept her up most of the night.

"This is the only place I work," he explained. "Unless you count Thursday and Friday nights at Low Places. I told you I've only been home a few weeks, but I've worked here since I was a kid and always helped out when I was home on leave."

Missy watched the change in his expression, the look in his eyes, and knew without question this place was someplace special to Lee. He loved this store, it was part of him.

"What are you doing tomorrow?" he asked.

"Um..." Missy shook her head. "Nothing specific. I thought of picking up some paint samples while I'm here and painting some test blocks at the house. See what I like."

"How about I help you with that in the morning, and you and the boys come out to the ranch in the afternoon?"

"The ranch?"

"My parents' place. We've got horses, a couple of real docile ponies, and a litter of beagle pups in the barn."

"Puppies!" Levi cried, twisting in Lee's hold enough he could clap.

Lee laughed. "Well, I've got one convinced."

"It won't be an inconvenience to your parents?"

"Nah." He squeezed her hand and slowed his steps so she would stop and turn toward him. "I told Mama about you last night, and I think she's itching to say hello. I'm sure she's told Dad by now."

"You told your mother about me?" she asked, realizing how foolish her tone sounded.

He hummed an affirmative and began walking again. "Of course I did. She wanted to know why I had such a fool grin on my face." He winked at her, and Missy smiled, looking away with a shake of her head.

"You're ridiculous."

"Maybe," he agreed.

They reached the front of the store, and Levi tried to wriggle free of Lee's arm. Lee released her hand so he could set down the squirming toddler, who immediately bolted for the display. Before they took another step, he had one of the tractors on the floor and was making sounds the best a three-year-old could like a tractor.

Lee circled his arm around her waist and drew her to his side. "I know you said you can't go to the show tonight, but I was thinking... we could still do dinner. Maude's is this real family-friendly place on Main Street, and I have it on good authority their kids' menu is awesome."

"You mean take the boys?"

"Well, sure." Lee let her go and walked to where Levi played and crouched down, showing Levi how he could attach one of the trailers they also had on the shelf. "I've only spent those few hours with them at the house."

Something about his words, or the way he said them, bloomed warm and comforting in Missy's chest and also made her skin prickle with panic. This wasn't about just her like it had been when she and Daniel dated. She had known that from the beginning but had been lost in the rush of being with Lee. Thayne's words rang back to her from the early morning hours.

"*Do you honestly, in your heart, in your head, believe a twenty-four-year-old guy wants to take on four kids not his own? Some of which he's not even old enough to have fathered if he wanted to?*"

"Y'all go out to dinner together, don't you?"

She blinked and refocused. Lee looked up at her but shifted his weight so he could sit on the floor beside Levi. Not having any idea what his naïve actions meant, Levi scrambled into Lee's lap and sat in the cradle of his folded legs, playing still with the tractor. Lee chuckled and ruffled Levi's blond hair as if the boy had spent hours —years—in his lap and such a thing was completely normal.

"Missy?"

She inhaled and willed back the tears, not for sadness, but for the realization Levi had never known a father figure, and yet, here he sat in Lee Henry's lap like he belonged. "Yes," she finally answered. "We used to go out every Friday night in Boston. The fun part was finding a new place to go."

"Well, then, Maude's will be your new place this week. Can't guarantee new restaurants for too long before travel would be required, though." Lee leaned forward so he could watch Levi over his shoulder while he played. Missy got caught up in watching him, watching how easily Levi had taken to Lee. After a few minutes, Lee looked up again. "What do you say?"

Missy blinked and tore her attention away from Levi to look at Lee. "I think dinner would be wonderful."

Lee had prepared himself all day for a dinner reminiscent of the ones he'd shared with his family, nephews and nieces included. Something between barely controlled chaos and a rock concert.

Dinner with the Coltons was surreal in comparison.

"Wyatt Emerson," Missy said, glancing down the table at her second eldest. "That steak may be rare, but not so rare it can run away. No need to rush."

Wyatt smiled, still chewing the chunk of steak in his cheek, and nodded. "Okay, Mama."

Even though they had waited twenty minutes for their orders to be taken, and another twenty before the food arrived because the Friday night crowd at Maude's was wall-to-wall, Missy's boys had remained exceptionally well behaved and quiet through the wait. Only Levi had fussed a bit, but a piece of buttered bread had quickly quieted him. Jeremiah worked diligently on coloring the activity sheet their waiter Riley had brought, and Jude and Wyatt battled each other in a self-created competition to see who could complete their word searches first, leaving Missy free to engage in adult conversation.

Shelley, Bea, and John Junior could take lessons in child rearing from Missy. Heck, he knew a few drill sergeants and one General Barajas who could learn a thing or two from Missy Colton.

Once Wyatt went back to his steak, Missy looked to Lee with a grin that spoke more of pride than irritation for her son. "I swear his stomach is a bottomless pit. He always eats like he hasn't seen food in a week."

"He's a growing boy." Lee cut into his steak, the same dinner Jude had ordered. "Mama said once John Junior hit double digits, she could barely keep food in the house. Then there was Ricky, Mark, and me. I think she's been cooking for the last twenty or so years."

"Between her trips to the ER."

Lee laughed loud enough that Edie and Elliot Jansen turned at their table to glance their way, smiles on their weathered faces. Lee waved, fork in hand, and they waved back. He nodded and winked at Missy. "Yes, between her trips to the ER."

Missy leaned toward him, the scent of her shampoo drifting to him. Lee shifted closer and tried to be inconspicuous as he inhaled. "How many times did your mama take *you* to the ER?"

Her lips mesmerized him. It had been an hour and seven minutes since they'd met in the parking lot and he'd kissed her without nearly the amount of enthusiasm he'd wanted to. When she arched her eyebrows, he realized he'd been staring rather than answering. Lee chuckled and grinned, looking away to find his tongue again.

"Ah...probably half a dozen times or so. But never just me. My brothers had a way of dragging me along in their shenanigans." As he talked, he unbuttoned the cuff of his shirt and rolled it up to his elbow. He tapped a scar in the shape of a hook near the point of his elbow. "This I got jumping from the hay loft with Mark and Ricky. Landed on a hoof hook lost in the hay. I was seven."

"Ouch." Missy touched the scar with her fingertip, and sparks danced up his arm.

He yanked the shirt higher above his elbow and twisted his arm so she could see the six-inch scar up the back. "Mark convinced me I could break the Mustang stallion Dad had bought in Oklahoma City. Had a pin for six weeks. I was thirteen." He glanced down the table. "Jude's age. Somehow, Jude seems a bit smarter than I was at that age."

"Mama, how do you spell mustang?" Wyatt asked, looking up from his word search.

"How do you think you spell it?"

"Is it m-a-h-s-t-a-g?"

"No," Missy answered with a barely-restrained smirk. "It's m-u-s-t-a-n-g."

"Oh..." Wyatt twisted his lips into an annoyed frown and went back to his word search.

Lee chuckled and took a drink from his sweet tea. "Close, just not quite."

Missy set her fork on the side of her plate and folded her hands in her lap. "This was such a good idea. I can't remember the last time I had fried catfish this good. Certainly not in Boston."

Lee reached under the edge of the table and took her hand, curling his fingers through hers. "Then we will have to make this a regular happening. The six of us—"

"Welcome home, son," came a deep, booming voice from behind him as a firm hand came down on his shoulder. Lee pushed back his chair to stand and face Pastor Oliver Nason, the lead pastor at Lee's church downtown. Not one to hold back, the big man embraced Lee, patting his back. "I didn't get a chance to welcome you home properly on Sunday."

"It's good to see you, sir," Lee said, stepping back from Pastor's hold. He motioned toward the table. "I'd like you to meet a friend of mine—"

"Evenin', Missy," Pastor said, tipping his head toward her with a touch of his fingers to the brim of his brown Stetson. "Evenin', boys."

The four Colton children called their various greetings, all going right back to their dinner

"Oh, you know Missy..."

"Sure. She and her boys have been coming regularly since she came to town. Missed you on Sunday, though," he said directly to Missy.

"Levi had a fever," she explained, smiling. "I didn't think it was worth getting half the congregation sick."

"Good to see he's feeling better," Pastor said with a chuckle as they all watched Levi take a big bite of baked macaroni and cheese. "See you on Sunday, then. You'll be able to enjoy our prodigal son as he returns to our worship team."

Missy's smile lit up and she looked at Lee, the sparkle in her eyes making his insides warm. "I look forward to it."

"Y'all enjoy the rest of your evening." Pastor Nason offered his hand to Lee, and with one final firm shake, headed out of Maude's.

"Look at that," Lee said, taking his seat again. He took Missy's hand and kissed her knuckles before holding it on the tabletop. "I'm guaranteed to see you tomorrow *and* Sunday. Can we begin booking next week?"

"You don't believe in too much of a good thing?"

"Not when that good thing is you, sweetheart."

CHAPTER NINE

Levi asked if he could take the tractor to bed with him.

I didn't have the heart to say no.

I'll send a picture when he falls asleep.

LEE SMILED WHEN HE READ THE TEXT, THEN SLID HIS THUMB ACROSS THE screen to open the chat program and text back.

I know a few things about boys. if they're under ten and over twenty, they love tractors. The only thing that changes is the size of the tractor.

Glad he and Jeremiah liked them.

Don't worry. I'll try to avoid anything ER-worthy. ;-)

Wasn't sure Jude and Wyatt would like the hats, though.

He hunched forward, sitting on the edge of the stage in Low

Places, phone in hand while he waited for her response. The honky-tonk would be packed in another half hour, and they were setup and ready to play, so he had a few minutes to enjoy her texts.

"Hey, Lee."

He looked up. Callie Hayden stood a few feet away from the stage, hands pushed into the back pockets of her skin-tight jeans and a band of bare stomach showed between the hem of her cropped sweater and waistband. She was definitely dressed for a night at the club; hair curled and make-up applied with a heavier hand than what she'd worn the night before as their waitress. Lee sat up and set his phone on his thigh, screen up.

"Hey, Callie. Got the night off, huh?"

She smiled and stepped closer. "Yep. I don't usually get weekend nights off, so I figured I'd better grab my chance to hear you play." She looked over her shoulder and around the sparsely occupied club. "Where's Mrs. Colton?"

Something about the way Callie used Missy's formal name scraped across Lee's nerves like sandpaper on the back of his neck. "Missy is at home with the boys," he answered, stressing her name just enough to make his point clear.

Callie looked back at him and smiled with more than just a greeting. It was an invitation, blatant and obvious. She took a step toward him and ran her tongue over her painted lower lip. "It's good to see you again, Lee. I've missed you and worried about you something terrible while you were over there. You can ask your mama; I asked about you a lot."

"She told me," he said with a nod. "I appreciate it, Callie."

"What are you going to do now that you're home for good?"

She took another step closer, and Lee strained his spine, leaning back a bit to create more space between them. "Same plan as always. I'm taking over a lot of the daily stuff at..." His phone vibrated against his thigh, and he glanced down, then finished his thought as he picked it up. "...the store helping Dad."

"I guess I meant more personal than that," Callie clarified, leaning at an angle like she was trying to see the phone. "You know, for you."

A photo appeared on his screen, a bit dark since Missy had taken it in an unlit room crouched beside Levi's bed. He was asleep on his side, his mouth open and smushed up a bit from the pillow. Hugged to his chest, with his arm draped over it like a precious stuffed toy, was the green John Deere tractor Lee had given him after dinner. The same one he'd played with at the store earlier that day. A match to the one Lee had brought for Jeremiah.

Lee smiled and chuckled.

"Who is that?" Callie asked, her tone pitched a little too high for a simple question.

Lee turned the phone out so Callie could fully see the picture. "Levi, Missy's youngest." He chuckled and looked at the picture again. "I gave him that tractor earlier tonight. She said he wanted to sleep with it."

Callie scowled and crossed her arms. "I just don't get you, Lee Henry. You could have any single girl in this town and some of the not-so-single girls, and you choose a woman with four kids and an ex-husband?"

Lee clenched his jaw and focused first on his response to Missy because Missy deserved his attention.

We have a sand pit in the backyard perfect for tractors.

While waiting for her response, Lee looked up again, keeping the phone in his hand this time. Callie still stared, arms crossed, head tilted. "First, Missy doesn't have an ex-husband. She's a widow." Callie's scowl softened somewhat, but not enough to make up for her comment as far as Lee was concerned. "Second, I'm not looking to *have* any girl, Callie. I'm intending to make Missy Colton and her boys a part of my life. Permanently."

Her lined and mascara-fanned eyes popped wide. Her mouth fell open and she stuttered to say something else, but his phone vibrated in his hand and Lee focused there instead.

Okay. I'll make sure. I know things should be starting there soon. Have a good show tonight. I do wish I was there.

I'll see you tomorrow.

Callie harrumphed, and he caught sight of her scuffed boots stomping away as he typed his response.

Tomorrow can't come soon enough.

Sweet dreams, sweetheart.

I'll be at the house by 10:00

See you then. Goodnight.

Lee closed the text program and slid his phone into his back pocket, hopping down from the edge of the stage. Callie was now on the other side of the dance floor, talking with some of her girlfriends he recognized from high school. Barbie Marks-Johnson had to be about seven months pregnant, with her second if Lee remembered right. She'd married Robbie Elkins—Ed's boy—their senior year of high school because she got pregnant, and divorced a year after the boy was born. Now she'd moved on to husband, and baby, number two with Phillip Johnson. Charlotte Perkins stood beside Callie, shaking her head while Callie talked, glancing in Lee's direction once with a deep frown.

He chuckled and used the edge of the stage as a leverage point to jump up rather than go around to the steps. Mark sat on one of the speakers, tuning his guitar, and looked up at the hard thunk of Lee's boots on the hollow-underneath stage.

"Callie is in rare form tonight," Mark said.

"Not so rare." Lee lifted his guitar from its stand and slid the strap over his head. "As I recall, this is pretty much Callie's form." He glanced in her direction but didn't linger long on the scene. "Time and distance sure has cleared my vision, brother."

"There might have been a time you wouldn't have minded her attention. You two did date for a few months."

"That was then." Lee focused on the sound each string made as he plucked it, making sure the Yamaha was in tune. "I'm looking for more than a few dates." He dropped his hand away from the guitar's neck and looked at his older brother. "Funny thing is, I didn't *know* that was what I was looking for. Not until..."

"Until you met Missy."

Lee nodded. "You think I'm crazy, too?"

"Nope." Mark set his guitar back in his stand. The bar was beginning to fill now and they'd start soon. "Yeah, so she's more my age than yours. She's got kids. If it don't matter to you, what should it matter to anyone else?"

Lee extended his hand to his brother, and Mark looked at it a minute before taking it in a firm shake. "Thank you," Lee said.

"I've always got your back. You know that."

Tomorrow can't come soon enough.

Sweet dreams, sweetheart.

I'll be at the house by 10:00

See you then. Goodnight.

Missy hit send and waited for the status bar to show the text was gone before she set the phone on the table where she sat. She'd come down to make a cup of tea after finally getting Jeremiah to bed. Her daredevil would have stayed up all night playing with his new tractor. The gift easily outdid every gift the boy had ever gotten, or so Jeremiah led her to believe.

She smiled, remembering the way Lee had beamed as much as the boys when he gave them the gifts. Wyatt had whooped and hollered over the black Rodeo Junior Stetson felt hat Lee gave him, and immediately slapped it on his head. Jude had been more reserved, but Missy knew her boy, and she knew he loved the dark tan Carson Stetson Lee had chosen for him. It took him ten minutes of intense study, taking in every angle and edge of the felt, before he placed it on his head.

He'd said a quiet "thank you, sir," and left the younger boys to their loud enthusiasm.

The three youngers had run into the house, shouting for their uncle and aunt so they could show off their gifts, and Susan had shown all the enthusiasm Thayne lacked. Especially when he heard they had been from Lee. The children were, thankfully, blind to their uncle's sour disposition, except for Jude. He'd hung back with Missy, and even offered a quiet "Uncle Thayne doesn't have to like 'em," bit of consolation.

Her heart hurt to know how much carefree childhood ignorance Jude had lost since his daddy died.

Missy couldn't recall a time she'd ridden such a rollercoaster of emotions. Things had been bad when Daniel died, and she'd gone from sad to sadder most of the time, but this was different. When she was with Lee, she felt alive and light. She was able to forget Thayne's sour attitude, and the obstacles seemed so much smaller. When she wasn't with Lee and she had to face down her brother and his arguments or the quiet when she had time to think, the lightness evaporated.

Like now. In a quiet house. Thayne and Susan had gone out as soon as she got home so she could watch Betsy, who had been asleep before they went out the door. They'd be gone at least another hour, and she intended to be in her room by then.

Yes, she fully intended to avoid her brother as much as possible.

Her phone buzzed and bounced on the table, and she picked it up.

> I loved being with you and the boys tonight. I don't think I said it before I left. I want you to know.

> They are great kids.

> No need to respond. I'm going on stage. Do me a favor and imagine me kissing you goodnight like I couldn't earlier.

Missy inhaled a deep breath and released it slowly out her lips. Heat crawled up her throat to her face, and she wished the hot tea she'd made was iced instead. Even when Lee kissed her with restraint, he had a way of making her bubbly and soft at the same time. Text messages were no different. He made her feel young again.

Never once since coming to Indian Prairie had she felt so isolated as she did sitting in the dimly lit kitchen by herself. She had family here, but not that she could talk to. Thayne was the problem, and Susan was the holder of the cattle prod pushing her toward Lee. In Boston, she'd had Miranda, her dearest friend who'd held her together after Daniel was gone. Miranda had been her college roommate, had been her friend the whole time she and Daniel dated, and had been their maid of honor at their wedding. The phone was in her hand, and her contacts open, before Missy had to think any more of it. The smartphone automatically switched to its Bluetooth programming and connected with her hearing aids, the only way she ever wanted to use a phone again.

It was later in Boston, but Miranda was a night owl. She picked up on the second ring.

"Missy?"

Missy smiled at Miranda's familiar, broad and flat Southy accent. "Hey. I'm not calling too late, am I?"

"Of course not. Charlie is working late, and the kids are in bed, so I've got my own little Netflix marathon going here. How are you? What's going on? Do you like being back in Oklahoma?"

"It feels familiar, more familiar than I thought it would." Missy sighed and chuckled. "I guess it's right what they say. You can take the girl out of Oklahoma, but you can't take Oklahoma out of the girl."

"Familiar. That's a good thing, right?"

"Sure. We're settling in fine. The kids like school, and we're moving into the house next week. You're still coming to visit this summer, right?"

"Wouldn't miss it for the world."

"Good, because I sure could use a friendly face."

"Uh oh." The sound of shuffling fabric carried through the phone, and Missy imagined Miranda moving into a different position amongst the plethora of blankets and comforters on her bed. It was, after all, March in Boston. "Talk to me. What's going on? What's wrong?"

"That's just it, Mira." Missy slumped in the wooden kitchen chair and stared out the window in the back door to the dark back-yard. "I guess I need to talk to someone separate from the situation."

"Okay. What's the situation?"

Missy drew in a slow, fortifying breath before she said, "I've met someone."

"No way!" Miranda cried, and Missy winced at the sheer volume of it shot directly into her ear by the aid connection. "So, tell me *all* about him."

"Well, um...his name is Lee—"

"Oh, I love it already. Homegrown, I bet."

Missy laughed, her best friend magically having the ability to lift her spirits from two thousand miles away. "He is from Oklahoma, yes. Born and raised here in Indian Prairie. He's military—Army— but he's separating in a few days. He owns, or I guess *will own*, a business with his dad. Family business." With each statement, Miranda offered an affirmation of some kind. "Oh, and he's a musician. Plays guitar. Sings."

"Dang," Miranda said, and Missy heard more shuffling. "That's a whole lot in the plus column. Is this serious?"

"I've only known him a week."

"So? Must be something if you're calling to tell me. Have you gone out together?"

"Yes. Last night just the two of us, then tonight we went to dinner with the boys."

"With the boys? Was that his idea or yours?"

"His."

Miranda hummed, and Missy wished they could have this conversation face-to-face. She'd see Miranda's honest opinion in her eyes. "Have you, you know..."

"God, no!" Missy protested. "I said I've only known him a week."

"Yeah, but it's been a while—"

"Miranda!"

Miranda laughed. "Okay, fine. Have you at least kissed him?"

"I don't think I can take it anymore. God help me, Missy, I'm dying to kiss you."

"Is this where it starts?"

"I sure as hell hope so, sweetheart."

The recollection brought a slow smile to Missy's lips, and she was glad at that point Miranda couldn't see her. She'd probably never let Missy live down a goofy grin. "Yes," she answered simply.

"That one word tells me all I need to know. Do I get to see a picture?"

"I don't have one—"

As she spoke, her phone vibrated again with an incoming text, and she tilted the screen. A thumbnail photo displayed on the screen, with part of a text from Lee.

> I lied. One more...I'm thinking of you.

She clicked on the thumbnail of the photo and it opened to fill the screen. It was a picture of Lee he'd clearly taken of himself, with the stage and the audience as a backdrop, the angle of the shot a testament to his attempt at taking a picture of himself while holding up his other hand to be seen in the shot. His index and middle fingers were curled to his palm, with his pointer, pinky, and thumb held high. He was grinning like a fool, but the sight of him set to flutter a thousand butterflies in her stomach.

"Missy? Where'd you go?"

"Hang on. I was saying I didn't have a picture of him, but...I guess I do."

"What, just now?"

"Yeah, hang on." Before she could tap options and save the photo, another popped into the text window. Another selfie, this time just a picture of him smiling.

> Mark says I'm acting like an idiot. I don't really care. I want you to know I'm thinking of you. See you in the morning.

"Well?"

"Hang on. I'm saving it. Do you have your phone handy?"

Miranda snorted. "Do I have my phone handy? Silly question."

> I'm thinking of you, too. Wish I were there.

> Wish I could give you that goodnight kiss

> you wanted me to think about.

> Maybe I'll make up for it with a hello kiss tomorrow.

She almost didn't hit send. Almost deleted it all and wrote something tamer, something appropriate for a thirty-something mother of four. Almost. Then she groaned and hit send, then immediately saved the photos, opened a new chat to Miranda, attached them, and hit send.

"Okay, two photos on their way."

"Will probably take a few minutes. Bad storm rolling through here, so there's been some lag. So, while I wait...what is it you're not telling me?"

"Am I that obvious?"

"Only to me, Missy. What's the problem?"

Missy huffed. "He's a friend of Thayne's. They served together. Thayne...Thayne doesn't approve of us dating. I guess I have my own reservations."

"Why? Oh, wait...phone just went off."

"I think you'll understand when you see the photos." Missy held her breath, waiting. The programmed twitters and blips of Miranda's cell phone carried through their connection. She heard the moment Miranda saw the photos...at least the first one.

"Holy crap..."

"Yeah," Missy said softly.

"Geez, Missy, he's *gorgeous!*"

"Of this I am aware. That's not the problem."

"What the heck could be the problem?" Miranda paused, probably as the second photo came through. "Nope. Not seeing a problem."

"You don't?"

"What...oh, is it supposed to be a problem he's younger than you? How old *is* he anyway?"

"Twenty-four."

Miranda whistled, then hummed in appreciation. "Nope, not seeing a problem at all. Hold on...you know what that hand sign he's making means, don't you?"

"Yeah," Missy said with a sigh, looking at the photo again. "My mother was nearly deaf, remember? We used some sign language."

"So, you know he's signing that he loves you—"

"It's just a sign."

"That means I love you. Missy, you didn't answer my question. Is this serious?"

Missy drew in a long breath and blew it out through pursed lips. She slumped back in her chair and crossed her legs, leaving her arms hanging in her lap. "After Daniel died, I had a few counseling sessions with our pastor. He told me once that a heart that has loved —truly loved, deeply loved—is more open to loving again. Do you think that's true?"

"I don't know. Missy, are you telling me you're *in love* with this guy?"

Missy huffed and shrugged, even though Miranda didn't see her. "I don't know what I'm telling you. I just know I am happy with him. I know I look forward to seeing him. I know when I think about next week, next month, whenever, I wonder how Lee will fit into my life."

"Damn, Missy..."

Her phone buzzed a new message, and Missy backed out of her text to Miranda, and back into Lee's.

Damn, woman.

She smiled.

CHAPTER TEN

Saturday's weather took a turn to the warm and muggy side, not enough to warrant anything as extreme as air conditioning, but enough to leave Missy drained after an hour of painting color patches on her bedroom walls. She'd long since discarded the long-sleeved button-up blouse she'd worn over her tank top, and her hair was now piled on top of her head in a haphazard mess of humidity-induced ringlets. With every window and door open in the house, the occasional cooling breeze blew through and left gooseflesh on her arms. She didn't mind; it refreshed more than anything else.

Jude and Wyatt's voices and laughter carried through the courtyard from the open doors in their bedrooms. She'd opted to leave Jeremiah and Levi with Susan when she offered, since she wasn't likely to get much done trying to watch out for Levi's curiosity and Jeremiah's daredevil antics. The house was nearly ready to move in, and the plan was to take up official residence the following weekend. Once they picked all the colors they wanted, Ed Elkins' crew would paint every room in the house, and after a visit from The Pool Doctor on Tuesday, the house would be ready.

She would have her own home again.

Missy finished the last four foot square block of color on her wall, set the disposable brush into the small sample can, and stepped back. She huffed a breath up her face, a vain attempt at cooling the sheen of perspiration. Sun streamed into the double french doors, casting blankets of light on the wall where she intended to set her bed. The double bed would look like a toddler's bed in the massive room, but their townhouse had been so small they had gotten used to the smaller size. Besides, what did she need with anything bigger?

"Which color do you like, Wy?" came Jude's voice through the open doors leading to the courtyard.

Missy turned to the open door and leaned her shoulder into the jamb, listening for a moment. She wanted the boys to feel at home here, so once each had chosen their rooms, she also let the older ones choose the colors of their walls. Only Levi didn't choose completely. She narrowed it down for him to three shades of blue, otherwise she feared he'd end up with blaze orange or John Deere green walls.

"Which do you like?" Wyatt asked.

"It doesn't matter which one I like. I already picked the color for my room. This is your room."

"What color did you pick?"

Missy smiled, knowing exactly what Wyatt tried to do. So did Jude, because he answered quickly.

"Nope, I'm not telling you until you pick. It's your room, Wyatt."

"I kinda like that one that's kinda grey. Not really though, like it could be blue, too."

"That's a good one," Jude said, his enthusiasm carrying through the courtyard.

Missy stepped away from the door and went back to the middle of the bedroom, staring at the half-dozen blocks of color. She'd tried just about every color family, from yellow, to a cool blue, to a warm, rich red. The yellow had been the color she was convinced she'd like best, but now that she saw it on the wall, she wasn't so sure.

"Hey there, pretty girl."

Missy jumped and turned, pressing her hand to her chest. "Goodness, Lee, you scared me."

"I'm sorry." He stepped into the bedroom, the thunk of his boots echoing in the empty space. "I figured I'd cut across the courtyard instead of come through the house."

"I was lost in my thoughts anyway." She motioned toward the painted wall. Lee crossed the room and came up behind her, standing close enough the cotton of his tee shirt brushed her arm. "I'm trying to decide on a color."

His fingertips brushed across her shoulders and the back of her neck, moving aside the tight ringlets that had escaped her clip, and his other hand snaked around her waist to rest flat against her stomach, pulling her back against him. Missy's heartbeat jumped and her tummy swirled at the touch, even before his warm lips kissed the column of her neck.

"I like the red one," he said against her skin before kissing again.

Missy tried to keep her eyes from fluttering, and the low moan from whispering up from her chest, but it didn't work. The hand that had brushed away her hair came around to her chest, his palm over her pounding heart. His calloused fingers found the pulse at the base of her throat.

"You do?" she managed to rasp out.

"It makes a great backdrop for you."

Missy turned in his hold, raising her arms so she could wrap them around him and draw him to her as soon as she faced him. She met his lips, determined to give him the hello kiss she'd promised the night before in her text. Missy had to toe up to get her arms around his shoulders, and to kiss him with the fervor she felt, but it was worth his undeniable and immediate response. Lee groaned into her open mouth, his arms high and firm around her body to press her to him, one hand against the dip between her shoulder blades, the other cupping the back of her head to deepen the kiss.

It had been a long time since Missy had kissed with such abandon, and part of her was pleased she remembered how. Open lips and warm tongues slid together, each contact a conduit that jump-started her pulse again, and again.

She didn't realize he moved them until her hips bumped the wall and Lee's body pressed against her. He took her head in his hands and held her in place, delving into her mouth, retreating, and returning until she nearly mewled in frustration. His belt buckle caught on the fabric of her top when he pressed with his hips, and Missy thought she might fly apart.

Just as abruptly as it began, Lee broke away from the kiss and leaned past her to rest his forehead on the wall, his palms flat against the plaster, his hot breath rapid against her shoulder. Missy tipped back her head, resting it beside his, fighting to steady her own breathing.

"Damn, woman," he said, echoing his text, following with a deep, low chuckle that reverberated through her where their bodies still touched.

Missy rolled her head against the wall to look sideways at him, grinning as soon as she saw his wide smile. Lee laughed louder, the sound echoing back from the bare walls. The laugh was contagious; Missy giggled and pushed against his chest, not putting any effort into actually putting distance between them.

"You're crazy."

Lee moved in front of her again, no longer laughing, a slow and sexy smile on his lips. "You are right, Missy Colton. I am crazy." He ran his finger along her jaw, watching the progression, until he came to her mouth. The way he stared and smoothed his thumb across her lip sent both a flush and a chill over her skin. "I am absolutely, unde-niably, and completely crazy for you."

The weight of his voice was a caress, and Missy turned into his fingers, the roughness of his hands tempered by the gentleness of his touch. "You've known me a week."

He hummed an affirmative, the pad of his thumb drawing down her lower lip, parting them. "Eight whole days." His gaze shifted to look her in the eyes. "Why are we taking so long?" He leaned in closer, his breath warm on her chin.

"Taking so long for what?"

"To get on with forever."

His lips pressed to hers, but this time she focused on the contact and not the bubbling flutter in her stomach that wanted. That was the only way to define it. She wanted. She wanted Lee. She wanted his touch. She wanted this. She wanted it to never stop.

She wanted it so much, it burned her eyes.

"Mom! Hey, Mom!"

The combined shouts of Jude and Wyatt coming down the house hallway forced them to step apart, and Missy quickly sidestepped around Lee to meet her sons at the open door leading into the hall. "What are you shouting about?"

"Lee is here," Wyatt answered, about half a decibel below shouting. He looked past Missy, and his smile broadened. "Hi, Lee!"

"Hey, boys." Lee stepped up beside her, his hand settling at the small of her back. "Are you ready to come out to the ranch?"

Wyatt nodded, but Jude looked toward Missy before answering. She smiled, and he smiled back. "Yeah, sure. Mom, do you need us to write down what colors we want?"

"Here." She reached around to her back pocket, her fingers brushing Lee's as she took out a black fine-point marker. "Take this and write your name on the color chip you want. I'm going to give all the chips to Mr. Elkins on Monday, and your rooms will be painted by Friday."

Wyatt let out a whoop and ran back down the hall. Jude started to follow but stopped a couple of steps away and looked back at Missy and Lee. He smiled, a slow mysterious grin that tugged more at one side of his mouth than the other, then headed away at a more sedate pace. When he was gone around the corner, Lee wrapped his arms around her waist.

"That boy has something on his mind."

"Mmmm..." was the only affirmation Missy offered, wondering herself about her eldest.

"So," Lee whispered near her ear. "Are you going with the red?"

"Okay, if I get turned around, I'll call."

"We're tough to miss." Lee's voice carried through the speaker system in the car, and Missy's phone routed through the Bluetooth setup. "If I don't see you within half an hour, I'll send Jude and Wy out as a search party."

She heard her boys' chuckle, followed by Lee's. They'd opted to ride with Lee to his family's ranch rather than come back to the house with Missy to pick up their little brothers. Missy turned into Thayne's driveway, the house feeling less like home every day she grew closer to having her own again, and put the Jeep in park.

"I have a decent sense of direction. You have to, living in Boston. Construction changed my route every other week."

Lee laughed. "Okay, sweetheart. See you in a little bit."

Missy disconnected the call and turned off the vehicle, climbing out. The morning had been warm, but the afternoon was cooling right down and the clouds threatened rain. She mentally reminded herself to grab sweatshirts for Jude and Wyatt before she left. Susan's car was in the spot parallel to Missy, but Thayne's truck wasn't anywhere in sight. Missy was both relieved to see her brother wasn't home and saddened to accept the reality of her relief. She didn't want to fight anymore, and with Thayne's attitude, the only way to avoid the fight was to avoid him.

She went through the front door and called out "I'm home!" Running footsteps upstairs told her where to head.

"Mama!" Levi cried, tearing out of the spare room he shared with his brothers, his new John Deere tractor in his arms.

"Quick, quick," she said, after giving him a quick hug and kissing

Jeremiah's head. "Get your shoes on, and grab sweatshirts, please. We're going to Lee's house, remember?"

"Puppies!" Levi squealed and ran right back into the bedroom.

"If we could tap into the energy of every three-year-old on the planet, we would never have a fuel shortage," Susan said from the other end of the hall.

Missy turned, chuckling. "It might slow them all down enough we might have a chance at keeping up."

Susan walked toward her, smiling. "How did the paint selection go?"

"I think we've got everything nailed down. I'm leaving the guest room and office for now. Time yet to figure that out." She stepped to the doorway to watch the boys, making sure they had socks on with their shoes. "Jude and Wyatt finalized their choices today, too."

Susan looked around the hall and down the stairs. "Speaking of..."

"They went on to the ranch with Lee. Sit down on the bed, Levi, and I'll get your shoes tied."

Missy went to the side of the bed where Levi plopped himself down, crouching so she could lace up his sneakers. Susan followed, standing just inside the door with her arms crossed.

"I get the impression your boys have taken a real liking to Lee."

Missy nodded, working on the second shoe.

"Wee gave me a taktor," Levi stated, as if the whole house didn't already know.

"It's an awesome tractor, too," Susan said to Levi, and he beamed. She looked to Missy as she stood. "I suppose that's a good thing since their mama has taken a real liking to him, too."

Heat crawled up Missy's throat, but she was neither inclined nor hesitant to deny Susan's observation. "Get a sweatshirt, sweetie. It's getting chilly, might rain."

"Yes, Mama."

"So..." Susan drew out, following Missy as she led them back into the hall and down the stairs while the boys finished getting ready. "Meeting the family today, huh? Nervous?"

"God, yes," Missy admitted, shaking her head. "Susan, I feel like I'm eighteen again meeting my boyfriend's parents for the first time."

"You're a bit old for a boyfriend, aren't you?" came Thayne's voice from near the kitchen when they hit the bottom of the stairs. Missy's gut instantly clenched and she stopped in the foyer, her hand on the banister, holding her breath as he came into the hall. "Did he ask you to go steady yet?"

"Thayne—" Susan began.

"I have a right to voice my own opinion in my own house," Thayne snapped, glaring at his wife for a moment before he turned to Missy.

"Yes, it is *your* house, Thayne," Missy reiterated. "You've been reminding me of such for days. Another week and you won't have to worry about it anymore."

"Missy, we're not rushing you out of the house," Susan began but didn't try to finish.

"Of course not," Missy said and went to the hall closet to get sweatshirts for Jude and Wyatt. While there, she took out the jacket Lee had let her keep after their date. "It's okay to admit it'll be easier for everyone with less tension in the house."

"There doesn't have to be any tension, Sissy."

Missy held up her hand to silence him. He loved to play the "Sissy" card when he didn't want to come across as a total ass. "I'm not doing this right now, Thayne. Thankfully, the little ones haven't noticed what's going on between us and I'd like to keep it that way."

Jeremiah came running down the stairs, with Levi following at a slower pace, hanging on to the railing with one hand, his beloved tractor tucked under the other arm. Jeremiah had his tractor, too, and both boys were ready to go.

"Head out to the Jeep," Missy instructed. "I'll be out in a couple of minutes to buckle you in."

She waited until both boys were well out of the house and the door shut behind them before she turned to her brother. Missy drew in a long, slow breath and released it, trying to find a center calm before she laid down the law.

"Thayne, this is the last time I'm speaking on this. I mean it. The last time. I acknowledge you have a strong opinion about my relationship with Lee, however misguided and unnecessary as it may be, but your opinion on it is irrelevant." He opened his mouth, but she shot up her hand; he scowled but didn't speak. "You've voiced it, and now you're done."

"I'm only against it because I love you, Sissy."

Missy shook her head and squinted her eyes. "See, that's what I don't understand. Why, if you love me, would you be so against me being happy again?"

"Because it's not going to last," Thayne snapped. "And how is that supposed to make you happy again?"

Missy closed her eyes and forced herself to release her clenched hands. She pressed her lips together and looked at her brother again. He scowled, but it didn't read of anger. Maybe regret, but either way, she didn't care.

"I never knew you were psychic, Thayne."

"I don't need to be psychic to see where it's going." He shook his head and sighed. "I'm just not wearing the same blinders you are."

"I'm deaf," Missy forced out, tamping down the thick emotion in her throat. "Not blind. I'm also not a fool, and I resent you considering me to be one." Missy turned away from him before he could say anything else, and strode to the door. "I don't know when we'll be home. Don't wait on dinner, Susan."

If either said anything more, she didn't hear it.

CHAPTER ELEVEN

"Hold your hand flat and let the carrot lay across your palm."

Wyatt tensed and started to draw back his arm as soon as Prince Charming dropped his head over the paddock fence railing, but Lee crouched behind him and guided his arm out again.

"Don't worry, he's not going to bite. There's a reason we call him Prince Charming."

Wyatt glanced over his shoulder to Lee, then to Jude, who was feeding his second carrot to Cinderella. Seeming to garner courage, Wyatt stretched out his hand and held it high enough Prince could reach the carrot. Prince tilted his head just a bit and used his long, floppy lips to work the carrot into his mouth. Wyatt laughed when the old gelding's whiskers wiggled on his hand.

At the prospect of treats, the other horses in the paddock meandered their way to the fence. In a couple minutes, Jude and Wyatt would have more horses to feed than they had hands.

"You got it now?"

Wyatt nodded and took another bit of carrot from the bowl Mama had provided. Lee stood from his crouch and tapped Wyatt on top of the black Stetson he wore. Both Jude and Wyatt had come out of their new house, ready to head for the ranch, wearing their Stetsons. The sight pleased Lee more than he had expected.

The sound of tires on gravel drew his attention, and he turned to see Missy's Cherokee coming down the driveway. "Your mom is here, guys. You keep feeding. Jude, don't let Jeremiah or Levi feed the horses alone, okay?"

"Sure," Jude answered, nodding.

Lee walked away from the paddock, confident none of the horses gathering around the fence would hurt any of the boys. He'd intentionally made sure only the oldest and gentlest of their stock were readily available to garner some young boy attention. He reached the edge of the driveway as she stopped, and opened the back passenger door to help Jeremiah from his car seat.

"Hey, buddy," he said, glancing at Missy as she slid from behind the steering wheel and headed for the other door for Levi. Her lips were pressed into a tight line, and she didn't look directly at him.

"We brought our tractors," Jeremiah informed him, holding up his.

"Awesome. Give me five minutes and I'll take you out to the sand pit. Best place ever to play with a tractor."

As soon as he had Jeremiah free, and set his feet on the ground, the boy was off running toward his older brothers. Lee shut the door and walked around the back of the Jeep so he could come at Missy without the open door being in the way.

"I wanna see the hohsies!" Levi shouted, bouncing in his chair.

"Go right to Jude, okay, buddy?" Lee said, getting the boy's attention. "He'll show you how."

Missy looked at Lee, wide eyed, and he caught the shine of barely-restrained tears. His gut clenched, but he smiled and laid his hand on her arm. "It's okay. They're nothing but a bunch of old plugs. Couldn't hurt a barn fly. I made sure, and I told Jude to watch him."

She nodded and finished freeing Levi. Just like his brother, as soon as his feet hit the ground he was off and running, tractor still in his arms. Before she could move away, Lee caught her arm and drew her back, the Jeep offering a small degree of privacy between them and the boys, and the main house.

"Hey..." he said softly, touching her jaw so she would look at him.

When she raised her eyes, a tear slipped free and ran down her cheek, caught in the edge of contact between her skin and his hand. Missy dropped her forehead to his chest and curled her arms into the space between them, still not saying a word. Lee wrapped his arms around her and held her, not sure what to expect. She didn't weep, she just stayed in his hold. After a few silent moments, Missy drew in a shuttered breath and raised her head again, the shine gone from her eyes, a tentative smile now curving her lips. Lee smoothed his thumbs over her cheeks and watched her expression, worry digging in his chest.

"Talk to me."

Missy shook her head and started to move away, but as gently as he could, he held her back.

"Sweetheart, tell me."

Missy swallowed and licked her lips, then met his gaze again. "Thayne. We got into it at the house."

Lee clenched his jaw, biting back every name that came to mind. He still didn't understand Thayne's attitude, and since Thayne wouldn't give him a straight answer, he doubted he would any time soon. But ranting about her brother would only add to Missy's heartache, and he refused to do that. Instead, he leaned in and pressed a kiss to the middle of her forehead, holding her there for a moment.

"I'm sorry," he said against her skin.

She shook her head within his hold, then drew back enough to look at him and laid her palms on his chest. "It's his problem. Not mine."

"It's *our* problem, sweetheart."

"Are you going to stay out there all afternoon, or are you going to bring that girl inside?" Mama called from the ranch porch.

Lee grinned and looked past Missy. Both his parents stood, side-by-side, waiting not so patiently. They'd asked his siblings and extended family to stay away for the day to not "overwhelm the poor girl", and right now Lee was thankful for his mother's wisdom.

"You ready for this?" he asked with a grin and a wink.

The spark was back in her blue eyes, a genuine smile on her lips. She tipped up her chin, and curled her fingers around his shirt collar, drawing him to her. "Kiss me one more time and I'll be ready for anything."

"Invitation gladly accepted."

Lee followed her lead and cupped her jaw in his hands. He kissed her, unable—or unwilling—to deny the momentary indulgence of deepening the kiss a few seconds longer than propriety would insist, and slipped his tongue past her lips for a decadent moment. The low, soft sound she made deep in her throat nearly stole his ability to stop.

"You drive me to insanity, woman," he whispered and laced his fingers through hers to lead her toward the house.

"Wee, can we see da puppies now?"

"Levi, don't be rude," Missy scolded, reaching for Levi to remove him from the space between her and Lee where he tried to scramble, more toward Lee than her.

"Jer'miah and me wanna see da puppies, Mama," Levi whispered, though not too quietly, climbing instead into her lap like a little monkey. For good measure, he smacked a wet kiss on her cheek. "Pwease, Mama. Can we see da puppies?"

Lee leaned closer, his arm behind her along the back of the

couch. "I did promise, Mama." He kissed her cheek and stood, snatching Levi from her lap as he did. "I'll be back in a bit." Lee tucked Levi under his arm like a sack of potatoes, bouncing him with each step, Levi giggling all the way out the door.

Leaving Missy alone with his parents.

They were nice people, good people; of that, Missy had no doubt. Both were in their mid-sixties or older, which implied Lee had been born when Erin Henry was at least in her forties, but both were the picture of good old-fashioned country living. Their skin may be wrinkled, and tan from the sun, but it glowed. Their eyes sparked, especially when they looked at each other, and their smiles said more than a thousand words ever could. They had greeted Lee with a kiss on the cheek, and Erin had embraced Missy like an old friend. John Henry was a quiet man and hadn't said much at all, but what he had said had been kind and friendly.

Not once since she'd arrived did she feel scrutinized or unwelcome. Given the same circumstances, she wasn't at all sure she would be as accepting.

Of course, she hadn't been left alone with his parents, and she knew parents well enough to know they weren't likely to press a point with their son around to temper their approach.

"He's such a sweet little boy," Erin Henry said, looking in the direction Lee had parted. She smiled at her husband, then at Missy. "Oh, Missy, you don't need to look so worried. Mr. Henry and I aren't going to pounce as soon as Lee is out of the room."

Missy laughed, but it didn't make her feel any better. She flipped some hair behind her ear, then realized how nervous it probably made her look, and clenched her hands in her lap. "Am I that obvious?"

"Only a little, bless your heart." Erin smiled and tilted her head. "Maybe if we just get things out in the air, we'll all feel better."

Missy swallowed and nodded, her cheeks suddenly cold from the drain of blood. "Okay," she managed to say without croaking.

Rather than launching into all the reasons why she didn't want

Missy with her baby boy, Erin scooted forward and stood from the couch. When her husband moved to follow suit, she waved him back. "John, you stay here. Lee will be back soon, I'm sure."

"Sure enough, darlin'," he said, and the warmth in his voice made Missy smile even as she stood.

Erin startled her by taking her hand and leading her from the parlor. The farmhouse was large and sprawling, reminding her a bit of her own new home, although the Henry home was designed of dark woods rather than stucco and plaster, and had to be at least a century old. Lee had said the Henry family had lived on this property for five generations, so it wouldn't surprise her if this was the original homestead. The house felt very much like a genuine home, warm and comforting. Erin led her through the house, up the central staircase, and down a hall with several doorways.

"Lee will probably protest that I've brought you to his bedroom without him—"

"Oh, I—"

Erin tut-tutted at her and waved her free hand. "It will only be a mild protest, I assure you. But I want you to see something."

Missy followed her lead, and when Erin opened one of the bedroom doors, Missy stepped inside. She had no real expectations, but the room was typical as far as she could define. Like perhaps it hadn't changed much since he left high school, which made sense knowing he had been away from home for much of the last several years. The bed was made, neat and tight, and there were no dirty clothes on the floor. He had a single window, and the curtains were open, letting in the afternoon sunlight. Aged posters of military planes and guitar chord charts hung on the walls, some curling at the edges.

His guitar case leaned against the wall at the foot of his bed, and his guitar sat in a stand beside the bed as if left there within easy reach. A desk sat in front of the window, on it a closed laptop and a stack of business textbooks. The room held the scent of wood and leather and his cologne, pleasant and calming.

Erin released her hand and crossed to a tall bureau. "It might seem strange to some, but I gave back to my son all the letters he wrote me while he was overseas. They mean a great deal to me." She turned, with a bundle of letters held to her chest. "But, I believe they can mean a great deal to him as well." Erin smiled, but there was a touch of melancholy to it. "Lee is my youngest, but in so many ways, he is much older than my other children."

Lee's mother held out the stack of envelopes, and Missy took them but only read the top envelope. An APO address was written in the upper left corner, Lee's handwriting was neat but heavy, the tip of the pen having left furrows in the thin paper. It was addressed to John and Erin Henry. Unsure of what Erin wanted of her, Missy looked to her again.

"I've prayed for the last six years for this time, Missy. For Lee to come home safe, once and for all." She looked up, her eyes glistening, but she smiled. "We almost lost him once, you know. Oh, you probably don't. I doubt he's told you. He doesn't talk about it much. He was in Kabul, and his unit took fire. Several men died. He was wounded and spent a month in a military hospital before they sent him back. He'll tell you it wasn't that serious, but you're a mother, so I know you understand."

Missy nodded, her throat tightening. She hadn't known him then, but her sudden panic at the thought he could have died was just as real.

Erin sighed, and took back the letters, returning them to the bureau. "You're probably wondering if I'll ever get to the point." She turned again, her gentle smile firmly in place. "I will admit when he told me about you I was surprised. I forgot, even if for a few moments, who my son is. I forgot he isn't the young boy who left Indian Prairie six years ago, he was just my baby boy again."

"I forget, too," Missy said before she gave herself a chance to rethink. "I mean..." She shook her head and huffed. "My brother Thayne is older than Lee, he's married with a little girl, and in my head, he's younger. I don't suppose that makes sense."

"Oh, it does. You see the same thing I do. When I consider Lee's heart, it doesn't surprise me in the least."

Missy recognized the distinctive stride of Lee's boots coming down the hall and looked to the door as he came into view. He stepped into the doorway and raised one arm, resting his wrist against the doorjamb. A slow, sexy smile turned his lips and Missy hoped the heat in her cheeks wasn't too obvious.

"Daddy said I'd probably find you two up here."

"No worries, sweetheart," Erin said with a soft chuckle. "I'm not showing Missy any nudie baby pictures." She looked at Missy and winked. "Yet."

Missy laughed as Erin left the room, patting her son's chest on the way out. Once she was out of sight, Lee moved away from the doorway, his hands now pushed deep into his jeans pockets.

"Where are the boys?" Missy asked.

"Rolling around in the hay with six playful puppies," Lee answered with a grin, crossing to his bureau. "I had to come change because one of the puppies got a little too excited. Give me a second, kay?"

Missy nodded, but before she answered, her voice stopped short in her throat when he reached his hand behind his neck and pulled his tee shirt over his head, revealing his back to her. With the tee shirt balled in his fist, he opened a drawer and removed another tee shirt.

"Jude is supervising," he kept explaining. "My brother Mark came home, too, so he's out there. He'll bring them in when he comes."

"Okay," she croaked out.

"Give me a minute to wash up." He headed for the open door leading to an attached bathroom.

From where she stood, she watched him stand at the sink, hunched over slightly while he lathered his hands and a washcloth. She didn't make the choice to walk toward the door, but once her feet started moving she didn't force herself to stop either. Missy stood in the doorway, her hand on the jamb and her cheek resting against her fingers. This close, and free of the sudden shock of his bare torso, Missy caught the slight puckering of skin and a long scar along his back right side. Another scar marred the back of his right shoulder, and a military emblem tattoo to the left of the upper scar.

Lee stilled, and Missy shifted her gaze, meeting his in the mirror. Heat infused her cheeks. "Sorry..." she whispered.

Lee shook his head. "Don't be." He unfolded the washcloth he'd been using and laid it on the rim of the sink to dry, then took a light blue hand towel from a rack on the wall and dried his face and chest. With the towel hung again, he drew his left arm across his chest and pointed over his shoulder to the tattoo. "That's the emblem of my division. The date underneath is a day we were attacked by Afghani rebels. Seven men were killed." He paused, swallowed, then raised his right arm and turned slightly so the light in the bathroom shined on the scar lower on his back. The position made his muscles bunch and lengthen, but also made the scar more prominent. "I was shot and hit with shrapnel from a fragment bomb."

"Your mama told me," Missy tried to say, but her throat was like the sands of Afghanistan, and she had to stop and try to swallow before she tried again. "She said you were hurt."

"I was," he said, but his tone was dismissive. "There were others hurt a lot worse than me."

"Yeah, but you're her baby boy," she said softly and smiled when he looked over his shoulder at her. "It's always different when it's someone you love."

Lee picked up the clean tee shirt he'd carried in with him and bounced it in his hand before shaking it out. "I'm sure she'll feel better when I'm officially separated."

"Of course." Missy drew in a slow breath while he pulled the clean shirt over his head. "So will I." When he met her gaze, she tipped her ear toward her shoulder and shrugged. "I don't like the thought of you not being here for me to accidentally run into every day."

Lee turned away from the sink and crossed to her, stepping into the tight space of the doorway, his hand settling at her waist. "Come here."

It required no thought to move toward him, or to lean into his touch when he laid his hand on her cheek, or to tip up her chin to accept his kiss. Sometimes it felt so simple, so natural, like this had been who they were for years...not days. He kissed her slow, deep, and warmth rolled through her.

"Mmmmm," he hummed against her mouth before drawing back to look into her eyes. "Making out with my girlfriend in my bedroom...every boy's fantasy."

Missy stepped back and into the bedroom, because with every kiss she was always left with the desire for more. She moved toward the guitar beside the bed and brushed her fingers across the strings near the top of the neck. The rich sound rolled through the room. "I think maybe I have your parents' blessing. At least your mother's."

"No question about it, sweetheart."

Missy looked over her shoulder at him. "Will you play for me?"

He stepped up behind her, his hand brushing her waist while he reached for the guitar with the other. With it free of the stand, he sat on the side of his bed, closer to the foot, and patted the mattress for her to sit beside him. She shifted around the neck and settled beside him so their thighs touched and the neck of the guitar was at an angle in front of her. Lee slid his fingers along the strings, his calloused fingertips rasping along the tiny, wire-wound grooves.

"Anything in particular you want to hear?"

Missy shook her head. "Whatever you want to sing."

He nodded and smiled. "Okay."

Lee began to play, and at first, Missy didn't recognize the tune. Perhaps he was just warming up, or trying to find the right lyrics. Then the music became familiar, and she smiled. A lot of singers had covered "Make You Feel My Love", but there was no doubt in Missy's mind at that moment Lee's version was now and would always be her favorite. Lee's focus was downward, his intent on his hands, but when he raised his head to sing looking at her, Missy's heart hitched.

"I know you haven't made your mind up yet, but I would never do you wrong. I've known it from the moment that we met, no doubt in my mind where you belong."

Lee leaned sideways and kissed her cheek before righting himself again, his hands never paused in their playing. Missy sat silent, willing away the blur in her eyes, while he finished the song. When done, he shifted the guitar to rest on his far thigh, the neck swinging out away from them, so he could move closer to her without it in the way. Lee braced his hand on the mattress behind her and leaned in for a kiss.

"I didn't mean to make you cry," he said softly, brushing his cheek along hers so he could whisper close to her ear.

Missy chuckled and rubbed her cheek to his, the sound of his late-day whiskers on her skin, a rustle made sharp and clear by her hearing aids. She brought up her hands and laid them along his sharp jaw before pulling back to look at him.

Something clicked in her heart—in her head—maybe in her soul, and without a doubt at that moment Missy had no more questions about what she felt for Lee Henry. She'd told Miranda she didn't know, and maybe just the night before she didn't. Now she did.

"I need to tell you something," she said, keeping her voice low to give herself the chance of getting the words out without cracking.

"Okay."

She focused on his lips when he spoke. It was an adaptive mechanism she'd made a habit over the last few years, a way to avoid the difficulty of speaking and looking someone in the eyes; especially when the words weren't easy. Staring at Lee's mouth was no hard task, but it gave her a focal point. Missy sniffed, unable to tamp down the tears anymore. She hoped he'd understand they weren't the bad kind of tears. If anything, she was afraid but she wasn't sad.

"When Daniel got sick, and we knew he didn't have long, we

promised we would never hold back saying what we felt. We taught the boys it was a good thing, a gift, to tell someone you loved them. No matter what. Even after Daniel was gone, I made sure they remembered." She sniffed again but didn't want to break her touch-point, her contact with him, to wipe away the tears.

Lee did it for her, stroking his thumb across her cheek. Missy swallowed and licked her dry lips.

"So, I'd be a hypocrite if I didn't do what I taught, right?"

For just a moment she let her gaze snap up to meet his, and the blatant emotion in his blue eyes curled warmth in her chest, fortifying her courage. Lee nodded but said nothing.

"Lee...I'm falling in love with you."

His hand left the bed and pressed to her side, his fingers a firm assurance. Missy blinked rapidly, clearing her vision again as new tears ran down her cheeks. "I know this is completely insane, and I know it's only been a week, but how long is it supposed to take?"

He swallowed before he answered, "One heartbeat."

Missy smiled and nodded, and just as abruptly shook her head, focusing again on his lips so she didn't have to see his eyes. "Don't think I'm—I'm not trying to push you into—"

His hard, insistent kiss stopped her. Without breaking the kiss, Lee moved his guitar from his lap and set it behind him, then held her with both hands and kissed her deeper. So deep she thought she'd faint from the heady effect. He left her breathless, her heart pounding, when he finally released her, a wide smile on his face.

"Oh, darlin'," he said through heavy breaths, "I'm not falling in love with you, I *am* in love with you. All the way." He kissed her again, open lips covering hers. She swayed, her head floating, when he pulled away. "I love you, Missy."

She laughed again, a giddy joy hitting her, and wrapped her arms around his neck, Lee dotting her cheek and throat with quick kisses. From somewhere in the house, she heard Jeremiah's laughter and knew the boys had returned; which meant they needed to go. She didn't want to, not yet, but she forced herself to sit back and pat again at her cheeks.

"You're beautiful," Lee said and stood to set his guitar back in its stand. Then he offered his hand and she took it, lacing her fingers through his, and came off the bed to walk out of the room together.

CHAPTER TWELVE

"An' we gotsta play wiff da puppies. Dey're Beegus. An' in a big, *huge* sandbox, and Wee letted me wide a hohsie wiff him!"

Missy smiled as she hit the bottom of the stairs, Levi's loudly animated tale carrying to her from the kitchen. She paused in the foyer, just outside the kitchen, to listen for a few moments before interrupting. They'd have to leave in the next few minutes to make it to church on time.

"Oh, Auntie Susan, the puppies were so cute," Jeremiah. "One of 'em kept climbing up on me and licking my nose. Lee said he picked me, and if Mama said so, we could have him after we move into our house."

"Yeah, an' Mama said yes!" Levi shouted.

"We have to pick a name for him, and Lee said we should think about it a long time because it'll be his name forever."

"Oh, that's a tough decision," Susan said, her tone lilting to show she was as excited as they boys. "Does everyone get a vote?"

"We're all going to pick one name," Jude explained, his voice sounding so much deeper in contrast to his little brothers, and

Missy's eyes misted at the idea her first baby was definitely growing up. "Then when everyone has given a name, we're going to vote."

"Sounds very fair."

"I wanna name him Zeke," Levi told her, his voice mumbled. Probably around a mouthful of pancake.

"Don't talk with your mouth full, Levi," Jude scolded.

Missy smiled. She blinked quickly to push back any telltale moisture in her eyes and stepped around the corner. Everyone sat around the kitchen table, working on a stack of pancakes Missy had made before going upstairs to change. Susan had added some eggs and sausage. Thayne sat at one end of the table, silent, his eyes shifting momentarily to Missy before he went back to eating.

"Everyone almost done?" Missy asked, setting her purse on the counter. Levi needed to change his shirt since she never let him eat breakfast in the shirt he'd wear to church, but other than that the boys looked cleaned up and presentable. Wyatt wore his new Stetson, and Missy dreaded having to tell him it would come off in church. "We need to leave soon."

"Almost, Mama," Wyatt answered, taking a long drink of juice. He wiped his mouth with a napkin and slid from his chair. "I gotta get my jacket."

"Take Levi with you," she asked. "His shirt is on his bed."

"Come on, Leviathan." Wyatt took hold of Levi's wrist as he passed and Levi hopped down from his chair, syrup on his chin. He giggled at the nickname Wyatt used, a nickname Lee had dubbed her youngest with while they spent the afternoon at the ranch, and followed out of the kitchen.

"Wipe his face, please, before the shirt goes on."

Wyatt called an "okay" from the hallway, and Missy turned back to her family. If all went according to plans, by the next Sunday they would be eating in their own kitchen before heading to church. Jude stood and picked up his plate, grabbing his brothers' plates as well, and took them to the sink. Jeremiah took one last long drink from his milk, and followed, picking up their glasses. Missy smiled, proud of her boys.

As soon as the boys were away from the table, Thayne set down his fork. "The way these boys went on, you'd think Lee Henry was their biggest hero." His tone reeked with sarcasm.

Jude paused at the sink, his plate held under the running water. Missy caught his hesitation and glared at Thayne. "Not now, Thayne," she forced through clenched teeth.

"Lee is wicked awesome," Jeremiah said, falling back on his Boston slang, completely oblivious to the tension between the adults in the room. He set the glasses on the sideboard and dashed from the room.

"Yeah, awesome." Thayne sat back and pushed away his plate. "We'll see how long the hero worship lasts."

"Thayne, don't..." Susan whispered.

Jude didn't move from the sink, and although his hands worked at rinsing the dishes, his gaze shifted between Missy and his uncle. Missy clenched her jaw and crossed her arms, taking two steps closer to the table.

"Why are you being so hurtful?" she begged to know, shaking her head. "You keep spouting it's because you don't want *me* to be hurt, but don't you get you're doing more harm than you accuse Lee of ever doing?"

"Better from me now than him later."

Missy shook her head and looked back to Jude, who had finished rinsing the dishes, but still stood at the sink, his hand on the edge, watching.

"Jude, honey, why don't you—"

"No, Mom. I want to hear," he said, his voice firm, then looked to his uncle. "Tell *me*, Uncle Thayne."

Missy shook her head again, this time out of desperation. "Thayne..."

He stared Missy down and pushed back his chair, standing. Susan said his name, her whisper cracking.

"The other boys are too young to understand any of this, but Jude is certainly old enough," he said, and his words cut to her heart.

"Old enough for what? You have *nothing* to base any of this on. At least nothing worth listening to."

"I know better than you think."

"How? You have failed to give me anything—"

"Know what, Uncle Thayne?" Jude asked again.

Thayne stared at Missy for another heartbeat before looking at Jude. "I'm trying to save your mother, and all of you, the embarrassment of the inevitable, Jude. Lee might seem great right now, but eventually, he'll be gone. Your mother doesn't see it, but I do."

"See what?"

Missy closed her eyes, tears squeezing free, and drew in a shaky breath. Her heart hurt, and she couldn't imagine anything Lee could say or do hurting as much as her brother's words. She heard her brother's steps and blinked open her eyes as he reached Jude and laid a hand on the boy's shoulder.

"Reality," he said. "Lee Henry is going to realize to have your mother, he's going to have to have a readymade family. Men his age don't want that."

Jude looked at Missy, his eyes large. Before she could say anything more, he pulled free of his uncle's hold and took off down the hall. The front door opened and slammed closed in his wake. Thayne turned toward her, and Missy shot up her hand.

"Don't. Speak. To me," she hissed out. "Don't you dare speak to me."

She took two steps backward before turning to stalk out of the kitchen. Thayne's attitude had frustrated her, worn on her, but now it just enraged her and broke her heart. Blood pounded in her ears, making the hearing aids feel like corks, and heat infused her face.

"Missy, wait!"

She ignored her sister-in-law's plea, heading straight for escape. Susan caught up with her as she reached the front door, and grabbed her arm. "Missy, please don't leave like this. Thayne is just—"

"What, Susan? *Worried* about me? Afraid I'll be hurt?" She wrenched her arm free of Susan's hold. "He's doing a crappy job of showing it." She grabbed the doorknob and opened the door. Tears ran down Susan's cheeks when Missy looked back. "Days, Susan. He has days left to be a sanctimonious jerk and trust me, if I could get out of this house before then I would. Once I'm gone..." She snapped shut her jaw and refused to spit the words on the tip of her tongue.

When she shut the door behind her, Missy swore a piece of her heart stayed behind. She stepped off the porch and turned toward the driveway, stopping short when she saw her oldest leaning back against the passenger front tire well, his jaw set and his arms crossed. His brothers were in the Jeep, buckled in, talking and smiling, ready to go and gracefully oblivious to the turmoil. Missy kept walking, swallowing hard, until she reached Jude.

"I'm sorry," she said softly so the boys wouldn't hear her over their chitchat. "I know you've heard us arguing, your uncle and I, but he shouldn't have..."

She didn't know how to finish, looking past the hood of the Jeep to the horizon beyond. The sky was light blue today and cloud-free. A beautiful Sunday. Missy's chest ached and she drew in a hard, ragged breath.

"Why does he think Lee would do that? They're friends, right? Does he think Lee would do that?"

Missy shrugged; a pathetic response, she knew. "I've asked him outright if he knows Lee to be that kind of man, and he only speaks in general terms." She looked at her son. "I wish I could say without question I know Lee isn't, but the truth is I've only known him a few days. It feels longer to me, but...I just can't imagine..." She trailed off again because she had to accept her own words.

She really didn't know Lee.

Missy laid her hand on Jude's arm, gently squeezing. "I'm sorry. If you and your brothers are hurt in any way, I'm so sorry."

With a heart so heavy it slowed her steps, Missy walked around the front of the Jeep to get behind the wheel. Jude was inside and buckled in before she started the engine. He didn't speak the whole drive across town to the church.

"I need to talk to you."

Lee looked up from the spaghetti pile of cords and wires he was trying to untangle to get his amp hooked to the church system. Jude stood just off the stage, hands shoved in his pockets. An uncharacteristic scowl pulled at his features.

Lee stood, dusted off his hands, and took a step toward him. "Sure."

He looked past Jude to the entrance of the church just in time to see Missy rush in, Levi on her hip, holding Jeremiah's hand, and Wyatt coming up behind. She looked frantically around the sanctuary, and when she saw Lee and Jude, she stopped short, wide-eyed.

Lee raised his hand, holding up one finger, just enough so she'd see everything was okay. She stayed where she stood, people shifting around her.

"Jude, what's wrong?" Lee asked, trying to sound calm.

"Do you care about my mom?"

Lee almost laughed, but tamped down the visceral reaction to what felt like a foolish question. Instead, he brought his hands together and worked his palms. "Jude, to say I care about your mom..." He shook his head, glanced to the back of the church again to see Missy ushering the boys into a pew, then looked back to Jude to look him in the eyes. "I love your mom, Jude. I love her with everything I am."

"You haven't known her very long."

"True, but it doesn't change the fact I love her."

Jude worked his jaw, his lips pressed together in a tight, white-rimmed line. He looked past Lee for a moment, then straight on again. "What about us?"

"Us? You mean you and your brothers?"

"Yeah," Jude answered, nearly cutting off Lee's question.

A tightness took over Lee's chest, squeezing his heart and lungs. It was the first time he'd consciously considered how he felt about the boys separate from Missy. Until that moment, they had been a whole for him, because with Missy came her sons. Lee had to swallow and take a moment to rub his fingers across his mouth before he could answer. Before he did, he crouched just enough to be eye-to-eye with Jude, which didn't require much since the boy was about to Lee's chin, and laid his hand on Jude's shoulder.

"Jude, you are a part of your mom. So are Wyatt, Jeremiah, and Levi. How could I not love you, too?"

Jude's chin trembled and he quickly looked away, sucking in a sharp breath. Lee didn't hesitate and pulled Jude to him in a hard embrace. Jude didn't take his hands from his pockets, but he didn't pull away and leaned into Lee. The last two years had been hard for Missy, and Lee had understood that, but he hadn't fully comprehended how hard it would have been for Jude. The oldest, he probably felt the weight of it all on his shoulders; old enough to understand, but too young to do much about it other than grow up fast. Whatever had put the idea into his head that...

Lee closed his eyes and clenched his jaw. Not whatever. *Whoever.*

"We good?" Lee asked, drawing back to put his hands on Jude's shoulders. Jude nodded and snuffed his nose with the side of his hand. Lee cleared his throat. "Look, ah, I realize you're the man in your house, Jude. I should have checked with you. Is all this okay with you?"

Jude swallowed, one final jerk of emotion pulling at his throat. He stared at Lee for a few moments, his eyes intense, then he nodded. "Yeah, it's okay. As long as you don't make her cry."

Lee smiled and laid his hand against the side of Jude's head, ruffling his blond hair. "Have no intention to, buddy. It's my job to make her smile. You, too."

Jude smiled, and some of the tension in Lee's chest released. Not completely, because whatever upset Jude like this wouldn't have left Missy unscathed. He swept his arm around Jude's narrow shoulders and led him toward the aisle leading to the pew where the rest of his family sat. Missy watched them walk toward her, blue eyes wide and shining. Since the three boys talked amongst each other, with wide grins, he suspected they had been shielded from the events of the morning.

"Hey, beautiful," Lee said as he reached the end of her pew. He leaned over and kissed her cheek, then kissed her lips for good measure. They tasted slightly of salt.

"Wee!" Levi shouted and scrambled across his mother's lap, reaching out his arms.

Lee swept him up and had to swallow hard against the sudden swell of emotion in his throat when the boy threw his arms around Lee's neck and squeezed as hard as a three-year-old could. Jude moved past his mom and brothers to sit at the far end of the row of Coltons, likely a common routine for them to keep the youngers in line during service.

Missy looked from Lee, down to Jude, and back again, all the questions playing through her eyes. Lee reached for her hand, and when she took it, he drew her up to stand with him. He set Levi on the pew, and the boy resumed his seat beside Jeremiah. People moved around them, talking and greeting each other like any Sunday morning.

"Everything is okay," he told her, leaning in enough so he knew his voice would override all the other noise. "I'm going to find out later what brought this on, but I want to make sure you understand something without question, okay?"

She nodded, her eyes watching his mouth. When he stopped talking, she looked up. Lee released her hand to wrap his arm behind her waist, pressing her back so she moved against him. He noted the tremble in her hands when she laid them on his upper arms, and her body was tense in his hold. She held a firm rein on the emotions he saw playing in her eyes.

"I love you," he told her, and repeated, "I *love* you. I love Jude, and Jeremiah, and Wyatt, and Levi. I just told Jude the same thing. I love them because they are part of you, and you are the rest of me."

Tears sprang to her eyes, but she smiled.

Lee smiled back, then looked to the boys. "Save me a seat, okay, guys?"

The three youngest nodded, Levi cheered, and Jude smiled. Missy's hands on his arms curled into a firmer hold. Lee pulled her tighter against him. "Hey..." She turned from looking at the boys to meet his gaze, and relief eased the tightness he'd had in his chest when he saw the spark in her eyes again. "I need to head up front. Are you staying for the cookout after service?"

"I'd planned to."

He grinned. "Good. You're sitting with us."

She smiled, and this time it went all the way to her eyes. "Okay."

"Kiss me before I go, but remember, this is church."

She giggled and leaned up to kiss him, and despite his chiding, he wanted to deepen the kiss. Missy was kerosene to his fire, even the slightest drop set him blazing. He hummed reluctantly and let her go, heading toward the pulpit so he could get wired before Pastor Nason began service.

He glanced back once, and met Missy's gaze, and smiled again.

"Thank you, God," he said quietly. "I have been blessed."

CHAPTER THIRTEEN

THE HENRY FAMILY, AND SUBSEQUENT ADJUNCTS WITH SPOUSES AND children, took up two tables in the fellowship hall, and Missy was sure that family alone was twenty percent of the entire congregation. In her family, there had only been her and Thayne, and Daniel had been an only child, so even combined holidays didn't come close to a church cookout with Lee's family. They were loud, and happy, and it wrapped around her like a warm blanket.

Her boys were enveloped into the fold like long lost cousins, each one sitting with Henry descendants near their age, and there were plenty. The only Henry children not married with kids were Mark and Lee. Even their sister Ellie, who fell in between Ricky and Lee, had married a couple years before and had given birth to a baby girl not five weeks earlier. There were two boys near Jude's age, a girl near Wyatt's age, and a cluster of kids ranging around Jeremiah and Levi. They had all met the day before at the ranch, so seeing the cousins again was like seeing old friends.

The oldest of the Henry grandchildren was Billy at sixteen, and he'd taken up a spot at the far end of the table with a pretty girl and possibly a couple of other friends. Missy hadn't quite squared away who belonged to who yet; the dinner the night before had been just as hectic and she felt pride in being able to recognize Lee's siblings versus their spouses. Her head spun with all the names, and she figured she'd need flash cards and pop quizzes to make sure she got them all straight. She'd always prided herself on her memory, but this was like trying to take a sip of water from a fire hydrant. Too much to process at once.

Best of all, her heart felt light and the anger of the morning was washed away, both from the wonderful church service and the people surrounding her. And they really did surround her. Ellie was on her left, baby Vanessa in her arms, and Mark was on her right.

"Scoot forward."

She turned at the sound of Lee's voice. He stood behind her a plate heaped with food in one hand, a plastic cup of lemonade in the other. Missy looked down at the wide bench she sat on that ran the length of the table, and did as Lee asked, moving so she sat closer to the edge. With a wide grin, he stepped over the bench one leg at a time, and settled to sit around and behind her so she was nestled between his thighs and he wrapped around her to set his plate on the red and white checkerboard plastic tablecloth. His chest pressed to her back, and as soon as he set down the cup of lemonade, he wrapped his arm around her waist.

"This is going to make a challenge of eating," she said over her shoulder.

Lee shifted closer, so they actually shared the spot on the bench pretty comfortably, and Missy was effectively wrapped in Lee Henry. "A risk I'm willing to take."

"I would have moved over, bro," Mark said with a chuckle.

"Nah, this is perfect." With his left arm still wrapped around her waist and his hand flat against her stomach, Lee used his right to work up a forkful of coleslaw. Before taking the chance of bringing the food to his mouth, he leaned in and spoke near her ear. "How are you doing in here? It's pretty loud."

Missy nodded, chuckling when he managed to get the slaw to his mouth without dropping any on either of them. "It's chaotic. My aids get confused about what they should focus on. Keep skipping programs on me."

"Would it be easier to take them out?" he asked, and she figured he couldn't help or didn't even notice he shifted his attention to her ears.

"No, not really. Yes, it'd quiet some of the conflicting noise, but I also wouldn't be able to hear clearly. I'd rather deal with the chaos than miss something important like the boys calling for me, or something. I'll just take them out as soon as I can and give my head a rest."

He nodded, seeming to consider the explanation.

"I have a feeling, though, in or out, I'd be able to hear you," she confessed.

Lee grinned, looking completely smug. "Yeah?"

"Oh, don't get all puff-chested." She nudged his abdomen with her elbow and he chuckled. "I mean, there's something about the tone of your voice that I hear easily. I noticed that the night we met. Even in the thumping and loud music at Low Places, I heard you."

"Well, just one more reason we are meant to be, sweetheart."

Missy leaned back into him and tilted her head to accept his kiss. He tasted sweet and tangy from the slaw. It was so easy to be lost in Lee Henry. Someone cleared their throat, and she felt Lee's grin before he drew back.

"I'm a little busy, Mark," Lee said, not taking his mouth too far from hers.

"Well, you might want to get un-busy. Pastor Nason is headed our way, and you might not want to get caught making out with your girlfriend at the church cookout. Most of us gave up on that at sixteen."

Lee cleared his throat and shifted, but didn't move from his spot wrapped around her. Missy rolled her lips together to hide her smile and faced forward to work on her plate of food. Pastor Nason did eventually make it their way, and greeted each member of the family, Missy included. And while he did perhaps linger a few moments longer studying Missy and Lee's sitting position, the smile on his face was honest and open, and Missy didn't sense any condescension toward them. If anything, she hoped what she saw was possibly approval.

When the food was eaten and paper plates stacked for clean up, Ellie turned to Missy, already holding out Vanessa. "Missy, could you hold her for a minute? I've held it as long as I can."

"Oh, sure." Missy set down her cup and opened her arms. She'd been dying to get her hands on the baby since Ellie sat down, but hadn't wanted to ask.

Vanessa was awake, but content, and didn't seem bothered at all at being held by someone else. Missy figured the baby had probably been passed around so many times with the size of the Henry family, that a new face was nothing to worry about. She settled the baby in her arms, the action feeling so familiar and so distant at the same time. In reality, it hadn't been so long since she'd cradled Levi, but it felt like years and years.

"She is absolutely adorable," Missy said to no one in particular.

Lee's arms came around her body, settling beneath where she snuggled Vanessa, and he rested his chin on her shoulder so he could look down at his baby niece. The girl had one tiny hand fisted against her cheek, big blue eyes staring up at them. She blinked slowly and let out a long-suffering sigh. Each blink took longer, and after just a few, she drifted off to sleep.

"She knows she's in good hands," Lee said low, his breath warm on her cheek before he kissed her skin.

"I've done this a few times."

Lee reached up his hand and brushed her hair away from her cheek. "Sweetheart, I don't mean to scare you..." She turned her head enough to look him in the eyes, and something about the way they looked back made her heart hitch. "but you look so beautiful in my arms, with a baby in yours."

He said it so low there wasn't a chance anyone else would hear, but the impact of his words sent a warm flush over her whole body, flooding her cheeks with heat.

Lee smiled and ran his fingertips across her cheekbone. "You're beautiful when you blush." The heat fluttered under her skin when he drew his touch from her cheek to the side of her throat. "It goes all the way down your throat."

Missy licked her lips and looked down at the baby. "It goes further than that..."

The arm around her waist tightened a tiny bit, and his fingers curled into the knit of her sweater. A low, rumbling groan vibrated through his chest and against her back, and Missy tried to hide her smirk.

"Woman, you drive me crazy."

"Okay, I'm back." Ellie returned and sat beside Missy, facing out away from the table. She looked down at her daughter in Missy's arms and smiled. "Wow, you're good."

"I've got some practice." Missy chuckled softly to not wake the baby. "It's been a bit, but after four boys you learn the tricks. Especially Jeremiah." She looked past Ellie to where her boys sat with some of the Henry cousins. "He kept me up all night when he was a baby, and I have a feeling that one is going to cause me many more sleepless nights when he's older."

Ellie smiled. "My husband loses sleep now, and that's just because she's a girl. Speaking of which, I've got to head home. Dean worked last night and probably will be waking up soon. Nessa likes to see her daddy." She snaked her arms through Missy's and took back her daughter. "Thanks so much."

"Sure, anytime."

As if on cue, people throughout the fellowship hall stood and began gathering the dirty plates, cups, and napkins. With a groan, Lee extricated himself from his position around her, one leg at a time. As soon as he was clear, Missy pivoted on the bench so her legs were on the outside, and he offered his hand to help her stand. When she gained her feet, Lee wrapped his arm around her waist and brought her against him.

"What are you doing the rest of the day?"

"Just about anything that doesn't require I go back to Thayne's," she said before really contemplating the words. She winced internally at the darkening of Lee's eyes.

"It's time Thayne and I had words again."

Missy shook her head and laid her hand on his chest, the feel of his heartbeat against her palm soothing in contrast to what she had felt earlier in the day. "No, Lee. Leave it be. I'm only living there a few more days, and then I don't need to deal with him every day."

"What did he say this morning to have Jude so worked up?"

Missy contemplated blowing off the confrontation, but the absolute resolve in Lee's eyes told her without question he wouldn't let it go so easy. She drew in a breath through her nose and released it. Despite her attempt to stay outwardly calm, her pulse kicked up before she even began the explanation. Lee slid his hand up her spine, drawing her closer in a comforting embrace.

"I'm ad-libbing, but the essence of it is he told Jude you wouldn't stay with me because you would eventually decide I wasn't worth taking on another man's four children."

The fingers against her back curled into the fabric of her sweater and his jaw tightened.

"Thankfully he didn't say it in front of the other children. I wish he'd had enough consideration not to say it to Jude, but..." Despite herself, hot tears blurred her vision.

"I now understand Jude's question this morning."

Missy blinked back the tears, willing them away, and looked into Lee's face. "What *did* he ask you?"

"He asked me if I cared about you. I told him I did more than that, I loved you." His lips, tense moments before, curled up into the slow, sexy grin she loved so much.

"Is that why you said what you did in the sanctuary?"

He nodded and hummed an affirmative. "I don't want you to ever question it. Promise me."

"Will you be upset if I say I can't help it?" She didn't wait for him to answer. "If I were on the outside of all this, looking in, I would think we were either crazy or delusional or both. Lee, we *met* less than ten days ago. Ten days. How can we—"

"Do you love me?"

Missy stared at his lips when he asked the question, her jaw working to find the answer. She finally just laughed and shrugged. "I do. The Good Lord help me, but I do."

He covered her hand with his, holding it firm to his chest. Pressed so hard, she could almost hear the thump-thump of his heart. "Do you feel that, Missy?"

She nodded.

"That beat is my love. You feel that beat and know you're feeling my love. Is that crazy?"

"No."

Lee grinned wide and smacked a loud, firm kiss to the middle of her forehead. "Then who cares if it's been ten days, ten weeks, or ten minutes? Let them think we're crazy. Let them doubt. But when we're old and gray, and still *crazy in love*, they'll have to admit we weren't crazy after all."

"I'll just be old before you," she couldn't help but slide in.

Lee shook his head, making a sound that said "No way" and wrapped both arms around her to link his hands behind her back. "Number only, sweetheart. Number only."

"We'll see."

"Are we going home now, Mama?" asked Jeremiah as he ran up to them, Levi on his heels.

"Actually," Lee said, turning to face the boys with one arm still behind her to hold her near. "I was thinking we should make a day of it."

"Make a day of what?" Jeremiah asked, his little forehead drawn tight in clear confusion.

"Make a day of fun. We could go to the baseball park over by the high school, then we'll go to Maude's for dinner—" At this, both Wyatt and Jeremiah cheered. "And...we could go get your puppy at the ranch before we go to the park."

Jeremiah and Wyatt bolted away to find their brothers and Missy laughed as she looked up at Lee. Her heart felt three times larger, filling up all the dark, empty spots she'd been harboring for the last two years. He looked down at her and grinned before kissing her.

It didn't matter what Thayne thought, what anyone thought. Maybe she would be hurt, but she didn't believe it, and until it happened she was going to enjoy every moment of bliss she could.

Daniel had made her promise before he let go, that she would be happy again someday. Just like Lee said there was no required time to fall in love, there was no required time she had to wait before she let love back in her life. She still thought they were crazy.

But she liked crazy.

CHAPTER FOURTEEN

"You think I'm crazy, too, don't you?"

Miranda's laughter carried through the Bluetooth connection, and Missy smiled. "Missy, this is *absolutely* crazy. Seriously cracked. But that doesn't mean it isn't the real thing. There's a reason there's a thing called love at first sight."

Missy set her phone on the kitchen counter so she could open one of the many boxes of dishes she'd brought over from storage that morning. The official move-in date wasn't until tomorrow, but she couldn't help getting a head start. The bulk of the large furniture and boxes would be dropped off in the morning, but until then she busied herself with the more mundane side of unpacking. Dishes. Pots. Pans.

It didn't feel mundane at all. It felt liberating.

"Is Thayne still giving you a hard time?"

"Nope," Missy said with a pop of the p. "He can't give me a hard time if I don't talk to him. I have managed to avoid him for the last six days except for one silent passing in the hallway yesterday morning."

"How long do you think this will go on?"

"Thayne is stubborn. And before you say anything, I know it runs in the family." She waited to hear Miranda's chuckle. "I think it will go on until he's either proven right or wrong. It'll take a little longer if he's proven wrong."

She heard the sound of tires on her gravel driveway and crossed the breakfast nook to look out the bay window looking out onto the front yard. Two *John Henry and Sons* trucks were parked beside her Jeep, and she grinned when she spotted Lee come around the front of one to meet up with a gentleman she didn't immediately recognize. Which meant he wasn't a Henry.

"I've got to go," she said, crossing the room again to retrieve her phone on her way to the front door. "My new appliances are here."

"You mean Lee is there, and it just so happens he has the new appliances."

"Maybe."

She picked up her phone just as the front door opened, and Lee bellowed "Woman!"

"Did he just call you *woman*?" Miranda gasped.

Missy chuckled. "Maybe. I'll call you later."

She barely got the call disconnected before Lee came through the foyer into the kitchen, and once he spotted her, crossed the room in four long strides to wrap her up in his arms for a kiss that lifted her off her feet. Missy squealed into the kiss, holding on to his shoulders until he set her down again. Breathless, she leaned back, his arms still firmly around her waist.

"Well, hello," she said on a huff. "Do you say hello to *all* your customers like that?"

"Only the pretty ones."

She popped her eyes open and dropped her jaw. Lee laughed and squeezed her a little tighter before letting go. "None as pretty as you, sweetheart." The door opened and closed again, and Lee turned to the gentleman coming in, who looked a bit sheepish, his middle-aged, weathered face a crimson red. Missy wondered if the opening and closing of the door had been for their benefit. "Missy, this is Scott Adams."

"Pleased to meet you, ma'am," Scott said with a tip of his head, his hat turning a slow circle between his hands.

"The same."

"Scott's going to help me get the old fixtures out and the new stuff in, then he'll go on back while I get them hooked up for you."

Missy leaned back into the edge of the counter and crossed her arms. "Soldier, musician, businessman...now plumber and electrician? I suppose you could change the oil in my car, too?"

Lee headed toward the door but looked back at her with a wink. "Oh, I can do more than that, sweetheart."

"You just keep giving me more and more reasons to keep you around."

He smiled wider and headed out the door, calling back "I can do laundry and barbecue a mean steak, too!"

Missy laughed and crossed the kitchen to the breakfast space so she would be out of their way.

The house hadn't come with any washer and dryer, so she'd picked out new high-capacity machines a few weeks prior since it took a bit for them to be delivered to Indian Prairie. John Henry and Sons sold the appliances, but only on a piece-by-piece basis since it didn't make sense for them to hold inventory. She'd also opted to switch out the refrigerator, stove, dishwasher, and garbage disposal before moving in since they were all several years old and with four boys, she needed heavy duty. A chest freezer was going into the laundry and storage room.

She didn't like to consider the "benefit" of a substantial life insurance policy left by Daniel, but it had been that policy that had allowed her to stay home with her children for the last several years and buy what she needed for the house without worry of how to pay. The sale of the townhouse in Boston had more than covered the outright purchase of the house here, the differences in property cost and values so radically different from Boston to Indian Prairie.

In a couple of years, some of the money would go to buying a car for Jude, and she had already established college funds for each of them. She'd always been prudent with her finances, even before Daniel's death, and it all paid off now...in as much as the financial gain from her husband's death could be considered a gain. With careful planning, she would be financially comfortable for a long while to come. Independent, though the idea of being alone didn't appeal nearly as much as it used to.

A thunk from the foyer preceded Scott backing his way into the kitchen, pulling a hand truck with her new chest freezer balanced on it. Lee walked with him, supporting the freezer.

"Laundry room?" he asked on his way past.

Missy nodded. "Do you need help?"

"Nope," he said with a wink as they passed. "Besides, you've got company." He ticked his head back toward the foyer, moving along with Scott. "I better not find out another man is trying to steal you away."

Missy scowled and shook her head as he disappeared around the corner to the storage room, and headed herself for the front door. She opened the door to a man carrying a large bouquet so large he had to carry it to the side so he could see.

"Good morning, ma'am. You Mrs. Missy Colton?" he asked, shifting the bouquet to hug it to his side so he could look at his order clipboard.

"Yes," Missy said, a bit in awe at the size of the bouquet. It had so many types of flowers she could only identify half of them, at most.

"Sign here, please."

She took the touchpad, looking away from the flowers only long enough to find the spot to sign, and exchanged the device for the vase. The young man tipped his head and tapped his cap brim before jogging back to his waiting van, *Tessa's Flowers and Gifts* painted on the side. Missy shifted the vase to try to see her way back into the house and managed to get to the kitchen counter without dropping it or running into anything. Once it was secure, she dug through the blooms to find the card.

When she read the note, her heart swelled with a mixture of happiness and sadness.

CONGRATULATIONS ON YOUR NEW HOME, OUR DARLING MISSY. GOD BLESS YOU AND THE BOYS, AND WE'LL SEE YOU SOON.
ALL OUR LOVE: MOM AND DAD COLTON

Missy smiled and blinked against her tears. She adored her in-laws and never could relate to people who whined and complained about their spouse's parents. Mom and Dad Colton had been a blessing during her marriage to Daniel, and an even greater blessing when they all lost him. They comforted each other in their shared loss and told Missy they were ecstatic she was coming back to Oklahoma. Her mother had died a couple of years after she and Daniel married, and her father three years later, and through it all they had been so loving and caring; so much so that she considered them truly more parents than in-laws.

She looked up from the card toward the door leading to where Lee and Scott's voices carried. How would they feel about her being involved with someone else? With the idea that another man might raise their grandchildren? Missy shook her head. She was jumping too far ahead. Yes, she loved Lee, but she wouldn't think yet of forever. That seemed a long way from "We met two weeks ago..."

Laughter carried from the storage room, both Lee's familiar sound and Scott's deeper chuckle. Missy set the card on the counter and followed the sound. She rounded the corner but stopped when she heard her name, and leaned against the wall just outside the door, out of sight but able to hear them.

"She seems like a mighty fine lady, Lee."

"Don't get any ideas," Lee said with another chuckle. "She's all mine."

This time Scott laughed. "Oh, no worry there. The way you two look at each other, I doubt she realized I was in the room."

There was a clank like perhaps a tool had been set down. "I never knew you to be so sentimental, Scott."

"Oh, thirty or so years of bein' with the woman you love can do that to a person. You'll see."

There was a slight scraping sound and soft grunts. Perhaps they were shifting the freezer into position.

"I have every intention," Lee said, sliding back into their previous conversation. "Thirty years. Forty years. All my years." Another clank. "Okay, let's get the washer and dryer in, then we'll work on getting the old appliances out."

"Sure 'nough, boss man."

Missy pushed away from the wall so she stood in the middle of the hall when Lee stepped out of the storage room. He pulled up short, then grinned. "Hey..." Then he narrowed his eyes, but they still sparkled with humor. "Flowers, huh? Who should I tell to stay away from my girl?"

Missy chuckled and shook her head. "No one. They are a house-warming bouquet from Daniel's parents."

"That was nice of them."

"They're good people. Um, I've got to get the boys from school and Levi from the sitter." She motioned between Lee and Scott. "You two okay here?"

Scott moved around them back into the kitchen, a bashful grin on his face. Missy got the impression Scott was probably much more romantic than Lee thought. Lee took her hand and leaned in to kiss her cheek, but touched her lips before he drew back. "Sure. We might even be done before you get back."

"Okay. I planned on going grocery shopping tonight. I have a refrigerator, freezer, and pantry to stock. Are you playing tonight?"

"Nope, took this week off with the move. I am all yours."

Missy smiled and canted her head. "You're so good to me."

"No, baby...you're so good to me." Lee leaned in for another kiss.

Scott cleared his throat behind them. "Sorry, ma'am. If I could ask you to please sign for delivery before you leave?"

"Oh, sure."

Scott held out his clipboard, and Missy released Lee's hand so she could accept it and his pen. She skimmed the invoice statement, then read it again. "This...I don't think this is right."

"What's wrong with it?" Lee asked, stepping closer to look over her shoulder. He shrugged. "Looks correct to me."

"Lee, this is considerably less than the total I expected."

He shrugged again and smacked a kiss on her cheek before walking past and into the kitchen, saying "Family discount."

"Family discount? What?" she called, following him.

"Family discount," he repeated and winked. "Don't you need to go get the boys?"

Missy squinted and pursed her lips as she went past him, heading for the door. "We aren't finished with this conversation, Mr. Henry."

Lee waved as she climbed in her Jeep.

"So, what's your method of attack?"

"Method of attack?" Missy asked, pushing her shopping cart through the automatic doors to the Food Pyramid. Levi fidgeted in the seat and Wyatt followed behind holding Jeremiah's hand. Jude walked ahead, scoping the bakery section.

"Yeah. Do you hit certain sections first? Work a list? What?"

Missy laughed and shook her head, her eyes sparkling with life. He loved it when she looked at him like that. "This trip? Aisle by aisle, cart by cart, because I'm pretty sure we're going to need more than one. I'm starting from scratch, flour to Fudgsicles."

"Fud'sickles!" Levi cheered, throwing his hands in the air.

"I probably should have gone with something else as an example," Missy said out the corner of her lips, looking at him sideways.

Lee laughed and stepped behind her to slide her out of the way so he could push the cart. "Okay, so let's hit the middle first for the non-perishables, then the outskirts for produce and frozen goods. But, only buy enough meat to get you a few days. I'll hook you up with the butcher in town. Much better meat."

"In my experience buying directly from a butcher is great, but more expensive."

"Not when you get the family discount." He winked at her. "Bea's husband owns the shop. Inherited it from his father."

Missy stopped walking and crossed her arms, one eyebrow tugging upward. "Yes, family discount. I recall wanting to speak to you about that."

"Nothing to talk about," Lee said, continuing into the first aisle. "As far as I'm concerned, and anyone else in the family, you *are* family, sweetheart. Semantics only."

"Semantics?" she called, catching up with him to place bags of flour and sugar in the cart.

Before she could slip away again, Lee snaked out his arm and yanked her to his side, leaning in to whisper in her ear. "Semantics. How long do you think I intend to wait for forever?"

That beautiful blush of hers crawled up her throat and bloomed in her cheeks. Then she smiled, a slow, sexy, flirty smirk that stirred his blood. "Well, then, Mr. Henry...I suppose you'll want to pick out your own breakfast cereal?"

"I like Cheerios," Wyatt said, walking up to them, apparently clueless to their flirtations.

"Mmmm," Lee said with a wink at the boy. "Me, too. Love 'em."

They made it three aisles before the cart was overflowing, and they needed to swap out. Lee left Missy and all the boys but Levi in the canned goods aisle to head to the front of the store. He was sure Bobby Jenkins, who managed the store, or one of the floor supervisors, would let them set aside the full cart until they were done. Especially knowing they'd probably have two more coming.

As Missy said, "Four boys eat a *lot* of food."

Wait until it's five...

He grinned at his own thoughts.

Sure enough, Brooke Johnson was in charge of the floor and she told him to leave the cart by the customer care window until they were done. With the cart parked, Lee hauled Levi out of the seat and settled the three-year-old on his hip to go claim another cart.

"Wee..." Levi said, a little lilt to his voice like he was leading into a question.

"Yeah?" Lee held Levi with one arm while he separated a cart from the row of carts with the other. He settled Levi into the seat and recognized the look of deep concentration on the preschooler's face. Lee set his hands on either side of the boy on the back of the seat and crouched down to be at eye level. "What's up, Leviathan?"

Levi touched his face. It was an innocent move, but the impact of it was a slam to his chest, and Levi looked at him with unfiltered honesty. "Will you come wive in our new house?"

Lee smiled, knowing the boy had no idea how close his question came to everything Lee wanted. Not so much the house, but the people in it. He'd live in a trailer if it were with Missy and the boys. "Do you think there's enough room for me?"

Levi nodded, blue eyes wide. "Uh huh. Dere's a whole udder bedwoom you can have. Or you can sweep in my woom. I gots bunkbeds."

"No way," Lee said with feigned awe.

Levi nodded with a child's enthusiasm. "Yup. It usta be mine and Jer'miah's beds, but he gots a new bed and his own woom."

"Do you like having your own room?" Lee straightened to swing the cart around and head toward the aisle where he'd left Missy.

Levi shrugged, but he didn't quite look convinced.

"Well, it didn't take long for the Widow Colton to whip you into domestication."

Lee stopped the cart when Callie stepped out of one of the aisles, a small basket draped on her arm, blocking his direct path. She walked around the front of the cart, trailing her fingers along the edge, until she stood adjacent to Levi, who didn't seem to take notice.

"Grocery shopping. Pushing around the baby. She lookin' for a new daddy for those boys?"

"Mind your tongue, Callie," Lee said through clenched teeth, glancing at Levi to make sure the boy wasn't paying attention. At three, it was doubtful he'd understand Callie's more subtle jabs, but he would understand if she got too blatant.

"My Daniel daddy lives in heabin," Levi said, raising his head to look at Callie and Lee's gut clenched.

"I know, sweetie," Callie said in a sticky sweet voice. She looked to Lee. "Like I said—"

"Enough—" he cut her off. Lee shifted his stance and braced his arms on the shopping cart handle. "Do you honestly think this b—" He stopped himself, and cleared his throat. "Do you honestly think this woman-scorned attitude is going to do you any good?"

The heads of at least two nearby shoppers turned briefly in their directions before they feigned a lack of interest and went back to their shopping. Lee clenched his jaw and curled his hands tighter around the cart handle. Levi patted his hand, tapping until Lee released his grip.

Callie scowled, her painted lips pulling together. "Do you think you're being fair to that woman? Eventually you're going to realize—"

"Sounds like you've been comparing notes with Thayne Bingham."

She cocked an eyebrow and shrugged. "Don't need to, but damn, how ironic. Anyone with a lick of sense knows this *whatever* it is you've got going with Widow Colton is wrong, and you'll figure it out eventually, too. Guys like you always do."

A moment of realization hit him, and Lee drew in a slow, calming breath through his nose. "This isn't about Missy and me. This is about Patty?"

Her smug grin slipped. "You're pretty low to bring up Patty."

"Why shouldn't I? You might not be saying her name, but you've brought her into this, not me." Lee closed his eyes and turned away, looking at Levi when he opened his eyes.

The boy's eyes shifted between Lee and Callie. Lee smiled and smoothed the boy's hair, and Levi smiled back. Not looking back at Callie, he finished the conversation. "I'm sorry Patty was hurt. But that was a different situation, and has nothing to do with Missy and me."

"How can you say that, Lee?" she called after him when he walked away.

He didn't answer, and pushed the cart forward to the next aisle, turning. And pulled up short to keep from hitting Missy. Her head was tilted to the side, her hand resting on the shelf beside a row of canned corn. As soon as he was in sight, Jude and Wyatt came to either side of the cart to empty the armloads of food goods they carried. Missy didn't move, didn't say anything, just stared at him, her features neither angry nor tense, almost too placid.

Lee stepped around the side of the cart to stand in front of her.

"Patty is Callie's older sister," he said, not waiting for her to ask or wanting to force her to ask. "She was involved a few years ago with a man..." He cleared his throat and pushed his hands into his pockets. "...with a younger man. She has two children and..." He winced, unable to get through the whole explanation without pausing. "Patty thought she'd have a future, and it left her pretty wrecked when it didn't work out."

Missy nodded and looked away long enough to complete the mundane task of placing several cans of corn in the quickly filling cart.

"So, like Thayne, Callie figures that will happen here, too," she stated, looking down at the cart rather than at him. "Like it did to her sister."

"I think so, yeah."

Missy chuckled, but it lacked all humor. "So, like Thayne, Callie is concerned for *my* wellbeing. Funny, I thought she was more interested in you."

"Sweetheart, look at me."

She did as he asked, but he couldn't read the stillness in her eyes.

"It wasn't me."

Missy was shaking her head before he finished. "I never thought it was," she insisted. "Not ever."

"Okay." Lee laid his hand against her cheek and leaned in to kiss her forehead. She tilted her chin down, moving into the touch "Okay," he said again.

CHAPTER FIFTEEN

Missy smiled and grunted as she slid one of her jam-packed suit-cases from the back of her Jeep. Lee grabbed two, one in each hand, and stepped back, carrying them effortlessly.

"This is all we had to take out of Thayne's, everything else is coming on a truck from the moving and storage place. I figured why stir up a hornet's nest if we didn't have to?"

Lee led the way toward the house. It was a gorgeous day for moving, with sunshine and a light breeze. Warm in the sun, but in the shade and in the house it was perfect. They stepped into the foyer, and the temperature from outside dropped ten degrees. With little to no furniture in the house yet, the sound of running boys' footsteps and laughter carried back to them.

"Are all these going to the bedrooms?" Lee asked, heading through the kitchen toward the bedroom hallway.

"The one in your left-hand goes to Jeremiah's room, the one in the right to my bedroom."

He nodded and headed down the hall while Missy made a stop in

Jude's bedroom to drop off the suitcase she dragged behind her. It was both Jude and Wyatt's things, but they'd divvy up later, just like the suitcase going to Jeremiah's room also had Levi's clothes. Once set in the corner of Jude's room so it would be out of the way when the furniture arrived, she sighed and continued to the back of the house to her bedroom. She'd managed to coordinate the delivery of her ordered furniture with the delivery of the stuff in storage, so "moving" would be one weekend, and one weekend only.

She found Lee standing in the middle of her cavernous bedroom, hands on hips, scrutinizing the paint job on the wall where she intended to set the bed. Missy had been a little reluctant to go with the red he recommended, thinking it was just too powerful a color for a bedroom, but once it was done she loved it. She tried to imagine her basic, small bedroom set in the big room, but the image was always overpowered by the imagination of a large, heavy-posted bed and long bureau. Substantial pieces befitting a room this size.

She figured another shopping trip was in her future.

"You were right," she said, stepping into the room to lean against the wall to the right of the door. "I didn't think red would work in here, but it does. It definitely does."

Lee turned when she spoke, and walked back to her, his eyes intent on her until he stood right in front of her. Missy had to tip up her chin to keep eye contact, and the way his lips ticked up at one corner made her skin warm. He raised a hand and ran his fingertip along her brow, smoothing away some waves that had escaped her clip.

"Makes an even better backdrop for you than I imagined," he said in a low, husky voice.

Missy's stomach tumbled. Each time they were close, each time he touched her or kissed her, her traitorous body reacted with more and more intensity. Soon, one touch and she might actually implode. Thoughts of propriety and temperance and taking things slow slipped away in the haze of sparking sensations his proximity and touch stirred in her, muddying her resolve.

"I don't think I've told you enough just how beautiful you are, sweetheart," Lee whispered, brushing his cheek against hers so his breath warmed her ears and her aids amplified his voice. "Beautiful. Tempting. Maybe too tempting."

She giggled. "Funny, I was just thinking much the same thing."

Lee drew back enough to look her in the eyes, his thumb stroking her cheek. He swallowed visibly and a small line dug in between his eyes like he were in deep thought, or deep examination.

"What?" she asked.

"Missy, I—"

"The delivery truck is here, Mama!" Wyatt yelled, tearing down the hallway toward the bedroom, his voice echoing in the empty halls.

"And the moving truck just pulled in," Jeremiah added, running along behind Wyatt.

They ran right past the bedroom to complete the circuit back to the front of the house. Missy laughed and shook her head. "I have a feeling they see this house more like a running track than a place to live."

Lee chuckled once and took a step back. "Let's go get this place filled up, huh?"

"Did you want to say something?"

"Nah," he said with a shake of his head, his lower lip curling out a little. "Nothing that can't wait until it's less hectic." He linked his fingers through hers and led her from the bedroom.

Missy barely sat down for the next few hours, and only caught glimpses of Lee as dozens of boxes and pieces of stored furniture filed into the house, along with new pieces being delivered and assembled, to fill the empty rooms of the house. It wasn't until nearly four when she finally had a moment to stop and pause and take a long breath. Feeling tired to her bones, she started the trek from the back of the house through the living space toward the kitchen. She heard her boys' voices, but they were on the other side of the house and only muted sounds, not anything distinguishable.

She came through the foyer into the kitchen as Lee shut the door to the refrigerator. He looked over his shoulder at her and grinned, then turned with two bottles of iced tea.

"Hey, pretty girl," he said, coming toward her with one bottle held out. "You as tired as me?"

Missy sighed and gladly took the cold bottle. "Exhausted." She took three deep swallows of the sweet tea and hummed in appreciation. "Oh, that's good."

He drained half his bottle. "So, where do we stand? Is everything here?"

Missy laughed and crossed to the small, round farmer's table she'd brought from Boston and sank into one of the familiar chairs, crossing her legs. "I have no idea." She shook her head and took another drink of sweet tea. "I mean, it *looks* like everything is here. I don't know if I'd even notice if anything is missing."

Lee sat adjacent to her and slid his hand across the table to take hers. "Well, if you need anything, I'll make sure you get it." He lifted her hand and kissed her knuckles.

Missy smiled and shifted forward with the idea of getting a kiss, but paused when she heard tires on the driveway. She twisted in her chair to look out the window behind her.

And groaned.

"It's Thayne."

"I'm surprised he wasn't here sooner, to be honest," Lee said, setting his bottle down with a thunk. "I mean, his sister moving into a new house. Me aside, I would have thought he'd be here to help."

Missy stood and sighed. "I asked him not to."

She was almost to the foyer, Lee two steps ahead of her, when Thayne flung open the front door so hard it bounced off the interior wall and stormed into the house.

"Thayne!" Missy cried in surprise.

He didn't acknowledge her, but in one fluid motion took a step toward Lee, drew back his arm, and swung. His doubled-fist contacted Lee's jaw with a crack that echoed in the smaller space, and Lee's head snapped to the side, but he didn't stumble.

"Thayne!" Missy shouted again.

"You son of a bitch," Thayne ground out, his fists now doubled at his side and he sucked in rapid breaths through his clenched teeth with such force, spittle formed on his lower lip.

Missy stared wide-eyed, unable to say anything at all. Lee righted himself and faced Thayne, bringing his knuckle up to his lip, blood marring his skin when he took it away again. He ran his tongue along his lip, staring at Thayne, the tableau playing out in slow motion for Missy.

"What is *wrong* with you?" Missy demanded, stepping toward the two men.

Thayne turned on her and held out his hand to keep her from getting any closer. "Stay out of this, Missy. This has nothing to do with you—"

"Like hell it doesn't!" She batted his hand out of the way. "You come into *my* house, with violence, and you say it's got nothing to do with me?"

"Fine," he snapped. "It's got everything to do with you, and the ass you chose over your family."

"I didn't choose him over you, you forced me out!"

"I'll deal with you later," he came back, leaving Missy slack-jawed and stunned.

"Hey!" Lee barked, stepping between Thayne and Missy. "I don't give a damn how pissed you are with me, or think you have a right to be, you'll show Missy respect."

Thayne drew back again for another punch, but before Missy could shout anything, Lee grabbed Thayne's arm, flipped him around, and had his chest to the wall with his arm leveraged up his back. "You always sucked at hand-to-hand, Thayne, so back down."

"Get off me, damn it!" Thayne shouted, his cheek to the stucco.

"Not until you calm down and quit swinging."

"Fine!"

Lee released Thayne and stepped back several feet so Thayne could turn without him being in arm's reach. Thayne's glare was murderous, and as much as she didn't want to give him an inch, Missy took a step back and crossed her arms over her body. Lee looked to her, his jaw locked, then back to Thayne.

"Who the hell do you think you are bringing up Patty to Callie?" Thayne demanded. "In *Food Pyramid*?"

Lee chuckled, a single, humorless sound, and shook his head. "You've got a hell of a lot of nerve acting put out over that. I won't lie and say you didn't come to mind a couple of times early on, but it just took me until yesterday to figure out what the hell your—and Callie's—problem has been with me all this time."

Missy scowled and looked from Thayne to Lee.

"What if word got back to Susan, you son of a bitch?"

Lee shook his head. "One, I didn't say anything about your affair with Patty Childing. I didn't mention *you* at all, Thayne."

Missy gasped. *Thayne...*

"Oh, God..." Missy whispered, unable to think of anything else.

"And besides that, Susan *knows* about Patty."

"Susan knows *what* about Patty Childing?"

In the chaos, Missy hadn't heard Susan's car and hadn't seen her sister-in-law come to the open front door, Betsy in her arms. A cold dread curled in her gut at the blanched expression on Susan's face.

"Geezus, Susan, I told you to stay home," Thayne growled.

"Last I checked you're my husband, not my daddy," Susan said back, her voice tight and strained. She took a step into the house, glaring hard at Thayne. "What is it I'm supposed to know about Patty Childing?"

"Nothing," Thayne answered quickly. "Lee's just—"

"You lying sack of—" Lee cut himself short, and pressed his lips together in a tight line. He set his hands at his waist and dropped his head forward, shaking it. When he spoke, he spoke to the floor, not Thayne. "You told me, you *swore* to me, you came clean with Susan before you proposed."

"Came clean for what?" Susan demanded, this time her voice quivering and tears welled in her eyes.

"Oh, God..." Missy whispered again, pressing her hand to her chest. Her stomach rolled and clenched hard.

Thayne lunged for Lee again, a sound like a primeval scream tearing from him. He slammed his hands into Lee's shoulder and shoved him back until Lee impacted with the opposite wall. Lee quickly gained the upper hand, looping his arms up through Thayne's to knock them free, then pivoted them both so Thayne was back to the wall instead. Lee pinned him there, Thayne bucking against his hold. Betsy wailed, her tiny voice tearing at Missy's heart.

"No!" Lee shouted. "I've had enough! Stop this, Thayne. You're scaring your daughter."

Lee shoved at Thayne's shoulders one last time and stepped back, touching his knuckles again to his split lip. He turned his back on Thayne and crossed the foyer to Missy, watching her. Missy's heart was in her throat and she couldn't swallow, doubted she could speak. She kept her hand to her chest, hoping to hold in her thundering heart.

"I'm sorry," Lee said softer. "I didn't realize until last night what Thayne's real issue is with you and me."

Missy looked past Lee to Thayne, who stood with his head hung forward, his fists clenched. She blinked against the burning in her eyes from staring so long and focused again on Lee.

"I'm glad you've figured it out," Susan forced through clenched teeth, coming toward them and away from her husband, Betsy still crying against her shoulder. "Now tell the rest of us."

"Lee..." Thayne warned.

"Damn it, Thayne," Lee ground out. "This is not my confession to make. Step up and come clean, man."

"Tell me!" Susan screamed.

Lee turned away from them and took a few steps, scrubbing his palms over his face before he turned back. The anguished twist to his mouth and shine in his eyes tore at Missy anew. She wanted to tell him no, don't say anything, but the words wouldn't come.

He glanced toward Thayne for only a moment before looking back at them. "Back when you and Thayne were dating, I heard rumors that Thayne was..." He stopped and swallowed. "He was dogging around with both you and Patty. Callie told me Patty was seeing this military man named Thayne, and I knew there weren't too many Thayne's on base. I put two and two together."

Susan's eyes were unnaturally large and shining, and her body shook as she tried to hold Betsy. "And?" she asked. The simple question demanded a truckload of answers.

"And I confronted him about it," Lee said with a shrug, but it was far from indifferent. "I told him it wasn't right. He told me he knew it was wrong, and planned on making a choice. The next week, he told me he'd ended it with Patty...and that he'd confessed everything to you when he saw you that weekend. And he'd proposed."

Tears ran down Susan's cheeks and she glared at Thayne. She shook harder now, so hard Missy stepped forward and took Betsy from her arms, with no resistance. Betsy still sniffled, dropping her head to Missy's shoulder.

"Damn it, Lee. Keep your mouth shut," Thayne practically growled.

"Fine, Thayne," Susan said, spinning around to face her husband. "Do your best friend a favor and let him off the hook. Grow some balls and tell the truth."

Thayne raised his head, and Missy swore he was ten again, and had been caught after breaking Mama's favorite cookie jar. He sucked in several deep breaths and finally pushed himself away from the wall. He took two steps toward his wife, and she took two steps back, her hands held up for him to keep his distance. Thayne stopped and let his arms hang limp at his side.

"Baby, I'm so sorry."

She shook her head and made a low sound in her throat. "You

can save your apologies, Thayne Bingham. Right now, you'd better be doin' nothing but telling me the truth."

Thayne slid a harsh look at Lee. "We're done after this."

"Your choice, Thayne," Lee said through tight lips. "Not mine. You did this. Every bit of this."

"Bull!"

Unable to take it anymore, Missy took a step toward Thayne. "You've got a hell of a lot of nerve," she snapped and he immediately shifted his glance from Lee to her. "You've been lashing out at Lee, at me, over *your* guilt and you still want to put this on him?"

"If he'd just—"

"What? Kept quiet a secret he didn't know was a secret?" Susan cut in. "Spill it, Thayne, if you have *any* hope of coming home."

His arguments stopped and his eyes widened, his shoulders dropping, and Missy figured he'd just figured out the real ramifications of his deceit.

Thayne swallowed and released a long breath before he began, his voice so low Missy could barely hear him, but she heard enough.

"I met Patty just a week or two before I met you, and we'd already gone out a couple of times before you and I..." He paused and shook his head, raising his hands in a contrite offering. "Baby, I screwed up. I knew I was wrong when we started getting serious, and I made my choice. I chose you."

"Only when Lee called you on it."

Thayne shook his head. "No, baby. No. Yeah, Lee asked me about it, and he told me what I already knew. I needed to fix it." He reached out for her. "I ended it with Patty and I chose you."

Susan sucked in sharp breaths through her nose, her arms crossed tight over her body. "Were you sleeping with both of us?"

"Baby—"

"Were you sleeping with both of us!" she screamed so loud Betsy jumped in Missy's hold and Missy turned her head away.

"Yes," he finally admitted.

The crack of Susan's hand across his cheek was enough to make

Missy flinch and she bundled Betsy closer, keeping the baby turned away from her parents so she wouldn't see. Thayne's head snapped to the side, but he didn't move otherwise.

"Why?" she asked.

Thayne shrugged and shook his head. "I was stupid. I didn't—"

"No! Why did you choose me?" Before he could answer, she threw another question. "Did you love her?"

Thayne swallowed and licked his lips, looking off toward the open door before looking at his wife again. "I thought maybe I loved her. But, I realized I loved you."

Missy looked at Lee, he had his arms crossed and his head down. Susan marched across the foyer until she stood in front of Lee.

"Now you tell me," she ordered. "What didn't he say?"

Lee looked Susan in the eyes, his entire expression grim. "I don't know much more."

"What'd he tell you?"

"Same thing. He knew he had to choose."

"Why did he tell *you* he chose me?"

Lee shifted his eyes to Thayne, but Susan stepped into his line of sight again. "Answer me, because I know he's not telling me everything."

Lee worked his jaw and slowly shook his head, cursing Thayne under his breath. "Damn it. This shouldn't be coming from me."

"You started this," Thayne hissed.

"I didn't, but if this finishes it, then fine." Lee turned his head toward Missy, holding her gaze a moment before saying so quietly she only saw the words on his lips, "I'm sorry for this." Then he focused again on Susan. "He told me he cared for Patty, but he had no interest in raising another man's kids."

Susan didn't say another word. With tears streaming down her cheeks, she went to Missy and took Betsy from her arms, then pivoted on the balls of her feet and left the house, slamming the front door behind her. Missy couldn't breathe, her lungs burning, until she finally had to suck in ragged air. She felt emotionally beaten up and knew what she felt was only a fraction of the pain Susan had to feel. She stood in the middle of her foyer, empty arms hanging at her side, staring at the front door with no idea what to do.

Then Thayne shoved past her, heading straight for Lee again. He swung, but Lee dodged it and lunged forward, wrapping his arms around Thayne's body until they both propelled across the foyer and slammed into an antique Queen Anne table she'd set across from the door for flowers. The table slammed into the wall, and both men stumbled sideways.

"Stop it!" Missy screamed. "Stop it!"

Both of them were yelling, everything they said a jumbled cacophony she couldn't decipher, just shouting and noise and chaos. Thayne shoved Lee's chest and they both went down, Lee landing on his back with a grunt. Thayne pinned him down and pulled back a fist.

"No!" Missy screamed.

"Uncle Thayne! No!"

Missy spun around, and gasped, her heart freezing in her chest. Jude stood in the doorway of the kitchen, Levi in his arms, her youngest with his lower lip out and his cheeks streaked with tears. A large bump, already tinged in blue, raised on his forehead.

"What happened?" she asked, rushing forward to take Levi from Jude. New tears bloomed in Levi's eyes and he sucked in a sob.

"I fallded down, Mama."

She heard scuffling behind her and she closed her eyes, clenching her jaw as she tried to comfort her baby boy.

"Is he okay?"

Missy spun around at the sound of Lee's voice, coming face-to-face with Lee and Thayne. "Get out."

"Missy—"

"Sissy—"

"I said go," she ground out, looking Lee in the eye because she was still too furious with her brother to even glance in his direction. "I can't have you—*this*—in my house in front of my children."

"I'm sorry," Lee said, and even though she believed him, she shook her head.

"I don't doubt that you are, but that doesn't change the fact the two of you were *fighting* in my house in front of my children." She metered each word carefully, intent on keeping her calm for the sake of the frightened, crying boy in her arms.

"Missy, you gotta understand—"

She turned her glare on her brother, and he stopped short, his lips pursed tight and he diverted his eyes. "There is nothing you can say that will ever, *ever* make me understand what I learned today, Thayne. Nothing you can say that will justify any of it."

Eyes burning, Missy looked to Lee again. He canted his head and shook it slowly. "Sweetheart..."

"Please," she begged. "You need to go." Missy stroked Levi's hair and shushed in his ear before shifting her focus to her brother. "*You* need to get your backside back home, and do some intense praying on the way there and hope God gives Susan enough grace to let you in the door." She curled her lips together and shook her head. "Because frankly, Thayne, were I in her place I sure as hell wouldn't."

Thayne's face pulled into an angry twist and he took a step back toward the entrance. He glared hard at Lee until he reached the door, then yanked it open and stormed out of the house, without bothering to close the door behind him. Moments later, the engine of his truck revved to life and the sound of tire on gravel faded as he tore out of the yard. Missy focused on Lee.

"I need you to go," she repeated.

She saw the argument in his eyes and the twitch of his lips as he shook his head. He ran his fingers across his lips and sucked in a sharp breath. "I'll go, but—"

"No, Lee. You just need to go."

He nodded and turned away, his boots echoing on the adobe tile. When he reached the open doorway, he stopped with his hand on the door handle. Lee paused and looked at her over his shoulder. His gaze shifted from her to Levi, and past her to where Jude still stood. Missy swallowed, her throat burning.

"I love you," he said. "That doesn't make up for this, but I can't leave without saying it."

Then he shut the door. Missy closed her eyes, tears squeezing free, and held her breath until she heard his truck pull away.

CHAPTER SIXTEEN

THE SUN WAS HALF BEHIND THE HORIZON, THE BLUE SKY STREAKED WITH orange and pink, when Lee pulled into the driveway at the ranch. He'd driven around for awhile, sorting his thoughts, but no answers came and he found himself sitting in the cab of a still truck staring at the living room lights of his parents' home.

He wanted, more than anything, to put the truck in drive, turn around, and head straight to Missy. The problem was, he didn't know if what he wanted was the best thing to do. Stay or go...which would be the worst screw-up?

Lee opened the truck door and stepped out, shutting it behind him with enough force the slam echoed across the prairie. He inhaled the cool evening air, and released it, folding his hands together across the Ford's hood, dropping his head forward. It probably looked like he was in prayer, and the assumption wouldn't be far from the truth.

The stillness of the evening broke with the sound of angry tires on gravel, and Lee looked up, his gut immediatcly dropping and his muscles clenched. Dust and stones kicked up in the wake of Thayne's truck, and he slid to a sharp stop behind Lee's F-150. Lee straightened and turned, but didn't step away from his bumper and focused on keeping calm. One fight was bad enough today and bad enough it was in front of Missy; going to blows with Thayne outside his Mama's house wasn't anything he was interested in.

Thayne was out of his truck, the door slamming behind him before the big Chevy rocked to a stop.

"This is the second time you've come at me today, Thayne," Lee said in warning. "I told you I'm done."

"She kicked me out, you son of a bitch!" Thayne yelled but stopped short of coming right at Lee. He stopped a few feet away, feet apart and fists clenched at his hips.

Lee shook his head. "Not my doing, man."

"If you hadn't—"

"If I hadn't *what*, exactly, Thayne?" Lee demanded. "If I hadn't told your wife what you should have told her years ago? If I hadn't assumed you'd told both me and her the truth?" He took a step away from the truck toward Thayne. "Or if I hadn't fallen in love with Missy and reminded you of *your* screw-up, *your* unfaithfulness, *your* lies, and *your* choices?" With each point, he jabbed a finger in the air at Thayne.

"This was never about me, this is about Missy! She deserved better than being used by you to get your rocks off because you figure she's lonely and desperate. She's not some damn easy—"

Lee swung before Thayne finished the thought, pain splintering up his arm from the impact of knuckles to jaw, and Thayne stumbled back into the grill of his truck. Before he could recover, Lee grabbed him by the front of his shirt and yanked him upright before slamming him back again.

"Stand down!"

Lee's reflexes knew the voice of General Aarón Barajas before his head had enough time to process the order, and he jumped back from Thayne, dropping his hands. He never heard the general's car, never acknowledged the sight of the big, commanding man coming around the side of Thayne's truck, and neither of them knew he was there until he barked his order. Thayne crumbled to one knee when Lee released him but quickly scrambled to stand again, his back to the truck grill.

"General," Lee said, panting out the rank. He couldn't form enough words, stuck in the surprise of seeing his commanding officer standing in his driveway dressed in jeans, boots, and a plaid shirt, to ask General Barajas why he was there.

General Barajas stepped deliberately to the space adjacent to them, looking between Lee and Thayne, his disapproval obvious in the lines around his eyes and mouth. He tucked his hands behind his back and looked from Lee to Thayne, and held his focus there.

"I'm assuming, Sergeant Bingham, you've got a damn good reason for what's going on here?"

Thayne opened his mouth, looking ready to justify his presence, but just as quickly he snapped his jaw shut with an audible clack of his teeth. He worked his lips for a moment, then looked forward, away from the general. "I believe so, sir."

"You fail to be convincing, Sergeant." General Barajas looked to Lee. "What's his damn good reason, Henry?"

Lee cleared his throat, eyes forward. "I fell in love with his sister, sir."

General Barajas barked a laugh that took Lee by surprise. He waved a dismissive hand in Thayne's direction. "Head on home, Sergeant. I'm sure the two of you can pick up beating the hell out of each other later."

Thayne had the good sense to nod, a sharp jerk of his head, and move around the side of the truck to get in. Neither of them was official military anymore—a fact that had evaded Lee's head while standing at attention in front of the general—but they both had the good sense to do as General Barajas ordered. Moments later, the truck revved to life and Thayne maneuvered around the general's car to back out of the driveway.

It wasn't until he was on the road that General Barajas looked at Lee. "That really what the fight was over?"

"Simplest terms, yes, sir." Lee nodded. "It's a lot more complicated than that, though."

"It always is."

"Is there something you need, sir?"

"Walk with me, Lee."

Lee blinked at the use of his given name, something he'd never heard the general use, and fell into step beside the big man to walk back toward his car. General Barajas went to the passenger's side, opened the door, and retrieved a manila envelope from the front seat, handing it to Lee once he shut the door.

"Your separation papers came across my desk this week. Thought I'd drop them by personally rather than send them in the mail."

"Thank you, sir." Lee accepted the envelope but left it unopened. There would be time later for reviewing the paperwork, but the result was the same. He was officially a civilian again.

The date of separation had come and gone that week, and he hadn't even noticed. The sun was nearly fully set, so Lee motioned for them to approach the house where the porch light had come on at dusk. Once in the circle of light, the general smirked.

"Looks like I missed round one."

Lee gingerly touched the corner of his mouth, split and sore from Thayne's earlier swing. "Rounds one and two, sir."

"Sergeant Bingham really doesn't want you dating his sister," General Barajas said with a lilt of humor Lee wasn't accustomed to. "Feel like telling me the whole story?"

"I'm afraid I'm a bit prejudiced on the matter, General, and my side might shine like conduct unbecoming for Thayne."

"I promise not to judge." General Barajas set his foot on one of the steps leading to the front porch and sat.

Feeling unaccustomed to such casualness from the man, Lee kept his feet and stood on the ground at the bottom of the steps. Doing his best to keep his personal judgments from the telling, Lee gave the general a field report for the last three weeks, and his final conclusion of Thayne's attitude, right down to his attack at the house.

When he finished, General Barajas said nothing for several moments and Lee debated whether he had said too much. Or, not enough. Finally, the general cleared his throat.

"You say you love this woman."

"Yes, sir," Lee answered without hesitation.

"You're taking on a mighty big load of responsibility, Henry," he said, standing again. General Barajas was eye-to-eye with Lee with boots on the ground, but up two steps, he towered over Lee. "You're absolutely sure about this?"

"No question in my mind, General."

"Taking on another man's children is—"

"With all due respect, sir," Lee said, cutting off the general, and immediately feeling the heat of embarrassment at the man's look. He stopped, cleared his throat, and set his resolve. "With all due respect, sir, I'm getting mighty sick of defending my love for Missy and her boys. I have never, and never will, see them as another man's children. They are Missy's, and if she'll have me, they'll be mine in every way that matters."

General Barajas came down the steps and set his hand on Lee's shoulder. "You've convinced me, son, but it seems to me the only one you need to convince is this Missy of yours."

The general reached into his back pocket and removed his wallet, opening it to show a photograph inside, framed in a circle of leather. He held out the wallet for Lee to see.

The photo was of a much younger Aarón Barajas, in his dress greens, seated beside a woman with dark hair and dark eyes. Around them stood three young men, most appearing to be in their late teens, and a young girl of maybe ten or eleven years old. The girl stood beside the general, her arms resting on his shoulder, a wide and happy smile on her lips. Of the three men, two stood behind the woman, a hand of each on her shoulder. The third, the oldest, stood back center, a more grim look on his face with his arms straight at his side.

"That is my Angeline," he said, touching the photo. "These are our children."

Lee squinted and looked at the general, who chuckled. "You are assuming right, son. I am not their original father, but I am their father. I'm only about two years older than Edward, the angry-looking one in the back. Where you have Thayne Bingham arguing against your relationship with his sister, I had Eddie, who hated the idea of his mother and me marrying."

"Wow..."

"Yes, a bit more extreme than your case, I think. Angeline was nearly eighteen years older than me." He folded the wallet and stuffed it back into his pocket. "We never had children between us, but those boys and little Annamarie were as loved by me as any father. And, eventually, Eddie came around. Which I am forever thankful for." General Barajas smiled. "Eddie was my best friend before I married his mother, and eventually he was again. When we lost Angeline, it was good to have my best friend."

"I'm sorry, sir."

General Barajas cleared his throat and stepped away from the porch. "We had over twenty wonderful years together; a fact I wouldn't trade for anything." With a chuckle, the general turned back to him. "Perhaps something smarter than the two of us encouraged me to bring you those papers, son. Maybe I had something you needed to hear."

"Not to convince me, sir, but the affirmation is greatly appreciated."

General Barajas nodded and sighed. "Bingham will come around. You do right by Missy, and he'll see straight."

"I hope so, sir." Lee nodded. "It'd be good to have my best friend again."

General Barajas started across the yard, his boots crunching the dry soil and gravel as he headed for his car. Lee fell into step beside him, and when they reached the driver's door, Lee extended his hand.

"Thank you, sir, for bringing the paperwork."

"You're welcome, son." He got in the car and rolled down the window before starting the engine. "I'll be looking for an invitation to the wedding."

Lee smiled. "Yes, sir."

The transmission clicked and engaged as he put the car in reverse, and then looked to Lee one last time. "One more suggestion, son. You're not just convincing a man of your good intentions toward his sister, but you're convincing a woman that despite her brother, you chose her. Do you see my point?"

Lee nodded and swallowed. "Yes, sir. I do. I intend to take care of that immediately."

"Good man," General Barajas said in parting, then turned on his lights and backed out of the driveway.

As soon as the lights disappeared down the road, Lee turned on his heels and ran for the house, taking the porch steps in one leap. "Mama!" he shouted as he bolted through the front door.

"Goodness, Lee Allan Franklin Henry," his mother scolded as she came down the hall from the kitchen, wiping her hands on a dish-towel. "What on earth is wrong? Oh, what happened to your lip?"

"Nothing to worry about, Mama." Lee took his mother's face in his hands and kissed her forehead. "But, I need a favor..."

"How is your head feeling now, sweetie?"

"S'ok, Mama," Levi said, snuggling down into his blankets. He made a great show of testing the mattress and fluffing the pillows of his "new" old bed. Once settled, he folded his arms on top of his chest over the quilt. "The fud'sickle helped."

Missy smiled and tucked the blankets in snugly around his body. "I'm glad. Nothing fixes bumps on the noggin like Fudgsicles. Good night, sweetheart." She leaned over and kissed his brow on the oppo-site side from the black and blue mark left by his full-speed impact with the tile. "Sweet dreams. Remember, your brothers are right next door and I'm down the hall, okay?"

When she stood, she looked to the top bunk of Levi's bed and paused at the haphazard way it had been made with some spare blankets and pillows, some clearly from the couch in the living room.

"Dat's for Wee," Levi explained.

Missy looked down at him, his face cast in a light glow from his tractor nightlight, the newest addition to his tractor obsession. "For Lee?"

Levi nodded and hummed. "I asked Wee to wive in our new house. He can have da top bunk."

Missy smiled, overwhelmed by the expansion of her heart in her chest. "That's very sweet of you, Levi."

He just smiled and turned to face the wall and the tractor he'd nestled between it and his side. Missy went to the door and paused one last time to look back at her youngest boy before closing the door only far enough to leave a one-inch space. She paused at Jeremiah's door, but his light was already off and he'd fallen asleep before she tucked him in. It had been a long, tiring day for all of them.

In more ways than one.

Missy sighed and headed down the hall toward the front of the house. There were still plenty of boxes to unpack, and she intended to take the house one room at a time, beginning with the kitchen. As she approached the laundry room, she paused at the faint sound of voices. Going on again, they grew easier to hear as she turned into the kitchen, and one was definitely Lee's. Missy crossed the kitchen and breakfast nook, dodging around boxes and chairs, through to the doorway to the foyer.

"Hold it good and tight, Jude," Lee instructed her oldest son, who knelt on the floor beside the flipped-over Queen Anne table, legs in the air. Jude had hold of one leg, his expression set with determination, while Lee examined the connection between the leg and the underside of the table. Wyatt knelt on the other side, a screwdriver in one hand, and a bottle of wood glue in the other. "I want that glue to set before we flip it over. Wy, can you hand me that clamp?"

Wyatt immediately set down the screwdriver and glue, and picked up a large c-clamp by his knee, handing it to Lee. "Here."

"Thanks, buddy."

Missy crossed her arms and leaned her shoulder into the doorway arch, watching the three while they were still unaware of her presence. Both Jude and Wyatt studied every move Lee made, shifting and leaning to get better views. Lee put small pieces of felt between the clamp and the wood and twisted the clamp into place. He'd also laid out a blanket for the table to sit on instead of the foyer tile.

"There. That should hold it firm until everything sets. We'll leave it upside down like this until tomorrow, probably. She'll be as strong as ever."

"Possibly stronger," Missy said.

All three turned and looked up, each with their own smile. Missy smiled back, unable to deny it.

"We helped Lee fix the table," Wyatt offered the obvious.

"I see that. Should be good as new."

"Maybe better," Jude said, and stood, picking up a couple of tools to carry them to the toolbox set off to the side. "Help me, Wy."

"Sure!" Wyatt scrambled to his feet and gathered the various tools, clamps, and rags scattered around the foyer.

Lee kept his gaze on her and moved from his knees to stand, wiping his hands on a rag he then tossed at Wyatt. The boys made quick work of picking up everything, done before Lee could make it to her.

"Do you want this in your truck, Lee?" Jude asked.

Only then did Lee look away from her, over his shoulder to Jude. "No. Put it in the storage room. I'm sure I'll need it again."

Jude smiled, wide and honest, and lifted the red metal box, lugging it past both of them with Wyatt right behind him. As soon as the boys were gone, Lee closed the space between them, standing close enough it would take no effort at all to reach out her hand and lay it on his chest.

"I didn't hear you arrive," she said finally.

Lee smiled. "Once the new pup is over here, you'll have nothing but notifications of arrival. He seems to be a howler."

"Great." She dragged out the word and rolled her eyes.

Lee raised his hand and laid it on her cheek, the subtle smell of glue and wood lingering on his skin. "I needed to work on making right what happened here earlier." His eyes darkened and his smile slipped, not enough to disappear, but enough to be noticed. "Missy, I'm sorry. I hate that Thayne brought our fight into this house."

Missy inhaled and tilted her head into his touch, looking up at him. "I was angry, but now I'm just sad. Sad about the whole thing, and sad over what it's doing to us. Thayne and me."

"Thayne is angry, but I have to believe it's more at himself than me, or what we have. He's stubborn, I've known him long enough to know that—"

"Runs in the family, so be warned," Missy said with a smile.

Lee's lighter smile returned and he chuckled. "I hadn't noticed," he teased. "I hope, I *pray*, he'll eventually get his head out of his backside and see things clear. But until then..." He raised his other hand and cradled her face between them. "I don't intend to wait for him to figure out what ails him."

"We all need time to figure things out." Missy swallowed and stepped back from him, turning to cross back to the table where they had sat that afternoon, just before Thayne's chaotic arrival. She sat in her chair, hands clenched in her lap, and looked back at Lee. "I know we've said a lot, and I'm not dismissing any of it because I meant every word, but—"

"No buts." Lee reached her in three long strides, and she gasped when he immediately dropped to his right knee in front of her chair, taking her hands. "Missy, I already have figured out everything I need to. I have no questions, no doubts. There is nothing we can't work out, as long as we're doing it together. All of us."

"I'm not saying we can't." Missy's eyes burned and she looked away, not quickly enough to stop a tear from escaping. "I like to talk brave, Lee, but I can't help but hear what Thayne keeps saying."

"What is it you keep hearing, Missy?"

His voice was so heavy, so strained, she couldn't help but look at him again. She swallowed hard, hating that she couldn't shut up the voice of doubt—or reason—depending on how she looked at it. Her hand trembled when she reached to touch his cheek, and she ran her thumb over the slight rough of his end-of-day whiskers. He'd stilled her heart the first time she saw him, so virile, young, and attractive. He still caught her by surprise when he turned his intense blue eyes on her and smiled at her like she was the only woman in the world that mattered to him. She wanted to believe it. Wanted to so much. But she saw reality when she looked at him. Youth. When she was his age, she had barely given birth to Jude; a far cry from raising teenagers or pre-teens. When she was his age, her plans were so different.

"If you can't even say it, how can you believe it?"

Missy pressed her lips together and swallowed, looking down at her other hand, still enveloped in his large, strong fingers. "It sounds so cold when I think it, so saying it would be so much worse. I know because it sounded so cold when you said it, even though you were repeating Thayne's words."

"Even though I've told you in my own words what you and the boys mean to me?"

Missy nodded, then shrugged and swiped a finger across her cheeks. "I'm sorry." She chuckled, but it was flat. "When you're here, everything seems so clear and right. Then you're not, and I get anxious and start thinking."

"Then I need to always be here."

With a fortifying breath in, Missy raised her head and looked him in the eyes again. "It's not that simple."

Without looking away from her, Lee shifted his weight onto his foot with the raised knee to reach into his front jeans pocket, removing a burgundy velvet pouch tied with a black rope thread. He worked the pouch open and tipped it up, dumping a silver ring into his palm. Missy's heart skipped, then immediately thundered into a full-on gallop and she caught her breath.

All she could manage to whisper was "Lee..."

He pinched the ring from his palm and lifted her hand in his to slide the ring onto her left ring finger. It was a delicate, definitely old band with engraving surrounding an opal, with a small diamond on each side.

"This was my grandmother's ring," he said, then paused to clear his throat. "You'd think with so many of us, someone would have claimed it by now for this purpose." He chuckled, and sandwiched her hand between both of his, lifting it so he could kiss her fingers before he looked at her again. "Mama said it was meant to be this way. I needed a ring, and Grandma and God provided."

She couldn't help the tremors that felt like they shook her right through her insides, and no matter how she tried, her throat just wouldn't work. Gooseflesh broke out over her skin and her nape tingled, and her blood felt like it had turned to champagne, bubbling in her veins. Lee shifted closer, still kneeling on one knee with the other raised leg along the side of her chair so he knelt as close as possible.

"Missy, I didn't rehearse this, so I'm kind of fumbling through here, I just know I can't get out right all the stuff in my head and my heart." He smiled, a gleam in his eyes that made her want to weep and laugh at the same time. "Please, Missy...let me be your husband. Let me be a father to your boys. Let me be a part of your life for the rest of...forever. Let me be here every day so you know how much I love you, and so you never again doubt it."

She swallowed and squeezed his hands, trying to quell the tremors in her own. "You're crazy," she whispered, shaking her head —an old and unwinnable argument.

He smiled wider. "Sure am. But if this is crazy, I don't ever want to be sane. Marry me, Missy."

Missy couldn't breathe, couldn't think straight. She was light-headed, but grounded to the chair at the same time. Finding strength in the contact, she held on tight to his touch. "Do you remember what I said when you asked me on our first date?"

Lee nodded, grinning. "I remember everything about every moment we've spent together since you loaned me your phone."

She slipped her hand from his and laid her palms against his cheeks. "I probably shouldn't, but I'm going to anyway."

Lee's smile spread slowly, but it took over his face, the light of it reaching straight into his eyes. He came off his knee to stand, pulling her up with him, and took her head in his hands to kiss her so deep she felt it in her toes. She leaned into him, a low, content sound curling in her chest while every sense came alive.

Lee punctuated the kiss with several quick, short ones until he wrapped his arms around her and squeezed, nearly lifting her off her feet. "God, I love you, Missy." Then he looked to the ceiling, and Missy thought she saw a shine in his eyes, and he whispered, "Thank you."

"Did she say yes?"

Missy jumped at the sound of Jude's voice, but Lee didn't seem all that surprised at the question. With her still in his embrace, he looked toward the kitchen and the hall leading to the bedrooms. Jude and Wyatt stood side-by-side, wide-eyed anticipation on their faces.

"She did," Lee answered, and both boys whooped.

"I'm waking up Jeremiah and Levi!" Wyatt shouted and took off down the hall, but Jude stayed in his spot, a smile on his face and his hands pushed into his pockets.

Missy looked from Jude to Lee. "Did they know?"

Lee motioned for Jude to join them, and he walked across the kitchen, still grinning, until he was close enough Lee could put his hand on Jude's shoulder. "It wouldn't have been right to ask if I didn't have the approval of the man of the house," Lee said and winked at Jude.

Tears ran down her cheeks unabated, but Missy had no control over them, or the swelling happiness in her chest. She stepped away from Lee to hug her son, having to tip her chin up since he'd grown. "Thank you," she whispered for only him to hear.

"We love you, Mom," Jude said and looked to Lee when Missy pulled back. "Lee loves you. It's good."

Missy laughed, despite wiping the tears from her cheeks. Seconds later, the combined shouts of three young boys came at them from down the hall. She was pretty sure no one was going to bed any time soon.

"Missy?" Lee called, rounding the hall corner from the boys' bedrooms to the main back hall. The door to her bedroom was open and light from the adjoined bath shined enough to cast a glow across the floor. Lee stepped through the bedroom door and moved halfway to the open bathroom door. "Missy, are you here?"

She stepped out of the bathroom and looked around the room until she saw him, and smiled. "Did you call me?" She spoke a fraction louder than usual.

Lee nodded and walked closer. "Just wondering where you got off to, that's all. I think Wyatt and Levi finally settled down. In the end, exhaustion won out."

Her focus was intent on his lips when he spoke. Although he often caught her watching him speak, this seemed more intent than usual, and he surreptitiously took a glance at her ears. Devoid of hearing aids. He took a step closer so he was more in the light, and tapped a finger near his own ear, arching his eyebrows.

Color bloomed in her cheeks and she laughed, a nervous giggle. "It's just been a long day, and after a while, my ears hurt. I needed a break. I can put them back—"

He grabbed her wrist before she could go back to the sink. "No. Leave them out if they're bothering you."

She startled when he spoke and stared at him. Lee scowled and canted his head, stepping closer to her. "What is it, sweetheart?"

Her smile was slow, and she looked up from his lips. "Remember I said I was sure I'd be able to hear you with or without the aids?" He nodded. "It's like everything else has the volume turned way down, but your voice cuts through the quiet. You sound different. Your voice is deeper, your accent stronger. I wonder why that would be." She shook her head and moved closer to him, her cool fingers at his jaw. "It's been a long time since I've heard a voice, anyone's voice, clearly without those darn things in my ears."

Her touch was a charge, firing his senses and in an instant, every part of him was aware of her. Lee released her wrist to set his hand on her waist and slide it around her body to draw her closer. She smiled, warm and beautiful, and just that smile made his heart beat harder and his breath catch.

"Tell me something," he said, and her smile ticked up like she enjoyed every word he spoke. She nodded and leaned into him. "Do you wear them when you make love, Missy?"

Her breath hitched and she tipped her head back to look him in the eyes. She licked her lips and shook her head slowly. "I haven't..." Her breath shuddered, and she looked away before meeting his eyes again. "I haven't been with anyone..."

Lee laid his hand on her cheek and slid his fingertips into her hair. She met his kiss with open lips, and her soft groan ricocheted through him as she welcomed his tongue along hers. Their first kiss had been the single most powerful kiss he'd ever shared to that point in his life, but every kiss and touch since had been more. And he wanted more. The kiss amped up, becoming a struggle between control and giving in to the tug and pull in his chest to give in to the want. Lee took her head in both hands, kissing her deep, his gut—his entire body—tensing when her hands slid over his stomach.

He didn't make the conscious decision to wrap his arms around her and lift her off the floor to carry her to the bed, yet every part of him was aware of every part of her. Lee laid her down and settled with her, every second of their kiss hazing his judgment, his resolve, sharpening his desire. The rapid thump of her heart beneath his hand, her breath on his neck, and the jolt of unadulterated arousal that shot through him when her delicate hand touched the skin beneath his tee shirt yanked him back to the reality of the moment.

With herculean effort, Lee forced his lips from the warm skin of her throat and he sucked in a hard breath, shifting up her body enough to brace his arms on the bed and rest his forehead on the pillow supporting her head. Missy's hands skimmed over his arms, touching his shoulders, throat, and cheek, her body pressing harder against him with every ragged breath she took.

"Damn, woman," he said with a huff, laughing despite the raging protest his body screamed against him to take her back in his arms and make love to her. "What you do to me..."

He opened his eyes to look at her, but her eyes were closed. Lee touched her cheek, her skin hot and flushed, and she nestled into the space between him and the bed, her face against his chest. Delicate fingers curled into his shirt as if she were hanging on, and Lee understood the need. He pressed a kiss to her warm forehead and slid his arm beneath her neck to support her. They lay there for several minutes, neither saying a thing, until he finally thought his heart had returned to its normal beat and he had some semblance of control again.

Only then, when he was fairly convinced he could behave like a gentleman, did he shift his weight so he could support himself on his elbow and look down at her curled beneath and against him. That view alone was enough to stir temptation again in his gut. Lee touched her cheek with his other hand, stroking her skin until her eyelids fluttered open and she looked at him.

"I want you like I have never wanted anyone or anything, Missy. I never knew it was possible to want to make love to someone as much as I want you."

She blinked, and he knew his frankness was probably a shock, but there was no hiding how much he wanted her. Not from him, not from her. Lee swallowed and smiled, taking in the beautiful blush in her cheeks that crept down her throat into the collar of her blouse, and he remembered her teasing comment a couple of weeks before, about just how far that blush went. Despite his resolve, desire rushed straight through him, screaming to be quelled.

Lee tried to meter his breathing and pressed a long kiss to her forehead, hoping it would be safer than the temptation of her lips. "But do you know what I want more than making love to my fiancée?"

She shook her head against the contact but didn't say anything. Lee pushed up again to look her in the eyes. He stroked his thumb across her lower lip. "I want to make love to my wife. Because it's her I plan on making love to for the rest of my life."

Missy smiled, and it was slow and sexy and smoldering, and he bet she had no idea what it did to him. "Then I suggest we not wait too long to get married."

Lee laughed and gave in to the temptation of kissing her mouth. "I could not agree with you more."

"Yeah?" she said softly, sounding unsure. "We ran head first into this engagement. You don't want to slow down for the wedding."

"No way." Lee ran his hand down her left arm until he reached her hand, then held it up so he could look at his grandmother's ring circling her finger. "I told you, sweetheart. I have no interest in waiting any longer than I have to for our forever to get started. Heck, if Pastor Nason would do it, I'd have him marry us tomorrow."

Missy smiled, a glint in her eyes that made him smile too. She had that effect on him; it was like she turned on the light in his soul. "You would?"

"I would. I want it all and I want it now. Call me greedy."

She shook her head. "Not greedy. I understand. I want it, too, and I'm done telling myself it's crazy, reckless, or foolish. I'm going to marry you, and I'm not going to apologize for it anymore."

"Good." Lee kissed the end of her nose. "I'm glad to hear it. Now, how do you feel about another four or five babies?"

Her eyes widened so big he was afraid they'd pop right out and her jaw dropped open. Lee laughed and rolled away from her onto his back. "Don't look so worried, sweetheart."

Missy sat up to sit with her legs curled under her beside him. The carefree light in her eyes had dimmed, and Lee immediately reached for her hand. "Hey, what's wrong?"

"Lee, what if I—" She seemed to choke on the last words, and shook her head. Then she cleared her throat before looking at him again. "You may be twenty-four, but I'm not. Nothing says I can't have more children, but nothing says I can either."

Lee sat up so they were eye-to-eye. "Then we let God decide, okay? Either way, we've got four boys down the hall who are likely to keep us hopping for years to come."

She stared at him, barely blinking, and Lee laid his hand on her cheek. "Missy, I mean it. We let God decide, okay?"

She nodded several times before finally saying, "Okay. We let God decide."

He swung his legs off the side of the bed and stood, walking around the foot to hold out his hand to her. "I tell you one thing, though. We are *definitely* getting a bigger bed."

Missy laughed and took his hand, letting him draw her off the bed. "I was thinking of that anyway. This one looks so small in here."

"I guess we're going shopping this week." With her hand in his, he walked toward the bedroom door. "Come on. Walk me to the door so I can say goodnight like a gentleman."

CHAPTER SEVENTEEN

"Are you absolutely sure your parents are as fine with this as you think they are?" Missy asked, stepping closer to Lee. He instinctively slid his arm around her waist and drew her to his side, smiling when he looked into her concerned eyes. "They just *met* me a week ago."

She was so beautiful. From the first time he saw her at Low Places he'd thought her beautiful, but there was something today about the glow in her cheeks and the spark in her eyes that had kept him mesmerized all morning and afternoon long. He'd caught himself more than once drifting away from Pastor Nason's sermon to study her profile while they sat in church. Maybe it was because she had done something different with her hair, or maybe it was something as visceral and spiritual as knowing she would soon be his wife.

Missy canted her head, beautiful color tinting her cheeks. "Are you going to answer me, or keep grinning like a crazy fool?"

"I might just do both." Lee chuckled at her sigh and snuggled in to kiss the side of her throat, loving the little tremor that moved through her when he did, before conceding to answer. "Yes, Mama and Daddy are more than fine. They love you."

"They barely know me."

Lee shrugged. "Sweetheart, some might say the same about us, but that doesn't mean I don't love you. Everything else will catch up."

With her held to his side, her hand resting on his chest over his heart, Lee took in the crowd of family filling the overflowing great room of his parents' home. Brothers and sisters sat in and on couches and chairs, and a couple of the older nephews and nieces had spots in corners. Most of the kids were in other rooms or outside, including their boys, who Lee had no doubt had found the puppies again.

It was Sunday afternoon, and except for those once-a-month Sundays when a meal was held at the church, the Henry clan gathered at the ranch. Sometimes Mama cooked, and sometimes on days like today, the meal was potluck with the main course of barbecue chicken and ribs coming from High Steaks and all the sides and desserts made and brought by the family. The house smelled of barbecue sauce, roasted potatoes, and baking bread, the last courtesy of Missy.

"What about everyone else?"

"*What* about everyone else," he repeated back, and chuckled at her exasperation. "No one matters but us, sweetheart. You, me, and the boys. Everyone else will catch up if they don't come along at the beginning." Worry lines started to appear between her eyes, but he quickly kissed the spot. "Nope, don't make that face. In truth, I believe they'll all be just as happy for us as Mama and Daddy."

She didn't argue anymore, and wrapped her arms around his body, laying her head to his shoulder. Lee kissed her hair and grinned. Minutes later, Mama, Shelley, and Bea came out from the kitchen and called everyone to eat. Children were gathered from outside and ordered to clean up before sitting at the table. The family was spread out at three tables and in two adjacent rooms, his parents having given up a long time before of ever having a single table for eating anymore. Only during the week, when it was the four of them

—Mama, Daddy, Lee, and Mark—did they use the small table in the kitchen.

It took a good half hour before everyone was seated, and John Sr. stood to say grace. With their heads bowed, Lee reached beneath the table and took Missy's hand, squeezing it gently. He had a great deal to be thankful for that day, and for every day going forward.

"I don't know if I'll ever get used to all the noise," Missy said, leaning toward him after a few minutes of trying to talk during the meal. "I can't differentiate anything other than you and your dad, since he's on the other side of me. Everything else is chaos."

Lee winced and laid his hand over hers on the table between them. "This is the Henry family. Loud. Loud. And did I mention loud?"

"You'd better get used to it, Missy," Bea said from the other side of Lee. "Every new grandbaby adds another stack of decibels."

"What did she say?" Missy asked.

"She said it gets louder with every grandbaby," he repeated, then grinned. "Which makes a great segue."

"For what?" Bea asked.

Instead of answering, Lee winked at Bea and pushed back his chair, standing. "Excuse me, everyone," he yelled out over the din. "Excuse me. Could I get everyone's attention?"

The talking quieted and all eyes at the main table turned to Lee. The kids didn't care much but had quieted enough not to be distract-ing. Lee cleared his throat and looked down at Missy, who stared at him with wide eyes and blushed cheeks. He reached for her hand and drew her up to stand beside him. Her grip on his fingers was firm and her skin was cold. Lee chuckled at the panic in her eyes, but not too loud to tease her too much.

"I'm going to get right to the point because if I make her stand here very long I think Missy might break my hand," he began, and her hold loosened, but he held her firm. Rather than looking at everyone at the table, Lee kept his attention on her. Blue eyes shined when she looked at him, and he fell in love all over again. Every time he looked at her. Her blush deepened, but her smile stilled his heart.

"So get to the point," Mark said across the table, humor lacing his tone. "We're hungry."

Several laughed, but Lee didn't look away from Missy. "Missy and I are getting married."

The instant uproar was enough to make even Lee cringe, and he saw on Missy's face the chaos it caused. She raised a hand to buffer her ear but didn't cover them completely, and laughed when he smiled.

"See?" he said, leaning in to speak near her ear so she could hear him. "No shouts of outrage, no declarations of argument. No threats to have me committed." He pursed his lips against her warm cheek. "We are no crazier than anyone else, sweetheart."

The noise didn't level out for the rest of the dinner, with either siblings or siblings-in-law shouting things down the length of the table, or coming down to congratulate them directly. Missy was hugged, kissed, and welcomed by every one of them, and with each, he saw the relaxation edging back into her face. After battling against Thayne since the beginning, he'd known his family would welcome her, and knew their grace would be what she needed.

"Have you talked dates?" Ellie asked once the table had been cleared and the family had again begun to disburse.

"We're going to talk with Pastor Nason tomorrow," Lee said, edging both Ellie and Missy toward a corner of the room where maybe the noise wouldn't be so loud. "But we're hoping next month."

Ellie gasped, her jaw-dropping. "Next month?" Then she chuckled and shook her head. "I guess you're not fooling around."

Lee looked at Missy and squeezed her hand. "I told Missy awhile back I didn't want to wait too long to start working on forever."

Ellie shook her head again. "You should write that in a song, little brother."

Lee grinned. "Maybe I will."

Missy startled and reached for her back pocket, taking out her phone. She looked at the screen, then at Lee. "I'm going to step outside to take this, okay?"

"Everything okay?"

"Oh, sure," she said with a nod, but her smile didn't quite convince him. Then she turned away and headed for the back door to the empty back patio.

"Damn, you are smitten."

Lee grinned wider, looking back to his sister. "Guilty as charged."

"Three weeks. You met her three weeks ago."

He nodded. "Yep. Twenty-three days ago today. And twenty-one days ago, I knew I intended to marry her."

"You're crazy."

"Maybe," he said with a shrug. "But, I'm okay with that."

After a few minutes without Missy, Lee slipped away to find her. She sat in the wooden bench swing his dad had built for his mom when Lee was a toddler, her phone in her hand, her hand in her lap, staring out across the fields behind the house. He caught the glisten of tears on her cheeks when he stepped around to sit beside her and reached for her hand.

"Hey, what's wrong?" he asked. "Who was on the phone?"

She looked at him and smiled, and despite the tears, the smile was sincere. "It was Daniel's parents. I called them earlier today before I left for church, but had to leave a message." New tears welled in her eyes.

"You told them..."

She nodded. "Just now." Missy smiled wider, and a new tear escaped. Lee swiped it away with his thumb, trying to figure out what the contradiction of smiles to tears meant. "I was more nervous about telling them than I was about you telling your family."

"And? What did they say?"

Her chin trembled when she spoke. "They asked a lot of questions about you, what kind of man you are. I told them in many ways you're like Daniel, but in many ways, you aren't." She inched closer and wrapped both her hands around Lee's one, working her thumb across his knuckles. "They asked how you feel about the boys, and I told them you love them. And they love you. I told them I will always love Daniel..." She raised her chin and looked at him. "But I love you with everything I am. I loved Daniel in a way I don't love you, and I love you in a way I didn't love him. Is that okay?"

"Of course it's okay," he answered quickly and kissed her temple.

She stayed leaned into him and Lee wrapped his arm around her shoulders to hold her close. After a moment in his hold, she chuckled. "Dad Colton said since my parents weren't here to vet you, it was his responsibility. They'll be here next weekend."

Lee chuckled and rubbed her shoulder. "I have a feeling they'll be harder to convince than anyone."

"Possibly." She sat back enough to look at him. "And they asked to come to the wedding."

"Of course," he said, frowning at the hesitation in her voice. "Sweetheart, I'm not the type of man who thinks now that you're with me everyone and everything you were before has to be shut out of your life. You are who you are because of Daniel, I believe that. I want to know about him. I want the boys to hear about him. I know he was a good man, a good husband, and a good father." The sudden tightening of his throat took him by surprise, but he swallowed past it and looked down at their joined hands on his thigh. "Baby, I want to be a dad to them as much as I can, but I know Daniel Colton will always be their father."

She smiled and curled into his side, tucking her legs up beside her so her knees were in his lap. "I love you, Lee. I think right now more than I ever have."

"Meet me for breakfast tomorrow before we go to see Pastor Nason," Lee said as he opened Missy's Jeep door.

"Sure. I drop the boys off at school just before eight. Where do you want to go?" She stood inside the open door space but didn't slide behind the wheel quite yet.

Lee moved in closer, his forearm resting on the top edge of the doorframe over her head. "Maude's is the best breakfast in town. And it's right down the street from the church."

"Okay, I can be there by maybe quarter past."

Lee smiled and leaned in to kiss her. A groan came from the backseat; which of her children it was she couldn't be sure.

"Are they always gonna kiss like that?" Jeremiah asked, which implied he was the groaner.

"Get used to it," Wyatt said. "You shoulda seen 'em last night." Then he proceeded to make kissy sounds.

Missy chuckled and Lee looked past her into the Jeep. "Yep, you'd better get used to it, because I intend to kiss your mama *a lot*," he stressed and smirked at the round of groans, followed by a very loud, adamant "Yuck!" from Levi.

Lee laughed, and despite their protests, came back to kiss her again; though this time he did hold back to a simple, but held, kiss to her lips. Then he let her slide behind the wheel and shut the door for her. Missy rolled down the window to say goodnight one last time. Then with a wave and a tap of his hand on the hood, Missy started the Jeep and turned it around to drive out of the yard.

The drive to the house was no more than ten or twelve minutes, and the boys in the backseat talked animatedly the whole way about puppies, horses, and their new cousins. That seemed to be the greatest of all treasures to them; the ready-made slew of new cousins they would inherit once she and Lee married.

Missy smiled.

She was still processing the reality of it all.

"You look happy, Mom."

Missy looked away from the road across the Jeep to Jude, who sat in the front passenger seat. In the dim light cast by the lights of the dashboard she saw his smile, and she smiled back. "I am, honey."

She glanced at the road and back to him. "How about you? You're okay with this?"

Jude nodded and looked over his shoulder to the backseat. His younger siblings were oblivious to their conversation, currently discussing names again for the puppy. Levi was chanting "Zeke! Zeke! Zeke!"

"Yeah, I'm good. We all are, Mom."

"You can tell me if you're not."

Jude nodded. "I know. But, we're good." He shrugged a single shoulder. "I like Lee. He's a good guy, and he makes you smile. And besides, they need a dad."

Missy's throat tightened and she focused on the road ahead for a few moments before she could talk again. "You all have a dad, honey."

"I know, but that's not what I mean. I mean you shouldn't have to do it alone." He shrugged again, apparently his newest form of expression. "And Lee is cool."

Missy smiled and turned down the road leading to their house. They had neighbors, but none too close, and she liked that. It was so different from Boston where they could hear the neighbors fighting if they stood in the right rooms of the townhouse. As she pulled into their driveway her stomach dropped.

"It's Uncle Thayne," Jude said.

"I see," she said with dread.

Thayne's truck was in the yard, and he stood outside of it, leaning against the tailgate, head down. Missy slowed as she approached, and put the Jeep in neutral under one of the buckeye trees. Before getting out, she took the keys from the ignition and handed them to Jude. "Take the boys inside, honey, and get them ready for bed. Okay?"

"You gonna be okay, Mom? Should I call Lee?"

"No," she said quickly, then smiled. "No, this is your uncle. He'll behave himself."

"He didn't ..."

"Yes, well, he will if he knows what's good for him." She smiled, hoping she was convincing, and opened the Jeep door to get out as Jude opened his side.

Thayne looked up, but didn't move away from his truck. Jude retrieved Levi from his car seat, and led the three youngers to the house, only glancing once at his uncle. Wyatt and Jeremiah waved to Thayne but continued to the house when Jude told them to move along. They hadn't seen the fighting the night before other than Levi, and Missy was fine with them being oblivious. The tension hung in the night air, and low anger curled in Missy's stomach for what her relationship with her brother had become at his doing.

She walked toward Thayne, arms crossed over her body, but waited until the boys were inside before she said anything. "Why are you here, Thayne? Lee isn't, so if you're looking for a fight—"

"I'm not," he cut off, but not with a sharp tone. If anything, he sounded defeated. He shook his head and stepped away from his truck, hands pushed into his front pockets. "I'm here to ask your forgiveness."

"For which part? For being a butthurt jerk the last three weeks, for saying things to Jude you knew would upset him in hopes of making your point, or for starting a fistfight in my home?"

Thayne worked his jaw and took a deep breath before answering. "For all of it." He shrugged. "I've spent the last twenty-four hours doing a lot of thinking. I'm not saying I don't think Lee will eventually hurt you, I don't know—"

"I thought this was an apology."

"It is. I didn't mean to hurt you. Or the kids. I don't want you hurt, by me, by Lee, by—"

"We're getting married," she snapped off.

Thayne's eyes widened, and he looked away before clearing his throat. "I guess I didn't see that coming."

"Obviously."

He nodded and sighed again. "Obviously. Look, it doesn't matter what I thought or why I thought it. I've screwed up seven ways to Sunday here, and I've got to start somewhere, Sissy."

Missy swallowed and looked out across the open prairie beside the house. Lightning bugs flickered in and out amongst the grass and the stars were sharp and clear in the sky. Everything was serene and calm, and it was enough to help her let go of some of the anger crawling beneath her skin.

"I can forgive, Thayne, but I'm not the only one you're going to need to ask."

"I know," he conceded. "I'm starting here, though. I know it's going to take a lot more to get Susan to forgive me if she ever does, but I need to know my sister already has."

Missy rolled her lips together and nodded. "Okay. But you need to stop this fight with Lee. It's not his fault you feel guilty over what you did, and it's not his fault you lied to your wife."

"I know."

"We *are* getting married, Thayne, so if you want to be a part of my life you're going to have to find a way to get over this." Suddenly, Missy was tired. Bone tired. She inhaled a deep breath of evening air and closed her eyes. "You were best friends, Thayne."

"I know," he repeated, nodding. "I know, Sissy. Like I said, I've spent the last day thinking. Hard."

"I pray so, Thayne. I don't think it's a good idea for you to come in. Not tonight. But, we'll keep talking, okay?"

He nodded, his head further down than up like he might be as emotionally drained as she was. Unable to hold on to the distance, Missy stepped to him and wrapped her arms around him. Thayne leaned into her, squeezing back, and whispered another apology. When he let her go, he didn't say another word but moved around to get in his truck. She stepped to the side when the engine revved to life, and walked to the front porch while he pulled away.

"We had a visitor when we got home."

Lee paused in stirring his coffee and looked across the table at Missy. She was spreading grape jelly on a slice of toast for Levi, her focus on the task and not looking at Lee.

"Who?" he asked, but his gut told him he already knew.

"Thayne," she answered and set the triangle of toast on Levi's plate. Lee waited until she looked up and across to him. "It's okay," she said with a strained smile. "He came to apologize." Missy took in a breath before adding, "I told him."

Lee raised his eyebrows and picked up his knife and fork to cut into his steak and eggs. "How did that go over?"

"He was genuinely surprised. I think despite all that came out, he still feels in his gut that things will go bad for us." She looked away, cutting her eggs with the side of her fork. "I can't say I don't understand his worry. If I were on the other end of this, I'd be worried too. Unless you're Cinderella or Sleeping Beauty, whirlwind romances don't often work out."

"Missy." She didn't look at him right away. "Missy, sweetheart." Then she tipped up her chin just enough to look at him through her lashes. "I admit I'd probably be worried, too, if my sister had come home and said she was marrying someone she'd just met. But, Thayne is taking it too far. Especially since he *knows* me."

The soft clearing of a throat made them both look up, and the sad, destroyed look in Susan Bingham's eyes made Lee's gut bottom out. She stood a couple steps from the end of the table in Maude's, Betsy on her hip. Her eyes were bloodshot, and she looked exhausted.

"Susan," Missy said, her voice laced with the same concern Lee felt.

Lee shoved back his chair to stand so Susan could sit and took the chair closer to the wall, now sitting right across from Levi. He winked at the boy, who tried to wink back while chewing on a bite of sausage.

Susan sank heavily into the chair Lee had vacated and sighed, shifting Betsy into her lap. She ran a hand over her messy hair and attempted a smile.

"Did I hear you right? Y'all are getting married?"

Missy smiled and nodded, her blue eyes shifting to Lee for a moment before she looked back to Susan. "Yes." She reached across the table and took Susan's hand. "Are you okay?"

Tears welled in Susan's eyes and she cuddled Betsy a little closer, her voice weak when she spoke. "No, I'm not. I'm tore up something terrible, Missy, and I just don't know what to do."

Lee sat sideways in the chair and leaned toward Susan, resting his elbows on his thighs. "Suz, for my part in this I'm so sorry."

She shook her head. "Don't you dare apologize, Lee Henry. This is Thayne's doing, and his doing only. You trusted him when he said he'd told me, and I trusted him that—" Her voice broke and she pressed her lips together, tears running down her cheeks. "The thing is I probably wouldn't have been near as mad if he'd told me back then he was seeing Patty than I am learning now he hid it for so long."

"He came to see me last night," Missy told her. "He apologized, and said he hoped he could fix it with you."

"I don't know yet. I just don't."

"Mama and Wee are getting' mawwied," Levi stated, clearly oblivious to their conversation. He smiled wide, chocolate milk on his upper lip. "Jude said dat means Wee can be my dad. Not my Daniel Daddy, though. Daniel Daddy lives in heaven. He'll be my Wee Daddy."

Lee reached across the narrow table and ruffled Levi's hair. "I can't wait, Leviathan."

Levi smiled again, showing some partially chewed toast and sausage, then went back to eating. Lee looked across to Missy, whose almost wistful smile spread warmth through him. He winked at her, and she smiled wider. It did his heart good to know the boys had talked about their engagement, and if Levi's choice of words were any indication, they were as excited for the future as him.

"I'm so happy for the both of you," Susan said, then sniffed and laughed. "I guess I didn't completely fail in the setup department, huh?"

Lee slid his hand across Susan's shoulders and leaned in to kiss her cheek. She tasted of salt, and he knew this wasn't the first time she'd cried today. "You win the prize for matchmaking," he promised and squeezed her shoulders.

CHAPTER EIGHTEEN

"Is everyone ready to have some fun tonight?"

Lee's question for the crowd, and their riotous roar of response greeted Missy when she opened the door to Low Places and stepped inside. It was well past sunset outside, and the neon and fluorescent lights inside the honkytonk seemed excessively bright. She blinked to adjust and stepped sideways to get out of the way of some people heading out to the parking lot.

"Did y'all miss me last week?" he asked, leaning forward to speak into his mic, but so his guitar wouldn't hit the stand. The crowd roared an unanimous "Yeah!" Lee chuckled and shook his head, taking the neck of his guitar in his hand so he could play a few quick notes, the fingers of his right hand moving so fast she couldn't follow them. "I'm not sure if you did or not."

The crowd roared again, and several lifted their mugs or bottles of liquor.

Lee grinned and looked out over the patrons. He changed when he was on stage; Missy had noticed the first time she saw him perform. He loved this. Being up there, singing and playing, was a part of him. He reveled in it, and she loved seeing the energy that practically emanated from him when he fed on the energy of the crowd. She saw it. She understood it.

And whether she would ever admit it aloud, she missed it.

"Well, I am celebrating tonight, so we are going to have a great time."

"What are you celebrating" someone shouted, a female. Probably one of Lee's many adoring fans.

"Good question." Lee paused in his picking to run his hand across his forehead, swiping away some of the sweat before it ran in his eyes. He clapped his hands together and rubbed his palms. "Well, where to start. I'm celebrating being home. For good." The crowd roared and he grinned. "I'm celebrating being a civilian again." Another cheer.

Missy stepped past the bar to stand on the edge of the main floor, which was three steps down, where tables and booths lined the outside and the center parquet floor was open for dancing in front of the raised stage. She stayed to the side, so she could see over the heads of the crowd but was out of the way for anyone going up and down the steps.

"And here's the big one. You ready for this?"

Cheering.

Lee leaned closer to the mic so his voice practically boomed through the speakers. "I'm getting married."

The response of the crowd was mixed, everything from cheers to cries of feigned distress from some of the female patrons, to one slurred-voiced man shouting "Don't do it!" Lee chuckled and played a bit more on the guitar. It was a familiar tune, the same he'd sung on their first date here. Missy smiled and leaned her hip into the wood railing, watching him work the audience.

"Oh, trust me, my friend," Lee said, speaking into the mic with his head turned in the direction of the drunken giver of advice. "If you had my woman, you wouldn't hesitate."

Heat crawled up Missy's neck and she shook her head. Yet, she enjoyed the swell of pride at his words.

"I met her right here in Low Places," Lee said, holding out his arm to point into the general space of the bar. "So, you never know where love is going to find you." By the time he finished his last sentence, both he and his band were already playing an upbeat dance song, the bass thumping in the air against her chest.

Once Lee began to sing, Missy took the steps down into the seating area and headed to the furthest table from the stage. She could hear just fine back here, and it was the most respite she could attain for her hearing aid enhanced ears. It was the same table she'd sat at two weeks earlier, the last time she'd been here with Lee, and not far from where she'd sat with Thayne and Susan three weeks earlier. The night they'd met.

It still stunned her when she quantified the time since he'd stepped into the hallway and asked her if she had some change for the payphone; three short, short weeks from strangers to soul mates, and at times she still questioned their sanity.

"What can I get you?" asked the waitress who approached the table, setting a napkin, glass of water, and bowl of popcorn in front of Missy.

"A Coke for now, thanks."

Becky, as her name tag said, nodded and headed back through the crowd. Most had broken off into pairs and danced the two-step or variations thereof all over the dance floor. From this table, she had a perfect view of Lee on stage, and settled in for the next half hour to enjoy watching him sing and play. They did a variety of songs, from boot-slapping dance to slow songs, and the enthusiasm from the crowd was infectious. After another half hour, Lee and the band performed "Don't Rock the Jukebox," and as he hit the last cord, he slipped the guitar strap over his head.

"We're going to take a breather," he announced, and the crowd clapped. "Feed the jukebox until then, and we'll be back."

The bar was only quiet for a few moments as he set aside his guitar before "No Shoes, No Shirt, No Problem" pounded through the speakers. The place seemed to be an unending hive of energy with the dance floor constantly full of people.

"Hey, darlin'."

Missy turned at the sound of Lee's voice behind her, just in time for him to reach the table, bend over, and kiss her hard and quick before he sank into the bench across from her.

"When did you get here?"

"Right about the time you announced you were getting married, and broke the heart of every woman in here."

Lee chuckled and sat sideways in the chair to put his back to the wall and stretched his legs the length of the long booth. Sweat darkened spots of his tee shirt and his dark hair spiked from it. On stage performer should be an Olympic event.

"Here you go, Lee," Becky said, returning to the table with a bottle of beer for him, and set Missy's Coke in front of her. "Y'all want anything to eat?"

"Mmm," Lee hummed. "Yeah, I'll take a cheeseburger. Chips, no fries. Missy?"

"No, I ate with the kids before I left."

Once Becky walked away again, Lee scooted from the booth and stepped to the end, holding out his hand. "Come dance with me."

"Aren't you tired?"

"Never so tired I can't dance with my wife." He winked as she slid from the booth.

"Not your wife yet, Lee Henry," she teased as she took his hand.

She gasped when instead of leading her to the floor, Lee tugged at her hand and yanked her against him, meeting her with a kiss. Missy didn't resist, and leaned into the kiss, slipping her arm around his neck to lace her fingers into his damp hair. He released her hand so he could wrap his arms around her, pressing his fingers against her back, and Missy acknowledged that undeniable shift in the kiss from "I'm glad to see you" to "I wish we were alone" when she parted her lips and his cool, bitter tongue tinged by his beer stroked against hers.

Lee groaned against her open mouth and brought his hands to her head, holding her to deepen the kiss. Her stomach fluttered and Missy held on, riding the wave of the kiss. Part of her felt the heat of embarrassment at kissing him so intently in the middle of a bar, but the tumble low in her belly and the flush over her skin made this the safest place to kiss him. Each time they kissed, it was more overwhelming, and she wondered if they would go another three weeks without imploding.

Lee slowed the tempo of the kiss, though she hoped he was as reluctant to stop as she, until he rested his forehead against hers, their warm breath mingling in the small space between their lips.

"Sweetheart, you have no idea how aware I am that we aren't married yet. If I could, I'd rectify that tonight."

Missy smiled and wrapped her arms around him. "Come on. Dance with me."

A new song began as they moved into the dance area, a fast-paced dance song that required Missy to remember every dance move and two-step she'd learned years before but hadn't put into practice much. She'd only gone dancing once in years, and that was the night she and Lee met. She was proud of herself for keeping up, and not tripping over her boots, by the time the song ended and the respite of a slower ballad began. Breathing hard, Missy willingly moved into Lee's arms as he drew her hand over his heart and pulled her close for the more sedate dancing.

"You're a tough woman to keep up with," he said with an out-of-breath chuckle.

"I was just thinking the same about you. I'm not used to this."

"I intend to dance with you often," he said and leaned in to press his cheek to hers, so his voice was near her ear when he spoke. His voice was heavy and as effective as a caress. "Fast and slow. All night."

Missy closed her eyes and rested her forehead on his chest, her heart pounding not just from the dance but the visceral reaction his words evoked.

"Have I told you lately how much I love you?" he said after a few moments of dancing slow when her heartbeat had leveled off and she breathed like a normal human being.

She smiled and tipped back her head to look at him. "Isn't that a song lyric?"

He grinned and shrugged. "I speak in song lyrics."

"Well, I think it's been nearly three hours since I heard it."

"Shame on me."

The song ended and Lee took her hand, leading her back toward their table where his burger had been delivered. He sat down and dug in with a ravenous vengeance. "Sorry," he mumbled around a mouthful of beef. "I didn't get a chance to eat lunch today, so I'm starving."

During his short break, half a dozen people came by the table and congratulated them, including one Missy suspected to be the drunken fan who warned Lee not to go through with it. He was rosy-cheeked and glassy-eyed, but he stumbled past and slurred out a "Con-Congratulashuns."

"So, Mama and Daddy all settled in?" he asked after devouring about half the burger. He sat back and stretched his legs out under the table, his knees bumping hers.

Missy nodded and stole a chip from his plate. "Yep. I picked them up and brought them back to the house so you can take them home later." She stole another chip and considered stealing his pickle. "I was late because I got a call from Miranda."

Lee's eyebrows popped up and he paused with a chip halfway to his mouth. "You've been trying to get ahold of her, right?"

"We've been playing phone tag, yeah."

"And?" He took another bite of the burger.

Missy winked and stole his pickle, and he chuckled. "And...she screamed for about three minutes and then said she would be here in three weeks to be my matron of honor, come hell or high water, to quote her. She promised she'd work it out, either way."

Lee chuckled and popped another chip into his mouth. "Good.

I'm glad she'll come." He reached across the table and took her hand, leaning over his plate so he could kiss her knuckles. "I can't wait to meet this woman. She sounds like a handful."

Missy sat back and crossed her legs, biting into the pickle. It was spicy, stronger than she expected, and she pulled a face. Lee's laugh boomed over the music.

"Sorry, sweetheart. I should have warned you."

"Yes, you should have," she tried to say while taking a drink of her Coke, which didn't help. The sweet just battled with the spicy, and not in a good way.

The song playing ended and no new song began. A short burst of feedback in the speakers indicated the on-stage mics were back on and Missy looked toward the stage. Mark and the other band members were already there, gathering their instruments and Mark stepped to the stage.

"Hey, Lee, quick molesting that fiancée of yours and get up here. These people paid to hear you sing."

The patrons clapped, the ones nearest them turning to look and smile. Lee wiped his fingers on his napkin and drank the last of his beer, then slid from the booth. With one more sound kiss on the lips, Lee headed for the stage.

Missy recognized the silver Taurus as soon as she turned into her driveway, and a strange swirl of both excitement and anxiety flipped her stomach. Lee's truck lights lit the front of the house as he pulled in behind her, and he turned them off as she opened her door.

"Who is that?" he asked, coming from the truck to meet up with her as she headed toward the porch.

"Jacob and Lydia," she answered, glancing at the car again to be sure she knew it. "Daniel's parents. I wasn't expecting them to head down until the morning." Lee stopped, and when she realized he wasn't walking with her, she also stopped and turned. "What?"

He was smiling, but it was a strange smile. "So, my parents and Daniel's parents have been hanging out for...maybe hours..." He arched his eyebrows and looked at her. "I'm not sure how I feel about that."

"You and me both," she said with a nervous chuckle.

Lee drew in a long breath through his nose and pushed his hands into his front pockets, staring at the house, a deep parallel of lines digging into his brow. Missy walked back to him, reaching up to touch his jaw so he'd look at her.

"Hey...what's up?"

"I knew they were coming," he said, with a slight shake of his head. "It wasn't until *this* moment I realized I'm going to try to convince the parents of my fiancée's deceased husband—who by all accounts was a good man, good husband, good son, and good father —I'm worthy of marrying the woman they consider a daughter." He looked at the house again. "I think it might be easier to convince Thayne."

Missy stepped in front of him so she was between him and the house, and toed up so she could lay her hands on his cheeks and kiss his chin. "Come on," she said and linked her hand through his. "We'll walk into the lion's den together."

He walked with her to the porch, and she paused to kiss him one last time before opening the door. "I love you," she whispered and stepped into the house. The sound of four mingled laughs drifted from the living room. "We're home," she called.

Missy went left through the foyer and headed toward the living room, Lee behind her, and met first with Lee's parents and Daniel's parents right behind. As ever, Lydia was the picture of a lady, dressed in linen pants and a pretty pink blouse, her silver hair styled perfectly. She always believed in looking her best. Jacob, a former military man like every man in Missy's life, carried himself straight and tall, eyes so much like Daniel's smiling when he saw her. Lydia rushed forward and enveloped Missy in a hug, and the tears that hit her didn't surprise Missy at all. She hadn't seen her in-laws in several months, and she missed them terribly.

"When did you get here, Mom?" Missy asked when Lydia released her.

"Oh, a couple of hours ago," Lydia answered and motioned back to John and Erin. "It was a nice night and we were restless, so we decided to come down tonight. John and Erin have been just wonderful." She sighed and turned back, looking straight at Lee with a wide smile. "I feel like we know you already, Lee."

Lee stepped forward and extended his hand. "It's a pleasure to meet you, Mrs. Colton."

"Oh, don't be silly," Lydia said with a giggle and opened her arms for a hug. "Like I said, we feel like we know you already."

Lee looked over Lydia's shoulder as he hugged her, meeting Missy's gaze. She smiled and winked, and mouthed, "See? Love you..."

"You seem to know your way fairly well around Missy's kitchen."

Lee paused in reaching for coffee cups in one of the upper cabinets and looked over his shoulder at Jacob Colton, who stood on the other side of the high kitchen counter. The mixed laughter of Missy, his mom, and Lydia Colton drifted from the living room.

He finished reaching for the mugs and set them on the counter beside the brewing coffee. "I helped her unpack it."

Jacob made a sound somewhere between dismissal and disbelief. As much as Lydia had welcomed them home with open arms—literally—Lee had known from the get-go that Jacob would be the hard sell. For all intents and purposes, Jacob Colton was Missy's father and like any daddy, he wouldn't let her marry any old schmuck who made promises and talked sweet. He intended to convince the man, but that didn't mean he didn't break out in a cold sweat at the thought.

Three tours in Kabul were easier than this.

He turned his back on the coffee maker, and leaned his hips against the counter, bending his arms back to rest the heels of his hands on the edge. "I'm here if I'm not working or sleeping," Lee told him, looking Jacob in the eye. "I come in the morning before work, and help her get the boys off to school, and sometimes I drop them off on my way to the store. I come here after work, and we all have dinner together. I help with homework. Wyatt is having trouble with fractions." Lee smiled and shifted to set his feet slightly apart and cross his arms. "After Jeremiah and Levi are in bed, I head home."

"You leave every night to come back every morning..." He said it as a statement, but Lee wondered if it weren't more a subtle accusation.

From anyone else, the implication might have bothered him, but he understood Jacob's view. Probably would have a very similar one if he were ever blessed with a daughter. "Yes, sir. Until the day Missy and I are married."

Jacob made a sound, somewhere between a grunt and an affirmation. "Sounds like you're a big part of their lives already."

"I'm trying to be, sir." Lee cut a hand through the air, palm up. "We aren't blind to the challenges created by our short..." He paused, struggling to find the right word. "...courtship and our decision to marry fairly quickly."

"*Fairly*?" Jacob said with a chuckle.

Lee matched it and stepped away from the counter to approach Jacob, the double-tiered counter/breakfast bar between them. "I know you have concerns, sir, and I am happy to answer any question you may have for me. Missy considers you and your wife like parents, your blessing is important to her. So, it's important to me."

Jacob, a formidable man whose stature and stance said military to Lee, nodded his head and although the set of his jaw was firm, Lee recognized a gentleness in his eyes especially when it came to Missy.

With a careful slowness that spoke to his age, Jacob Colton eased onto one of the tall bar stools on the other side of the counter. He linked his hands and leaned forward.

"You may regret saying that, son."

"I've yet to regret anything when it comes to Missy, sir."

Jacob nodded. "How old are you, Lee?"

"Twenty-four, sir."

"You are a very young man if you don't mind me saying so."

"Admittedly," Lee said, canting his head. "Not much I can do about that, sir, but I hope you don't hold it against me."

"That stands to be seen, son. The fact of the matter is you are taking on a family, and not a small family. You're taking on *our* family. Our grandchildren. You must understand you have tough shoes to fill."

"Yes, sir," Lee said with a nod. "All I can offer is my commitment to Missy and the boys."

Jacob's mouth tipped up in a very small, subtle grin. "What are your plans now that you're a civilian?"

Before he could answer, shuffled footsteps in the hall coming from the bedroom caught his attention. Lee turned as Levi appeared in the kitchen doorway, rubbing his half-lid eyes. Lee crossed to him and crouched down so he was eye-to-eye with the boy.

"What's up, Leviathan?" he asked. "You shouldn't be out of bed."

Levi didn't say anything. Instead, he stumbled into Lee and wrapped his arms around Lee's neck, curling into him with his eyes fully shut. He doubted Levi was even actually awake, and stood, scooping the boy up with him, one arm under Levi's legs to hold him close. Levi slumped in his hold, his head on Lee's shoulder and his arms hanging limp.

"I'll be right back," he said to Jacob and carried Levi back down the hallway to his bedroom at the other end near the master bedroom.

The bedroom door was open and Levi's nightlight still glowing, but his blankets had been tossed back and his pillow was on the floor. With Levi still slumped on his shoulder, Lee crouched to pick up the pillow with his free hand and set it back on the bed. With the pillow back in place, Lee tipped Levi off his shoulder and laid him down. It wasn't until he tugged the blankets over Levi did the boy open his eyes. He smiled a sleepy grin.

"Hi, Wee," he said, his voice heavy with sleep.

"Hey," Lee said. "You try to stay in bed now, okay?"

"Okay." Levi nodded, his eyes already half-closed again. "I wuv you, Wee."

Lee grinned and leaned over to kiss Levi's forehead. "Love you, too, Leviathan. See you in the morning."

When he stood and turned, he stopped short when he saw Jacob Colton standing in the hall just outside the bedroom, hands pushed into his slacks pockets. Lee stepped out and pulled the door almost shut, leaving an inch or so open so the light of the hall spilled into the room.

Silently, they turned together and headed back toward the kitchen. When they neared Jude's door, it creaked open and Jude stood in the doorway, his hair rumpled and looking half-asleep as well.

"Hey, Grandpa," Jude mumbled and squinted at Lee. "Everything okay?"

"Yeah, your little brother was wandering the halls, that's all," Lee told him. "What's got you guys awake so late?"

Jude grinned, but it was sloppy since he was still sleepy. "Don't know. Guess we're all kinda excited Grandma and Grandpa are here."

"We'll be here all weekend, Jude," Jacob said with a smile to his oldest grandson.

Jude nodded and mumbled an "Okay," before shutting the door again. Lee waited at the door until he heard the thump of the boy hitting the mattress. They headed back to the kitchen, and Lee went to the coffee maker to pour out a carafe of decaffeinated coffee for everyone. Jacob didn't return to his stool but waited for Lee to finish.

"To answer your earlier question, sir, I'm taking over the hardware and supply store my father opened thirty-five years ago. I've been working there since I was big enough to carry a box of nails, and I'm currently studying management. My father has well earned his retirement." He smiled over his shoulder at Jacob before turning with the tray of coffee, mugs, and fixings in hand.

"You don't need to answer another question for me, Lee," Jacob said, his slightly clouded eyes misty. "Seeing you just now with our boys was all the convincing necessary. I needed to know, above all else, you'll take care of them. I saw it in your eyes you'd do anything for them. Wouldn't you."

The last was not a question, but Lee nodded in answer. "Yes, sir." Lee set the tray down again because he felt his next promise was worth his full attention. "Mr. Colton, I want you to know I will never diminish your son's existence in their lives. He was and is and always will be their father, and they will grow up knowing that. I have already told Missy I want to know about Daniel, and neither she nor the boys should ever, ever feel they can't remember him." Lee took a deep breath and blew it out his mouth. "I can't be their natural father, but in Daniel's absence, I intend to be the best father I can be to them."

By the time he finished, Jacob looked away and sniffed, but the moisture in his eyes never fell. He nodded when he looked back at Lee. "I believe that, son," he said, his voice rough. "You have my blessing."

CHAPTER NINETEEN

"So, when do I get to meet this gorgeous hunk of man you've been bragging about for the last six weeks?"

Missy laughed and glanced across the interior of Lee's truck at Miranda Carlisle, her best friend in the world. They joked they were the ying to each other's yang. Where Missy was blond, fair skinned, freckled, and blue eyed, Miranda had hair black like a raven's wing spun into long, shiny curls, skin as creamy as milk chocolate, and eyes like dark roast coffee.

"Have I really been bragging?"

Miranda laughed and waved her hand. "Well, maybe not. But how can you not talk about Mr. Tall, Dark, and Crazy Handsome without sounding like you're bragging?"

Missy grinned. She'd been smiling since she caught sight of Miranda at the luggage claim turnstile in the Tulsa Airport, and had already laughed so much on the drive home her sides ached. It felt so good to see her friend again and reminded her of how much Miranda was missed in her life.

"To answer your question," she said as she turned into her driveway and saw her Jeep parked under the biggest buckeye tree.

"You can meet him as soon as we're inside. He kept Levi for the day and picked up the boys from school so I could drive into Tulsa to get you."

"Is that why you have this pickup?"

Missy nodded. "He wouldn't be able to commute four boys in here, so we traded off for the day."

Miranda snorted. "I can't ever get Charlie to pick up the kids, and he made 'em."

Missy laughed and brought the truck to a stop. "Leave your bags. We'll get them later."

"This is the house you bought?" Miranda didn't wait for the answer. "Nice! But, there's nothing around. Where is the nearest neighbor?"

"Half a mile. And that's fine with me."

They came together in front of the Ford and Missy led the way to the house. As soon as she opened the front door, she heard footsteps running toward her, the shrill puppy barking of Zeke, their beagle pup who had moved home the week before, and the combined sonic boom volume of her two youngest shouting, "Mama's home!"

They met her in the foyer, and their enthusiasm quickly shifted to "Auntie Miranda!" which came out more like "Auntie M'anda" from Levi.

Miranda humphed when both Jeremiah and Levi flung themselves at her, Jeremiah hugging her hips while Levi wrapped himself around her leg. "What do you feed these boys out here? I swear they've grown a foot since you left Boston."

Zeke ran around them, barking and bouncing until Missy had to snap her fingers and shush him. He immediately planted his fuzzy butt on the tile and sat still. Thanks to exceptional training by Lee before the puppy left his litter.

"Wait until you see Jude. I just had to go buy him all new jeans because his were becoming high waters. They must be this way..." She motioned for Miranda to follow, and once she detangled Levi from her leg, they turned into the kitchen.

Jude and Wyatt sat at the kitchen table, both hunched over their textbooks, and Lee sat between them, leaning more toward Wyatt, who had a look of consternation on his face. Fractions. Wyatt hated fractions.

"We're home, just in case you didn't hear."

Lee looked up and smiled, and Missy's stomach did a pleasant flip. She doubted she would ever get over how handsome she found him, even with some random flecks of sawdust in his hair, probably from the wood mill behind the store, and the late-day dark scruff shadowing his jaw. Maybe more so for it. The only time she found him even more appealing was when he had a guitar in his hands. He pushed back his chair and stood, and she fully appreciated the fit of his worn jeans over his slim hips and the way his tee shirt sleeves hugged his biceps and the dark blue material accentuated his upper body. Long and lanky, he was enough to make her melt.

"Good God Almighty," Miranda said low, hopefully only loud enough for Missy to hear.

"We heard. Wy is almost done with his last problem." Lee came around behind Jude's chair and straight to her, taking her jaw in his hands to kiss her. He tasted of the sweet tea on the table. "Glad you're home," he said against her lips.

Flushed and hot, Missy cleared her throat and looked to Miranda, whose head was tipped back so she could look up at Lee, her dark eyes wide, and her glossed lips parted, staring without shame.

"Lee, this is my best friend in the entire world, Miranda Carlisle. Miranda, this is my—" She stopped, grinned, and took a quick breath. "This is Lee Henry."

"It's okay, sweetheart. I *am* yours," he said to her with a wink before he extended his hand to Miranda. "I'm happy to finally meet you. I feel like I know you a bit already."

Miranda hummed and shook her head, taking his offered hand. "I don't think I have heard nearly enough about you, Mr. Lee Henry."

"Hey, Aunt Miranda," Jude said, coming to stand beside Lee. He easily lined up to Lee's shoulder.

"Dang," Miranda said and opened her arms to hug Jude. "You're right, Missy. He's grown a foot, at least."

Finally, Wyatt joined them and hugged Miranda. Lee asked him and Jude to come out to the truck so they could bring in Miranda's bags and take them to the guest room at the end of the hall. Levi and Jeremiah were already gone, Zeke with them, their voices in play carrying from their bedrooms. Alone again with Miranda, Missy turned to her friend with a grin.

"Go ahead."

"Good heavens, girl," Miranda declared, fanning her face with her hand. "I mean, I saw those selfies you sent but they did not—in *any* way—prepare me for that beautiful specimen of a man. How old did you say he is?"

Missy cleared her throat and stepped to the side of the table so she could watch Lee and the boys through the large front window. "Twenty-four. Insane, isn't it?" She turned back to face Miranda. "You don't have to tell me it's insane, I know it is, but..." She shrugged and shook her head. "I don't care anymore. I'm happy, Miranda." Despite herself, her eyes welled and she swiped away an errant tear with a small chuckle. "I'm happier than I've been in years."

"I know," Miranda said, her expression and smile softer than the teasing of moments before. "I saw it when I saw you at the airport. I see it every time I look at you. And *dang*, I saw it when he kissed you. You practically glow." Miranda sighed and pressed a hand to her chest. "It's been a very long time since Charlie looked at me like that." Then she pulled a comical scowl and tilted her head. "Heck, I don't know if Charlie *ever* looked at me like that."

The boys came back inside, and Jude and Wyatt headed down the hall with Miranda's bags, barely dodging Levi as he tore back into the kitchen and straight for Miranda.

"Auntie M'anda, know what?"

"What?"

"Onwy free more sweeps until Mama and Wee are getting' mawwide." He held up his hand, and using his other hand, bent over his pinky and thumb so his three middle fingers were extended, then held his hand out to Miranda.

"I know," Miranda said with exaggerated enthusiasm to match Levi's natural enthusiasm.

Missy looked around, realizing Lee hadn't come back in with the boys. While Levi entertained Miranda with tales of their new puppy Zeke, Missy stepped back to the window and glanced outside. Lee was a few feet from the house, his phone to his ear, his head tilted forward in conversation. He was pacing a four-foot strip, his back to the house so she couldn't see his face, but she saw him stop and shake his head, looking up at the sky.

"Something wrong?" Miranda asked behind her.

"I don't know," Missy said absently, crossing her arms over her body. She sighed. "I hope it's nothing."

"Are you and Thayne speaking yet?"

Missy turned from the window, not wanting to get caught standing there staring at him. "We're speaking, but it's still strained. He's talked to me a few times, but he's yet to speak with Lee. We invited him to the wedding, of course, but I'm afraid he hasn't given up his resentment yet. He blames Lee for the possible breakup of his marriage."

"By what I hear, Thayne couldn't keep it in his pants, and his choice to lie through his teeth is breaking up his marriage."

Missy sighed and shrugged while she shook her head. "He doesn't see it that way."

"Speaking of keeping it in his pants, you and Lee seriously haven't..." She wagged her eyebrows and grinned, crossing her arms so she could tap her fingers on her elbow, her body language already arguing whatever Missy said in answer.

Missy smiled and chuckled. "No, we haven't."

"Wow. I didn't think people stuck to those kinds of ideals anymore."

"They do. *We* do. Not to say I haven't been sorely tempted." A flash of memories of every time Lee had kissed her with overwhelming intensity, or pressed her to his aroused body, or whispered in her ear how much he wanted her and couldn't wait to make love to her, hit her in a wave of heat that threatened to set her cheeks on fire.

"Don't get me wrong. I think it's kind of amazing. Maybe more people should stick to their guns like that, and we wouldn't have so many issues in this world."

The front door opened, and Missy watched the kitchen archway until Lee appeared, sliding his phone into his back pocket as he walked. He looked in Missy's direction, holding his stare on her, and her stomach did a nervous flip.

"What?" she asked.

Lee pushed his hands into his back pockets, the stance drawing his shoulders back, and leaned one shoulder into the doorframe. "Miranda, would you mind giving Missy and me a few minutes?" Lee asked, looking at Miranda.

Miranda exchanged looks with Missy, and after Missy nodded it was okay, she looked down at Levi. "What say you give me the grand tour of the house, huh? Starting with your room."

"Okay!" Levi declared and took her hand, leading her through the kitchen.

As soon as they were down the hall, Missy stepped to Lee, standing close enough the conversation would be between them alone. "What's wrong?" she asked again.

"Mama just called. Frantic."

Missy gasped. "Is someone hurt?"

"You," he said with a pop of one eyebrow. "Or so she thought."

"Me? Why would she think I was hurt?"

Lee let go of a long, frustrated sigh and pushed away from the wall.

"Because that's what she was told." He cut a hand through the air, palm down. "I don't know the whole story, or how it got started, but I guess the ambulance went through town today. Somehow, the whole thing turned into a steaming pile of convoluted gossip relayed to my father at the store, and then to Mama, that had us breaking up, and you rushed to the hospital because you slit your wrists or some such foolishness."

Missy stared for a good three beats of her heart before she could blink and try to process the information. "Oh, my God. Your poor mama."

Lee smiled and looked back at her. "All that, and you're worried about Mama."

"Well, of course I am. She isn't upset *now*, is she?"

"Well, she's upset now for a different reason. Over people starting stupid rumors and being unable to stay out of our lives." He chuckled and shook his head. "She wasn't worried you'd tried to kill yourself. She ignored that part and said she knew there wasn't anything short of an act of God that would separate us. She was just worried you were the one in the ambulance." He slid his gaze toward her and smirked. "Because of another rumor."

Missy arched her eyebrows. "*Another* rumor? Goodness, don't people have better things to do with their time?"

"*They* don't think so. You came from a small town. You know how it is."

Missy huffed and crossed her arms. "Still baffles the mind."

"No argument." He came back to where she stood and set his hands on her hips, moving her back until she was between him and the wall, his body not an inch from hers. Missy ticked up her chin to look him in the face and smiled. "Seems she heard a rumor a couple of days back that you were pregnant."

"Pregnant?" Missy shrilled, then slapped her hand over her mouth.

Lee inhaled and let it go, doing well not to tease her about her outburst, even though she saw in his eyes he wanted to. All he did was tug her hands away from her mouth with a smirk on his lips, then kiss her palm.

"Yes, pregnant. She didn't say anything then because she figured if you were, we'd tell her in our own time. Though..." He canted his head and squinted one eye, making a clicking sound in his cheek. "... she did express in the telling of the story that she was *pretty sure* we knew better."

Missy smiled and gave into the smallest temptation of sliding her fingers beneath the hem of his tee shirt so she could feel the warmth of his skin. Lee's eyelids slid low and a muscle jumped along his jaw when he clenched his teeth. She couldn't help it; knowing she had such an effect on him was empowering.

"I don't understand the connection," she said, watching the play of reactions across his face.

Lee opened his eyes and moved his hands from her waist to the wall on either side of her head, leaning into her from mid-chest to mid-thigh. A small smile ticked up his lips. "She was afraid, if it were true, that something was wrong with you or the baby, and her heart broke a bit at the idea."

"I feel terrible..."

"Don't. I assured her, without question, you are perfectly fine, to ignore the rumors, we *do* know better, and I promised when there is a new Henry on the way, she will be the first to know."

"Do you think the gossipmongers will ever leave us be?"

"Not until a juicier story comes along." He moved in closer until his mouth hovered over hers. Missy tipped up her chin, teasing him just a little with a light brush of her lips. "Or, maybe once we're Mr. and Mrs. Henry."

"Three more sleeps..." Missy whispered, mimicking her youngest.

She felt Lee's grin. "Three more sleeps," he repeated, "until we don't have to sleep alone."

The deep, caressing timber of his voice made Missy's heart flutter and she toed up to brush his lips again. He kissed her with an open mouth, drawing a low purr from her throat.

"Do they do this a lot, Levi?" Miranda asked from behind Lee somewhere.

Lee chuckled and broke the kiss, smiling down at Missy. She smiled back.

"Awl da time," Levi said with youthful frustration and sighed much heavier than called for.

"Yeah, it's gross," added Wyatt.

Lee gave her one last, quick kiss before stepping away so she could see Miranda standing in the kitchen, holding Levi's hand on one side and Wyatt's on the other. Miranda was grinning like a Cheshire cat and winked at Missy.

"And I told you I intend to kiss your mama all the time, so get used to it." He wagged a finger in their direction and grinned at the faces they pulled. "Tell you what. Give me twenty minutes to shower and get the smell of molasses feed and wood chips off me, and we'll head out for dinner."

"Sounds good to me," Miranda said. "I grabbed a sausage sandwich and iced coffee from a Dunkin' Donuts in Logan before the plane took off, but that ran out on me a couple of hours ago."

"I won't be long. Boys, go get washed up." Lee started across the kitchen, the boys leading the charge down the hall, and just before he disappeared around the corner, he reached behind his neck and grabbed the collar of his tee shirt, yanking it over his head to reveal his bare, muscled back. The overhead kitchen lights highlighted the tattoo on the back of his right shoulder that showed the emblem of his unit, with the date they had been bombed in Kabul. The day he nearly died and didn't talk about much. She hadn't ever been one to find tattoos sexy...until Lee Henry.

It took all Missy had not to follow.

Three sleeps. Three sleeps. It was her new mantra.

Miranda hummed in appreciation. "Very nice. Very nice indeed. You are a very lucky woman, Missy Colton."

"Don't I know it."

"But, I thought he wasn't living here."

"He's not." Missy went to the table and closed Jude and Wyatt's textbooks and picked up their glasses, hoping the activity would help keep her distracted. "But, he will be in a few days. He moved much of his stuff over in the last day or two, so he has clothes in the bedroom."

Miranda leaned against the counter edge, arms crossed, while Missy opened the dishwasher to set the cups inside. "You seriously haven't..." She cleared her throat.

"No," Missy answered, turning back with a grin. "We haven't."

"Okay, if you say so." She ticked her head to the side and shrugged. "I'd say your loss, but I'm thinking it's more everyone else's loss. At least every red-blooded female in Indian Prairie, Oklahoma."

"No, Miranda. Put away the phone," Missy said with a long groan, her elbow set on the table so she could hold her forehead in her hand.

Lee chuckled, but ignored her protest, already reaching across the table to retrieve the phone from Miranda. "Now, come on. I had to sit through Mama telling every embarrassing story she could think of from my diaper rash to my first girlfriend at six. I've earned the right to see some old photos of you."

"Here you go, hot stuff," Miranda said, laying the phone in his palm. "Lucky for Missy, I planned ahead and created a very special album just of her. I thought we might have a sharing moment or two."

"I hate you..." Missy hissed, but her smile made the statement unconvincing.

Lee sat back and draped his arm behind her chair, holding the phone in his other hand so he could scroll through with his thumb. "Come on, baby. You can give me the commentary."

Missy sighed and sat up, dropping her hands in her lap. She leaned closer so she could see the phone in his palm. The first several were various shots of Missy and Miranda, always in the middle of some group of people or party, looking like the center of it. He'd learned from Missy before Miranda arrived that the women's friendship went back to their freshman year at Bentley University in Waltham, just outside of Boston. Miranda was Boston-born and bred, and the two had been placed as roommates. Which all meant Miranda had a lot of stories and had been sharing since they got to the restaurant.

With each scroll, Missy would give a quick rundown of where they were and what they were doing. Thus far, nothing too embarrassing. He scrolled again, and a picture of a young Missy standing with a tall man with light brown hair and green eyes, their arms around each other. Both were looking at the camera with wide smiles.

"That's Daniel," Missy said, her voice dropping slightly. "Um, I think that was a couple of months after we were engaged."

Lee set the phone on the table so he could pinch out his fingers on the screen and magnify the image without taking his arm from behind Missy's shoulders. He picked up the phone again and studied the face of Daniel Colton.

"Hmmm...I see a lot of him in Jude, I think. In the eyes. Definitely Jeremiah." He looked at Missy and smiled, winking. "But Wyatt and Levi take after you."

Missy smiled and leaned in to kiss his cheek. Lee pulled her closer so her shoulder was against his side and she laid her hand on his thigh while he continued to flip. There were more pictures of Daniel, and despite his logical mind telling him in a small voice this man may have loved Missy once but was gone and she was his, he still felt a twinge of jealousy each time he saw the way Missy looked at Daniel, or Daniel looked at her. There was clear and obvious love in their eyes.

Then he flipped to a picture that made him stop. The picture was blurry because of the low light, and light flares in various colors distorting the image, but it was most definitely of Missy standing on a stage behind a mic, her hands curled around the stand. Her eyes were closed and her lips were open as she sang.

"Hold up," Lee said, sitting up straighter. "What's this?"

Missy groaned and tilted her head. "My misspent youth."

"What picture?" Miranda asked, and Lee turned the phone so she could see. "Oh, right...nothing misspent about it. Missy was the female lead singer for this campus band."

Lee looked to Missy, wide-eyed, and arched his eyebrows. "Why is it you have never mentioned you sing?"

"Because I don't *sing*," she said, shaking her head. "I *sang*. Not anymore."

"Why not?"

"Yeah, chickie," Miranda said, her tone saying she might have asked this question before. "Why not?"

"Because..." Missy looked between the two of them and huffed. "Because I got married, and had babies, and..." She stopped, her pressed lips ticking into a small frown. "I started to go deaf."

"Losing your hearing doesn't mean you lose your voice," Lee said.

"It does when you can't hear yourself right," she answered. "I don't...I don't sound right when I try to sing with—" She motioned toward her ears.

"Mama sings great," Jude said from the other side of the table beside Miranda. Lee almost laughed at Missy's look of utter betrayal. "She used to sing to us a lot."

Lee looked to Missy again and she shook her head. "No. Don't even ask. The answer is no."

"Is there anything else I can get you?"

Lee chuckled at Missy's persistence before he looked up at Callie. If there were other options in Indian Prairie other than High Steaks for a decent meal with a large group, he'd have gladly gone to avoid the possibility of having Callie as their waitress, but fate fought them and they ended up with her table. She'd been completely civil, if not cold, and as long as it remained that way, he was fine.

"No, thanks."

Callie didn't bother to glance around the table before she took the bill from her apron and set it on the table by Lee's plate, turned on her heels, and walked away. Miranda arched her eyebrows and made a dismissive sound in her throat.

"What bunched her panties?"

"It's a long, sordid story, but in a nutshell...us," Missy said and took a final sip of her sweet tea.

Miranda looked at Lee. "Old girlfriend?"

"Technically, yes, but that's not the problem. Let's just leave it at that. Come on, boys. Pack it up."

Their chairs scraped across the wood floor as they all stood. Lee picked up Levi, who looked almost ready to nod off, and took Jeremiah's hand as they left the restaurant. In the parking lot, they divided again between Missy's Jeep and his pick-up, with Jude and Wyatt riding with him back to the house. They'd already gone hunting twice for a decent vehicle large enough to accommodate a family of six or more, but short of some of the minivans at Essex Honda, they hadn't found anything yet. Missy could fit fine with her and the boys in the Cherokee, but beyond that, they were relegated to separate vehicles.

When they got to the house, the boys climbed out of their respective vehicles and headed for the front door. They had orders to let Zeke out as soon as they came home from anywhere, so that was their number one priority. Miranda followed, and by the time Lee came up alongside the Jeep, she was already in the house.

"Your friend is a smart woman. Considerate, too," Lee said, stepping up beside Missy. "Giving me a few private moments to say goodnight to my bride-to-be."

Missy smiled and shut her door, leaning back against the vehicle. A breeze came through the prairie, warm as spring approached, and stirred her blond hair around her face. The air smelled of fresh grass and distant trees.

"Yeah, she's great like that." Missy reached for him and took ahold of his shirt, tugging him to her. "Kiss me before I go crazy."

Lee had a half-second to smirk before their lips came together, and like every other time they kissed, his desire for her was instant and overpowering. Lee kissed her with hunger, with need, and leaving no question how much he wanted her, and her response left no question to him she felt the same. The only sound in the night was their hungry whispers and moans and the slide of their open mouths seeking something they couldn't yet have. Missy raised her arms to circle his neck, her fingers bunching in his short hair, each tug a shot of arousal straight through him. Lee pressed his hands to her sides and found the hem of her sweater. His palms scraped across her bare sides, feeling the ridge of her ribs, the silk of her skin, and the satin band of her bra.

Lee groaned and kissed her harder.

He buried his face into the column of her neck, sucking and kissing at the rapid pulse point at the base of her throat, her moan vibrating against his lips. Her arms tightened and her rapid breath warmed his skin when she pressed her cheek to his, and Lee forced himself to pull his hands from her body and wrap her in his arms. Only then did he hear her whispers.

"Three more sleeps. Three more sleeps. Three more sleeps."

He started to laugh, and in moments, Missy shook in his hold with her own giggles. She let her head fall back to rest on the driver's window, her eyes heavy-lidded, her lips shining in the moonlight. "It's the only way I'm going to make it," she said in a low, sexy voice that sparked over his live-wire nerves. "Three more nights and I don't have to kiss you goodnight and watch you leave. Three more nights before I can kiss you and not make myself stop." She tipped her chin in the offer of another kiss, and Lee took it, tossing a bit of gasoline on the fire. "Three more nights until I don't have to lie in that new, big bed of ours by myself, wanting you with me so much I ache." She slid her hands to his hips and drew him closer, and Lee thought he'd ignite right there. "I ache so much it hurts, Lee."

He clenched his jaw and swallowed, trying to content himself with nuzzling his nose against her throat. "I don't know how people make it through long engagements."

She chuckled softly and sighed, tilting her head into his touch so her hair brushed his forehead. "They don't." Missy stroked his jaw, her eyes fixed on his mouth. "Wanting to marry you now has nothing to do with wanting to be with you, Lee. I guess I've adopted your desire to start forever as soon as possible. I wouldn't want to wait."

Lee cupped her face in his hands and stroked her skin, waiting until her eyes shifted up and she looked at him. "Darlin', you are the best thing that ever happened to me and I can't wait for Saturday so I can proudly say you are my wife. And I am your husband. I love you."

She smiled and he moved in for one more long, but much more sedate, kiss before reluctantly letting her go. He stood in his spot until she reached the front door and glanced back at him one more time before going inside, then attempted to walk to his truck.

Three more sleeps. Three more sleeps. Three more sleeps.

If he managed to sleep at all.

CHAPTER TWENTY

Missy leaned sideways in her chair to bring herself against his side and looked up at him, and Lee's chest tightened. She took his breath away. Her silk dress, skimmed over her body like whiskey cream, accentuating every feminine curve, driving him to complete distraction every time she moved. It was modest, giving only a hint of her collarbone at her throat and a dip of her breasts, falling a few inches below her knees, but to him, it was the most enticing dress any woman had ever worn. Ever. Her blond hair was piled at her crown in delicate curls, bits of pearls and baby's breath woven through it, and simple cream-colored pearls in her ears and at her throat. Dear God, there had never been a more beautiful bride.

His bride.

His wife.

"Not in about fifteen minutes," she answered with a smile that warmed him through.

"Then I am already failing as a husband." Lee slid his hand down her spine and along the small of her back until he could lay his fingers around her far hip and pull her closer. He pressed a kiss to her cheek, just in front of her ear, then inhaled the delicate scent clinging to her skin that was intrinsically Missy. She tucked her head into his touch and hummed, rubbing her cheek against his.

"Damn, woman, but you are driving me crazy. It was all I could do not to kiss you when you reached the altar."

She laughed softly. "I think you made that clear when you kissed me *before* Pastor Nason managed to finish saying 'you may now kiss your wife.'"

"I can only be expected to have so much patience."

Missy brought her fingers to his jaw and tipped back her head to offer her lips, a gift he willingly took, and kissed her with probably less restraint than he should have mustered while still at his wedding reception.

Miranda cleared her throat on the other side of Missy. "Save it for later, you two. You're embarrassing your children."

Lee grinned against Missy's mouth and consented to draw back, winking at Miranda on her other side. "Wouldn't want that."

He had to sit back when Levi showed up, squirming his way between them with his new medallion in his palm, the string holding it looped around his neck.

"It's da coowest, Mama," Levi declared, holding out the medallion for Missy as if she hadn't seen it already.

"I know," she said but made a show of lifting the medallion from his palm and examining the Colton crest on the side facing up. She then turned it over so the Henry crest showed. "It's beautiful, Levi. Did you understand what Lee meant when he gave it to you?"

Levi nodded with such exuberance his carefully combed hair fell across his forehead. He looked from Missy to Lee and grinned. "It means dat I'mma Colton but I'mma Henwy too. I have two dads, jus' like Jude tol'me. A Daniel Daddy and a Wee Daddy. Fowever."

Lee wrapped his arms around the boy and kissed his hair. Not for the first time, he fought back the tightening in his throat and the pressure around his heart; an overwhelming swell of pride, love, and all-out joy he'd been filled with since the moment Missy stepped into the church with Jude and the other boys. They had "given" her to him, and had been part of each step of the ceremony. The medallions had been Lee's symbolic pledge to them that as much as he was there to marry their mother, he was there to promise them he would be the best father he could, and he would love them as his children forever. Levi threw his little arms around Lee's neck and squeezed before letting go just as quickly to run off and join his brothers further down the head table.

They had made it through most of the rituals for the ceremony and reception. The toasts had been made, the first dances had been danced, the food had been served, and the cake had been cut. Now, all Lee wanted more than anything was to slip away and be alone with his wife.

His wife.

Every time the two words came to mind, Lee found himself grinning like a fool. Six months before he had been in the armpit of the Middle East, sweating and cleaning sand from places it had no place being. He just wanted to be home. If someone had told him, "When you get home, you are going to meet this beautiful woman with four amazing sons, and you are going to fall instantly and completely in love with her," he probably would have laughed and told them to drink another beer. Now, he couldn't—didn't want to—imagine what he'd be doing without her.

She and the boys had become his life in a moment.

"You're smiling."

Lee turned at the sound of her voice. "So are you."

She smiled wider. "I can't seem to help it."

Lee canted his head. "Neither can I, sweetheart."

Mark tapped his shoulder, and Lee turned in his seat to look at his best man seated beside him. "It's about time, bro," Mark said, extending his wrist so Lee could see his watch.

"Got it."

"Time for what?" Missy asked.

Lee scooted back his chair and stood, kissing her cheek and taking her hand as he did. "Come with me."

She followed without question, and he held her hand as he led her along behind the others seated at the head table until they reached the end and could skirt around. Mark was already to the small stage setup in the hall with some instruments already set out. Lee's band had played off and on during the evening, with a hired DJ filling in the gaps. The band was necessary for Lee to spring his surprise. He led Missy to the dance floor until they were a few feet from the stage and in the center of everyone's attention. Only then did he release her hand.

"Stay right here," he told her, and kissed her quick, grinning at her wide-eyed look of confusion before he went to the stage. "Hand 'er to me, Mark."

Mark was already on his way, stepping to the edge of the stage, Lee's Yamaha in hand. Lee took the guitar by the neck and slipped the leather strap over his head, settling it on the shoulders of his dress uniform. The stiff cuffs of the Class-A jacket complicated playing, but not enough to stop him.

"Thanks," he said to his brother and turned back to face his wife as he quickly ran his fingers and pick over the strings to make sure the instrument was in tune.

She stood still just where he had left her, hands held together in front of her with her fingers laced, her beautifully enticing blush staining her cheeks, but an equally beautiful and enticing smile bowed her lips. As he walked back to her, she tilted her head, and as soon as he was near enough she asked softly, "What are you up to, Lee Henry?"

Lee grinned and bent forward so he could kiss her without hitting her with the guitar, and began to strum when he moved back. No one spoke at any of the tables surrounding the dance floor. The reception hall was small, and he figured most would be able to hear him without the necessity of a microphone, but that didn't matter. The only one who needed to hear him was her.

His wife.

His life.

In a heartbeat, the swell of emotion he'd held at bay all day hit him with choking force. Lee chuckled, but it was just to break the grip on his throat and looked down at his hands for a moment to rein it in again. He'd done damn good keeping back the physical evidence of the waves of overpowering, blessed happiness, but this moment might be his undoing. To find his focus, he sniffed and just kept playing. Finally, Lee huffed and looked up again into Missy's tear-sparkling blue eyes.

And it was almost his undoing.

His wife.

"Ah, so..." He cleared his throat and paused his playing to snuff his nose, and tried again. "So, a few weeks back I was talking with Ellie and I told her I didn't want to wait too long to start working on forever with you."

Missy smiled and curled her lips together, a tear slipping from one eye. Lee knew he had to keep going if he was going to get it out. He scanned the gathering of guests quickly until he saw the table where his sister and other siblings sat with their parents. Ellie smiled and blew him a kiss and Lee winked back.

"She was teasing at the time, but she said I should write my words into a song. I told her I just might." He drew in a breath and huffed it out. "So, I did."

Missy pressed her hand to her chest and mouthed, "I love you."

"I love you, too, sweetheart," he said and then began to play in earnest.

He had to cycle through the beginning melody three times before he trusted his voice to work, and even then, it was a gamble. He swallowed, looked Missy in the eyes, and began to sing. "Before you, I never even looked for love. Before you, I never imagine forever. Tomorrow was tomorrow, and I'd get there someday. Then there you were, my gift straight from God above." He strummed down, but brought his hand up before drawing the pick across the strings again, and pointed upward. "Now I can't imagine forever without thinking of you. Now, I wonder how long I wanted what you've given to me."

He kicked up the tempo, thankful for a diversion from the swell in his chest. Lee plucked the strings and strummed with all his heart, and led into the chorus.

"I can't waste a day waiting for forever. Woman, what's taking so long? Come on, come on, let's get on with forever. Your love is the only thing I want. Your heart, the only prize to win. Forever, the only think I need for tomorrow. Forever together with you."

Missy brushed trembling fingers across her cheeks, but the smile on her lips told him all he needed to know. He played the bridge, repeated the melody, and went into the final verse.

"They call us crazy, they call us fools, because only fools fall in love. For you, I'll be a fool now 'til forever. Let's start our forever—together—Today. You won't have to wait to know my heart. It's been yours since my forever started. Looking into your eyes.

"I can't waste a day waiting for forever. Woman, what's taking so long? Come on, come on, let's get on with forever. Your love is the only thing I want. Your heart, the only prize to win. Forever, the only think I need for tomorrow. Forever together with you."

As he finished the second run of the chorus, Lee eased his playing and softened his tone until the last sentence was more intimately between them than anyone else in the hall. It wasn't for them, it was for her.

As he finished, Missy came to him, her cheeks streaked. He lifted the guitar away and off his neck in time for Mark to take it from him before she was in his arms. Lee pressed his hands to her back and held her so tight she had to wrap her arms around his neck, and he kissed her the way he'd wanted to since Pastor Nason gave him permission to "now kiss his wife". He might have kissed her before he was told to, but he was proud of the restraint he'd shown at the time.

Only when the cheering and applauding became too distracting did he pull back and smile down at her. Missy swallowed and smoothed her fingers across his cheeks, the contact slick, and he realized they were his own tears. Missy embraced him again, and he pressed his cheek to hers, only drawing back when he caught the high squeal of feedback from her hearing aids.

"I love you so much, Lee," she whispered, her fingers stroking the back of his head. He caught the crack in her voic and held her tighter. "I feel like Cinderella. How did I ever get so lucky?"

Lee chuckled and kissed the bit of exposed skin at her collarbone before straightening so he could see her face. "Missy, I'm the lucky one. In so many ways."

Once the exuberance of their guests died a bit, the DJ started some music; a slow song, which worked for Lee because he had no interest in letting her go. It was the song "When You Say Nothing At All" as sung by Allison Krauss, his favorite version. As the music slowly began, and Allison sang, Lee wrapped his arms fully around Missy and held her close. They moved together in a slow dance, and he didn't care much at all if, or how many, people joined them on the floor. They were just polite company, as far as he was concerned.

Halfway through the first run of the chorus, Missy stopped dancing and moved away from him enough to make him pause. She looked up at him for a moment, a strange, searching look in her eyes.

"What?" he asked, and her stare shifted to his lips. With the music, it was likely she wouldn't be able to hear him speak so low.

She smiled, a different smile than she'd had all day. Like she'd thought of something she liked. Then she stepped out of his arms, and while holding his gaze, she reached to each ear and removed the small bud. Lee watched, perplexed, until she opened the flap of the pocket on his jacket and dropped the hearing aids inside, and moved into his arms again. Before he could ask what she was doing, and why, Missy slipped her hand behind his head and drew him down so her lips were near his ear.

And she began to sing.

Lee's heart squeezed hard in his chest, and he held his breath.

Her voice was like an angel's, pure and clear, unadulterated. A voice meant to sing praises, not honkytonk country. Lee folded her in his arms and stopped dancing, wanting only to hear the words she meant for him and him alone.

"You say it best when you say nothing at all."

The lyrics ended, and she stopped singing, but Lee couldn't let her go. He knew, he understood, her reluctance to sing anymore once she'd begun to lose her hearing, and knew this was a gift. He wanted to hold her closer, tighter, but had to concede to pressing kisses to her cheek, jaw, and finally her lips. When he looked into her eyes again, they shined with questions.

Lee took her face in his hands, smoothing his thumbs across her soft skin, and nodded. "Beautiful," was all he could say. "Beautiful."

"We are very bad hosts," Missy said through hitched breaths. Lee's lips found the spot on her neck that sent jolts of desire straight through her, making her weak in the knees.

"It's our party," Lee said through a groan against her throat. "We can make out in the coat room if we want to."

She laughed, but the sound was lost in her gasp when his hand slid over her breast, a contact they had denied until that day, and now it was like gasoline on a bonfire. At that moment, she didn't know how she would make it the hour-long drive to Tulsa and their hotel for the next three days without bursting into flames.

Lee growled her name, his fingers digging into her hips to pull her hard against him, and left no doubt he wanted her with as much desperation as she wanted him. He took her jaws in his hands, kissing her deep and hard until her head swam. When he abruptly pulled back, Missy gasped and opened her eyes to look into his face. Their rapid breath mingled in the space between them and the dark, heavy look in her husband's eyes made her heart pound harder.

Her husband.

Missy smiled.

"We need to go," Lee said with a lopsided grin, "or I can't be held responsible for my actions."

Missy laughed and ran her thumb across his wet lips, shining with the gloss she had been wearing before they snuck off to the coat room for what they'd intended to be just a few minutes alone away from the crowd. "You won't get any argument from me, Mr. Henry."

"Then let's go say our goodbyes and get out of here, Mrs. Henry."

Missy smiled and tried to straighten her dress when Lee stepped back from her, tugging his blue dress jacket firmer over his hips. He had the advantage of short hair, but Missy was pretty sure her hair was a mess. She tried to pat it into place, but before she managed to get it under control, Lee brushed her hands aside and felt in her hair for the few pins that held it in place.

"Lee—"

"I like it down," he said, his only argument as he pulled the last pin free and her hair fell loose around her shoulders.

"Everyone is going to know we were in here making out like teenagers," she protested, her cheeks already warm.

Lee laughed and reached for her hand. "Because the fact we've been missing for fifteen minutes from our own wedding reception won't give us away."

He led the way to the door and made a theatrical show of glancing up and down the hall before they left the coatroom. Missy giggled at his antics and they jogged together toward one of the doors leading to the reception hall. Just as he reached for the door handle, it opened outward toward them and they stopped short. Thayne raised his head and looked between them.

Thayne cleared his throat. "Congratulations," he said simply.

Still holding Lee's hand, Missy stepped closer to him and curled her other hand in the bed of his elbow. "Thank you, Thayne. Thank you for coming."

He nodded and shoved his hands into his pockets. "Of course.

You're my sister." Thayne swallowed and looked at Lee, his jaw twitching before he added, "and my best friend. At least, I hope maybe someday I can say that again."

Lee squeezed her hand. "Yeah, I hope so, too."

"We'll, ah...we'll talk when you get back."

Lee nodded, and Missy held her breath when he extended his right hand. Thayne looked at it for only a moment before he took it and they shook hands. Missy released Lee and went to her brother, wrapping her arms around him.

"Thank you," she whispered before stepping away.

Thayne nodded and stepped to the side so they could go back into the hall. "They're looking for you." He turned away and headed down the hall toward the exit.

They stood together until Thayne was out of sight, then Lee slid his arm across her shoulder and brought her to his side, kissing her forehead. "We'll be fine," he said. "He's got things to work through, but we'll be fine. I promise."

Missy nodded and looked up at her husband. "I know."

"So, what do you say we go in there one last time, make our rounds, and then get out of here, huh?"

She smiled and turned into him, reaching up to lay her hand along his cheek. "The sooner the better. I need to make love to my husband."

Lee groaned and leaned in for a kiss. "And let forever begin..."

CHAPTER TWENTY-ONE

3 Years Later...

"Melissa Henry," Lee burst out, his hands slamming into the maternity wing nurse's station as he tried to stop himself.

The nurse jumped and looked up. "I'm sorry?" she asked.

"Missy Henry," he said again. "I got a call from my son. She would have come in within the last fifteen to twenty minutes."

"Oh, yes. Just a minute, Mr. Henry. I'll let Doctor Milliken know you're here." She picked up the phone and pressed an extension.

Lee stepped away from the counter and turned on his heels, shoving his fingers through his hair. His heart pounded like a runaway train in his chest, threatening to bust right through his ribs.

"Dad!"

Lee spun at the sound of Jude's voice, and bolted to meet his son halfway down the hall. Jude's girlfriend Beth ran behind him. Jude met him in a hard hug, and after the assurance his son was there—and thus so was Missy—Lee pulled back and gripped Jude's upper arms.

"What happened? Where is she?"

Jude shook his head, and when he spoke, his voice wavered. "She was fine. We were in the kitchen doing homework, and she was starting dinner. Then she just...yelled...and collapsed, and she said her water broke. We got her in the car and came straight here. I don't know where she is."

"Where are the other boys?"

"At the house. Wy stayed in charge, and Uncle Thayne and Aunt Susan were on their way."

Lee nodded and kept one hand on Jude's shoulder, his arm parallel with the floor to do it since they stood eye-to-eye, and ran his other hand over his mouth. He heard footsteps approaching behind them and turned just as a middle-aged man in a white coat, Dr. Milliken embroidered over his left chest, approached them. He had on a surgical cap and booties over his shoes.

"Mr. Henry?" he asked, extending his hand.

Lee took it, but only out of an automatic response. "Where is my wife?" he asked, trying hard not to grab the man and shake the answer out of him.

"Mrs. Henry is in labor and delivery now. She experienced a sudden onset of full labor, which we call precipitous labor, and was seven centimeters dilated when she arrived twenty minutes ago. I expect the pushing stage to begin within the next few minutes."

Lee huffed and swallowed, trying desperately to calm the panic that sat bitter in the back of his throat. "Is she okay? Is the baby okay?"

Dr. Milliken smiled. "She's fine. This is Missy's fifth child. Her body knows exactly what it's doing."

"Sixth," Lee corrected, his heart squeezing a bit. "She lost a baby last year in her fourth month."

Dr. Milliken's features softened. "Missy is at thirty-eight weeks, which by all definitions is considered full-term. The baby's heartbeat is strong, and all your wife's vital signs are good. You've been through this before—"

"*I* haven't," Lee said with a nervous chuckle.

Dr. Milliken smiled, seeming to understand. "She's simply having a baby, and if you want to be there with her, I consider you change."

A nurse joined them and touched Lee's arm. "If you come with me, sir, I'll take you to her."

Lee turned to Jude before leaving and laid his hand on his eldest son's shoulder again. "I'll come tell you as soon as I can."

Jude nodded, his features tense. "Okay. We'll be here."

Lee rushed to change into scrubs and clean up so he could be with Missy, his hands moving as fast as his heart. Finally, he stepped out of the changing room where the nurse waited, and with a smile she led him down the hall toward delivery. As they opened the door, he heard the argument going on between Missy and Dr. Milliken.

"You need to be ready to push, Missy," Dr. Milliken said in a calm, even-tempered voice.

"No!" she ground out through clenched teeth. "Not until my husband is here."

Lee pushed past the nurse to the side of the delivery table so Missy could see him, and immediately her tense features relaxed. "I'm here, sweetheart. I'm here."

"Oh, thank God," she whispered, her hand flailing to find him, but the words immediately became a groan. "Oh, God!"

"Push now, Missy," Dr. Milliken ordered. "Push!"

The entire Henry/Colton/Bingham clan came to their feet in the maternity ward waiting room when Lee came down the hall. Levi bolted free of Susan's lap and ran for him, and Lee scooped up the six-year-old as soon as he was close, continuing down the hall to everyone who waited.

"She's doing great," he said before anyone asked. "Missy's asleep right now, but everything is fine. Things moved along pretty quickly once I got here." He laughed a bit, remembering Missy's insistence that he be there before their baby was born.

"Well?" Mama asked, a smile on her face now that she knew everyone was fine.

Lee smiled wider and set Levi on his feet. "We have a baby girl."

Everyone cheered their happiness, and Mama came to him to hug him and kiss his cheek, then one by one the rest did the same. Levi stayed close to Lee, his arms wrapped around Lee's leg and his cheek against Lee's thigh. Having his mom collapse, then his big brother rush her out to the hospital, had to be terrifying for the boy, so Lee didn't make him step away.

"And?" Mama asked. When Lee shook his head, she huffed. "The details, Lee. The details!"

"Oh, right. Seven pounds, four ounces, and she was twenty inches long. All healthy, all good. She's got a great set of lungs." He chuckled and laid his hand casually on Levi's back to soothe the boy. "Her name is Faith Joy Henry." With each part of his daughter's name, Lee's chest filled more and his smile grew until his cheeks ached.

He talked a few minutes more with everyone, but when he said they wouldn't be able to see Missy or the baby that evening, they began to disburse with promises of visiting in the morning. Lee crouched so he could look Levi in the eye and gave the boy a firm hug before holding him away so they could talk.

"Your mama is okay," he told Levi. "She had a baby, just like she had Jude, and Wyatt, and Jeremiah, and you. Okay?"

Levi nodded, but tears shined in his eyes. "I got scared when she fell down."

"I'm sure you did, and it's okay you were scared. I would have been scared too, if I were home. I was more scared because I wasn't."

Levi just nodded, his chin quivering. Lee kissed Levi's forehead and hugged him again. "You're going to go home with Uncle Thayne and Aunt Susan, okay? You boys can stay there tonight." He said the last to Jude and Wyatt, who stood side-by-side and nearly shoulder-to-shoulder.

Jude nodded. "I have to take Beth home first. Then I'll be there."

"Thank you, Beth," Lee said to Jude's girlfriend of nearly a year. Lee had been concerned about them being so serious at only sixteen, but they also seemed good for each other and with each other, so he and Missy were just watching for now. "Missy told me how you kept the boys calm. We appreciate it."

"Of course, Mr. Henry," Beth said, blushing. "Anything I can do to help, too, once Mrs. Henry comes home. I'm happy to."

Everyone else said their goodbyes, leaving Lee with the kids and Thayne and Susan. It had taken months for the two of them to reconcile after Lee and Missy married, but with a lot of work and devotion, they had a strong marriage again and were working on a baby brother or sister for Betsy. Lee and Thayne had patched their beaten and bruised friendship after time as well, once Thayne seemed to accept Lee meant every word he said about his love and commitment to Missy and their boys, and Thayne also realized he had mislaid the blame for his broken marriage.

"Thank you, guys," Lee said as he approached them, "for picking up the kids and bringing them. It would have been too much for Jude to try to keep them calm *and* get his mom here."

Susan hugged Lee, squeezing tight. "Of course," she said as she stepped back. "Anything. We're so happy for you two. A girl! Missy always wished for a girl."

Lee grinned. He had heard most men wished for a son to carry on his name, but he had four sons and there were enough Henry grandchildren there was no risk of the name falling away. The idea of a little girl filled him up and made him a special kind of happy.

"We'd hoped but would have been happy with another boy. Not like we don't have enough tractors and baseball bats to go around."

Susan smiled and looked to Thayne. "Let's go. Lee wants to get back to Missy."

One more round of hugs and everyone moved down the hall to

the elevators, leaving Lee alone. Once they were gone, he pushed his hands into his pockets and went down the hall to the room number they'd given him where they'd be moving Missy.

The door was open slightly, but the room beyond was mostly dark. As he pushed open the door, he heard Missy's beautiful voice singing a lullaby, and he eased back the privacy curtain. Lee had to stop and take a slow, steadying breath and swallow the lump in his throat at the sight of his wife holding his baby girl, nursing Faith as she sang.

Missy looked up and smiled. "Hey, Daddy."

"Hey, Mama," he said in a rough whisper and moved to the bedside, perching on the edge near Missy's hip.

Faith's tiny hand was outside the blue and pink striped blanket the hospital had bundled her in, and Lee rubbed his pinky finger across her tiny, tiny knuckles. Even though she never took her focus from her meal, her precious fingers wrapped around his pinky and Lee thought for sure his heart would implode. He leaned forward and pressed a kiss to the top of Faith's fuzzy head, covered with thick, dark hair, then braced his hand on the raised head of the bed so he could lean in further and kiss his wife. She smiled before she accepted the kiss, and smiled wider when he sat back down.

"How are you feeling?" he asked.

"Tired," she said, sighing as she looked down at Faith. "Sore, of course, but not too bad. They've given me something for the discomfort." Missy looked at him again. "They said I can probably go home the day after tomorrow since she was born so late in the day."

"The boys will be glad to hear it. Levi is a little scared."

Missy frowned. "Awww, poor baby. I know he was scared."

"I think they all were. Beth said she would come help."

Missy smiled. "She's a sweet girl."

Lee sat for the next few minutes watching Missy feed the baby and listening to her sing softly. She'd grown less self-conscious about her singing since they'd married, though she still wouldn't do it in public no matter how many times he'd asked her to sing with him and the band. Though, these days, he spent fewer and fewer evenings at Low Places, playing maybe once a month, because he preferred to be home with his family. When she was done, she tucked Faith's blanket around her and held her out.

"Here, Daddy."

He'd held many of his nephews and nieces when they were this small and new, but it was a different world entirely when the tiny, precious bundle in his arms was his daughter. Lee adjusted her in the cradle of his arm and held her high on his chest. Big blue eyes blinked slowly and she released a long, shuddered breath.

"Hey there, pretty girl," Lee said softly and her little eyes shifted, maybe trying to focus on the source of her daddy's voice. "You are going to be the most loved little girl in the entire world."

Lee marveled at the delicate beauty of his daughter for several minutes, and when he looked up he realized Missy had drifted off to sleep. Her blond curls had been pulled back during her labor and now fell around her face in mussed waves, her beautiful features relaxed in sleep. Her hearing aids were on the bedside table in a container for safekeeping. Lee inhaled a long, slow breath and released it through his nose, reaching out to carefully run his finger along her cheek.

With his wife asleep beside him, and his baby girl asleep in his arms, Lee tipped back his head and closed his eyes. "Thank you," he whispered in a heartfelt prayer. "Thank you for my life."

THE END OF THE TELLING, BUT FAR FROM THE END OF THE STORY...

THE STORY OF HANK AND MAXINE...

The year was 1969, and it was spring in Massachusetts. Jewell Maxine Bingham Brow—known by her friends as Maxine—had been widowed for about two years, raising her four sons alone. Her youngest was nine years old, her oldest twenty, nearly twenty-one.

Her second son, Mark, came home one day and told her he had a buddy who had a birthday coming up. Hank had only been home from Viet Nam, where he served in Saigon, for about six months and had no immediate family in Massachusetts. Mark asked if his mom could bake a cake for his friend, and maybe Hank could come hang out for a while for his twenty-first birthday. Hank and Mark played country music together around town. She said sure. After all, he was just another young kid coming through the house. Pretty common when she had four boys.

So, she baked him a carrot spice cake and young Hank Hughes came for the evening.

The telling of events over the next nineteen days varies by who told the story. My mother claimed Hank was the pursuer, and my daddy said there was no pursuing involved, they just clicked. My brother Mark tells of how long it took before he figured out why on some nights when Hank wasn't around to go out, his mom always went out, too. The one thing that is agreed upon is that in nineteen days, Hank Hughes and Maxine Brow met, fell in love, dated, even broke up, found their way back to each other, and married.

Yes, married. Less than three weeks after they met, they were Mr. and Mrs. Henry Hughes.

The rumors were rampant, of course. In 1969, it was scandalous for a thirty-nine-year-old woman to be involved with—let alone marry—a twenty-one-year-old man. Gossip ranged from Mama being pregnant to threatening to slit her wrists if he didn't marry her. Mark, whom you might think would have been against it, too (Who would think a guy would be okay with his mom and his best friend getting hitched?), was their staunchest supporter. It wasn't easy, from what I've heard, but it was worth it. Two years later (now, don't go doing the math on me), I was born. Mama was advised not to have any more children, having had a miscarriage before me, so I was the only child of their union.

So, I grew up hearing about this whirlwind love story between my parents. Was their marriage perfect? Far from it, but what marriage is? All I knew was my parents loved each other. I saw it when they would hold hands while my dad drove, or the way my mom would smile when he teased her. I heard it when my mother told me the story, her version at least. I saw it when my daddy took care of her when she got sick, and how he felt the moment she passed, even though he wasn't with her. He was on his way, rushing to be there, when she slipped away.

He lost a piece of his soul.

Is it any wonder I write romance?

There are small things laced into *Feel My Love* that are very close to their relationship. There are things I've flipped, reversed, or tweaked to make this story original. It would take another twenty pages for me to list them all, but I'll hit a few.

Like Lee, my daddy was a country music singer. He was the youngest of seven children, but he was not from Oklahoma. He was born and raised in Maine, and like Lee, he was a country boy. It was my mama who was from Oklahoma; Indiahoma, just like Missy.

The name Lee Henry is a variation of my father's real name. Henry Leroy Hughes.

Like Missy, my mama was a widow with four sons. She was also going deaf, just like Missy, which I always found very ironic because my daddy was a musician. She still could hear his music, though. At that time hearing aids hadn't come nearly as far as they are now, and she hated wearing them. So, I grew up knowing to look my mother in the eye when I spoke and to make sure I spoke clearly and enunciated every word. She didn't give in to hearing aids until she was in her sixties.

I also have the same condition that caused my mom to lose her hearing.

The name Missy isn't from my mother's name, but what I thought for a long time was my grandmother's, since my mom didn't like the name Jewell. That, and I've already named a heroine after my mom in a different book. I thought for a long time my grandmother's name was Melissa Mae Bingham, and Bingham is Missy's maiden name. I learned since releasing *Feel My Love* that my grandmother's name was Minerva Mae and her nickname was Lucy. But by then, Missy was solidified in my mind and I didn't want to change it.

My father's family was very accepting of my mother, and by what I understand they never questioned his decision to marry a woman so much older than him, nor how quickly they married. Of course, they didn't meet Mama until after she and Daddy were married. In *Feel My Love*, Thayne kind of represents all the people who pressured my parents and told them they were wrong. In 2014, there isn't nearly the same stigma with age differences as there was then.

I like to say my mother was a Cougar before it was cool to be a Cougar.

I purposefully made Lee and Missy very much the opposites physically to my parents. I had to do that for my own sanity. I mean, whether they are the basis or not, this is still a romance, and what person would *ever* want to imagine their parents in an intimate situation? Hank Hughes was a solid, stocky man of average height with blond, wavy hair. He was so muscled at times in his life, that he couldn't scratch the top of his head because his muscles prevented his arms from bending that far.

I describe Lee Henry as being tall, and while well-muscled and defined, he is far more lanky and lean than my dad. He also has dark hair and a darker skin tone. This made it easy to separate Lee Henry from Hank Hughes.

Jewell Bingham was the opposite of Missy. She had dark, short hair and a different build, so again, it was easier for me to make Missy blond and fair. My mama couldn't "carry a note in a bucket", as she often said, so to make Missy her own person, I gave her a beautiful voice. The voice my mama always wished she had.

I'm not even sure how many times I used my parents as inspiration or guides for what I wrote. I would need to itemize every detail, every element, to find those comparisons. So, if you want to know how some element of their story compares to the true-life tale, I'm open to questions. Email me at Gail@GailDelaney.com, and I'll be happy to explain further.

I said it before, but I'll say it again: This is not intended to be a mirrored telling of their courtship. I couldn't do that since I wasn't born yet.

I hope you enjoyed the story as much as I enjoyed telling it.

ABOUT THE AUTHOR

Gail R. Delaney is a multi-published, award-winning author of romance in multiple sub-genres, including contemporary romance, romantic suspense, and epic science fiction romance. She always wrote stories as a kid through her teens, but didn't decide to write 'for publication' until her early twenties after the death of her mother. While helping her father go through her mother's papers, she found a box her mother kept with everything Gail had ever written—from book reports to short stories. It was then she realized her mother saw her as a writer, and it was time to live up to her mother's vision.

You can find out more about Gail R. Delaney's body of work at:

http://www.GailDelaney.com

ALSO BY GAIL R. DELANEY

Contemporary Romance

Something Better

Precious Things

Fools Rush In

Baker Street Legacy

Book One: My Dear Branson

Book Two: The Empty Chair

Book Three: Indefinite Doubt

Coming Soon

THE FUTURE POSSIBLE SAGA

PART ONE: THE PHOENIX REBELLION

BOOK ONE: REVOLUTION

BOOK TWO: OUTCASTS

BOOK THREE: GAINING GROUND

BOOK FOUR: END GAME

PART TWO: PHOENIX RISING

BOOK ONE: JANUS

BOOK TWO: TRIAD

BOOK THREE: STASIS

BOOK FOUR: LIBER